CONTROL

Powerless Earth - Book Two

Paul McMurrough

This is a work of fiction. Names, characters, places, and incidents either are the product of the author's imagination or are used fictitiously. Any resemblance to actual persons, living or dead, events, or locales is entirely coincidental.

British Library Cataloguing-in-Publication Data

A catalogue record for this book is available from the British Library

First paperback edition June 2022

ISBN: 9781838066048

.

Control is book two of the Powerless Earth series.
It is set one day after the end of book one, Reliance.
For continuity and your enjoyment, I would suggest
that you read Reliance before reading this story.

###

An Garda Síochána
is the national police service of the Republic of Ireland.
Also referred to as the **Gardaí** or "**the Guards**"

PROLOGUE

Conor Tobin had been a typical eighteen-year-old; fun loving, gregarious and outgoing. He was an excellent student, and could hold his own in most sports, but he was most at home on the water, being a competition sailor and keen canoeist.

That all changed eight days ago, the day before the power went off, the day he killed his best friend Eamon. Since then, he'd barely spoken a word, other than to lament the situation and confess his guilt.

Conor, Eamon, and two other friends had been out on the lake with their kayaks, as they did most Saturdays. It was a beautiful still day. The only disturbance on the mirror-calm water was from the rhythmic slapping of paddles.

As they approached the shore, after a couple of hours on the lake, the inevitable horseplay started. There was splashing with paddles, shoulder-to-shoulder jostling for position, and half-hearted attempts at rolling each other's boats.

Eamon had made Conor his target, for no other reason than he was in the nearest boat. From his position at the front of the group, he purposely scooped and flicked paddles of water directly into Conor's face with every-other stroke.

"Right, that's enough!"

Splash.

"Stop it, will ye!"

Splash.

Eamon laughed, ignoring Conor's protests, and flicked his paddle again. "Ah, is pretty-boy's hair getting wet?"

Conor took pride in his well-kept blond hair, and his mates took every opportunity to rib him about it.

The splashing and messing continued all the way back to the small jetty and slipway. With his fringe now pasted to his forehead, Conor fumed silently. He was the first to exit the water and drag his boat up onto the grass next to their trailer. Returning to the water's edge, where Eamon was wrestling himself out of his life jacket, Conor snatched his friend's paddle and with a mischievous laugh jumped onto the nearby jetty. He dangled the paddle out over the edge.

"Ah come on, don't be a prick," said Eamon, with a pleading tilt of his head.

Conor smiled and shrugged, and with a flick of his wrist, tossed the paddle off the end of the jetty. It hit the water and glided a little before lulling to a stop, half submerged, about ten feet out. He jumped down from the jetty, laughing hysterically as Eamon approached, shaking his head and smiling a promise of revenge at his closest friend. He stepped up onto the jetty and without breaking stride, dived off the end to retrieve his paddle.

About twelve inches below the surface, a broken branch, the width of a thumb, swayed gently with the current, trying in vain to free itself from the silt and mud, to continue its journey downstream. It did not free itself, and at the exact instant that Eamon — who'd dived off this same jetty a thousand times before — entered the water, the branch became a spear. For that split second, it aligned perfectly with Eamon's entry into the water. The tip of the trapped branch — sharpened to a point from where it had separated from its mother tree — reached up through the cold murky water at a forty-five degree angle.

There was little or no resistance as it pierced the soft tissue of Eamon's left eye, nor as it travelled deep into his brain before finally snapping in two.

Eamon died instantly, his body floating gently to the surface beside his bobbing paddle.

CHAPTER ONE

Dermot O'Connor lifted one of the dust-covered slats of the venetian blinds with the tip of his finger and peered through the window at the car idling outside. Two figures exited the beat-up 4x4 and looked up and down the street before striding purposefully towards Dermot's front door. Three loud raps echoed through the small entrance hall.

Dermot let out an irritated sigh and waited for the inevitable inquisition from his elderly father.

"Who's that at the door, Dermot?"

"It's okay. It's for me!" shouted Dermot, loud enough for his father to hear him in the back room.

"Don't open that door unless you know who it is," came the reply.

His father, now ninety-four, lived in a constant state of paranoia, as he'd done for most of his life. He'd taught Dermot from an early age to be suspicious of everyone, particularly the authorities. Every knock on the door could be *the one* — the Gardaí, the army, or even British agents. The latter would surely cause an international incident, if British forces were to carry out an operation on Irish soil, but they'd done it before.

You can't win a war from behind bars, was one of his father's frequent sayings.

"I told you, it's for me, da. Don't worry about it!" shouted Dermot as he bent to unlock the bolt at the bottom of the door. He did the same with the upper bolt and swung the door open with a rusty squeal.

His two visitors stood side-by-side, one facing outward, surveying the street of small terrace houses, the other with his hand raised preparing to knock again.

"Boss," said the first man, with a curt nod. His brother also turned and repeated the greeting before resuming his unnecessary surveillance duties.

The identical twins were difficult to tell apart, except when they opened their mouths. Joseph Kilpatrick, the older of the two by five minutes, had lost two front teeth in a fight on his first day in prison. His two assailants were unaware of his paramilitary connections at the time, but before the day was out, they'd been thoroughly educated and soon joined Joseph in the hospital wing, where they out-stayed him by some weeks.

Since his release, as part of the Good Friday Agreement, Joseph had become Dermot's right-hand man. They would meet every Friday in the back room of a local bar, along with a small group of other volunteers and supporters. At a secluded booth, they'd discuss the matters of the week. As the years passed, after the official end of the armed campaign in 2005, the *matters of the week* turned more to sport and world affairs than the campaign against the British establishment.

The size of his group also dwindled with time, although the Kilpatricks and a few other old-school members remained loyal. Occasionally, some new blood would join the group. Young, impressionable teenagers, angry at the world and flattered by the invite to join this secret club. The whispered tales of the struggle against the British occupation and the senior role that their leader had played would quickly seduce them.

"Boys," said Dermot, returning the nod. "Wait in the car. I'll be out in a minute."

Dermot closed the door again and lifted his green, waxed jacket from its usual spot on the banister at the bottom of the stairs. He patted the pocket, which bulged slightly. He never left the house without his grandfather's blackjack — a lead-filled thick leather pouch with a heavy-stitched leather handle — it was only about five inches long, but in the right hands it was lethal. A peaked cap completed his horse-trainer-like look.

"I'm heading out for a couple of hours, da," he said, as he poked his head into his father's bedroom.

Dermot Senior sat in bed reading a newspaper, which was over a week old. Not that it mattered, by the time he'd reached the bottom of a page he would've forgotten it all anyway. He rested his over-sized magnifying glass on the bed and looked up.

"Can you turn that light on? I can hardly see this," he said.

"Da, the power's out, remember?" said Dermot, rolling his eyes, then immediately feeling guilty.

"Huh? Oh yeah, right. Have you tried the fuse box?"

"No, it's out everywhere," explained Dermot for the hundredth time. "Why don't you sit out here? There's better light from the window."

"Aye, I might."

"Do you need a hand?" asked Dermot, knowing the reply.

"No, I don't need a hand. What do ye take me for, an invalid?"

I take you for a ninety-four-year-old pain in the ass, thought Dermot.

"Alright. I'll see if I can find a shop open anywhere and bring in some groceries," said Dermot as he turned and headed for the door, lifting a small sports bag from the chair on his way.

Anthony, the younger of the Kilpatrick brothers, held the back door open and ushered Dermot into the car. In his self-appointed role as bodyguard, all that was missing was for him to put his finger on his ear and talk into his cuff. In older times, such a blatant show of hierarchy would've been impossible, but Dermot secretly enjoyed the show of respect.

"So, what'd you find out?" asked Dermot, as the driver, a cousin of the Kilpatricks, pulled away from the curb.

"Yeah, it's true. Grinnley's ripping people off," said Joseph. "He's charging crazy prices for everything in the shop. Like €10 for a tin of beans, or a loaf of stale bread. He's even letting people pay with jewellery or other valuables."

Dermot shook his head and chewed on the inside of his bottom lip. "And how's that going down?"

"Not well. There's a crowd building outside. Some people are desperate, and prepared to hand over whatever they have just to get food for their family. Anyone who complains is soon sent on their way by his two sons. One of them has a shotgun."

"Well, let's have a chat with Mr Grinnley," said Dermot, making eye contact with the driver through the rear-view mirror.

The driver nodded and pulled out onto the near-deserted road into town.

Dermot turned back to Joseph. "Did you talk to Barry Doyle?"

"Yes, he has diesel, but there's an army patrol stationed at his place and they're only allowing Barry to give fuel to emergency vehicles," said Joseph.

"How many soldiers are there?"

"Just one jeep, two soldiers."

Dermot bobbed his head, pursing his lips in thought.

It was only a short drive to Grinnley's convenience store and as they rounded the final bend, Dermot could see the crowd that Joseph had reported. Those who hadn't yet entered the shop queued in a semi-orderly line which led from a row of temporary wire fence panels, the type you see around a building site, which had been hastily erected around the front of the shop. Dermot assumed that the burly youth manning the make-shift barrier was one of Grinnley's sons.

"Boss," said the driver, nodding towards a police car which was parked a couple of hundred yards from the shop. "The Guards are here."

The silhouette of the patrol car's two occupants could be seen through the back window.

"Pull in just in front of them," said Dermot.

Dermot saw his young driver's raised eyebrows in the mirror.

"It's okay, just pull in. I'll have a word with them," said Dermot calmly.

As the car eased to a stop a short distance from the Garda patrol car, Dermot placed the sports bag at his feet and pushed it under the seat in front of him, before stepping out into the morning sun. He instructed the others to stay in the car.

Seeing him approach, the two officers exited their car.

"Dermie O'Connor," said one of the two police officers with a tinge of derision, which wasn't lost on Dermot. He was the younger of the two, but his Sergent stripes made him the more senior. Dermot ignored him and directed his attention to the other, older officer, whom he knew.

"Thomas," said Dermot in greeting.

"Mr O'Connor," said the older officer in a much more respectful tone, which was more to Dermot's liking.

Dermot had been well known to the local authorities — more so in his earlier years — and had often been questioned on various matters, although never charged with any offence. After the ceasefire in the late 90s and during the arms decommissioning, his position as Quartermaster for the Donegal Brigade of the Provisional IRA became somewhat of an open secret.

"What can we do for you?" asked the Sergent.

"I'm just here to see what's going on," said Dermot with a smile.

"And what concern is it of yours?" asked the Sergent.

Dermot studied the younger man for a long moment, then looked to the other officer before slowly returning his gaze to the Sergent.

"Some members of the community have asked me to come and talk with Mr Grinnley," said Dermot with a glance down the road towards the growing crowd. "To see if I can help defuse the situation."

"So, you're a community worker now are you?" asked the Sergent, eyebrows raised.

"Something like that."

"Well, everything's under control here, so no need for you to get involved," said the Sergent.

Dermot frowned and rested both hands in the pockets of his jacket. He looked to the crowd outside the shop, then back to the Sergent. "Oh, so you've got everything under control from back here, have you?"

The colour began to rise on the Sergent's face.

"We've been told to keep our distance Dermot, we don't have the manpower..." said Thomas, before being cut off by a glare from his Sergent.

"Yeah, I thought so," said Dermot. "That's why you should head on to more important things and let us resolve this at the community level."

"We'll be going nowhere, and you'll do well to stay out of it," spat the Sergent, as he turned and headed back into his patrol car. "Let's go," he said to his partner, before falling into his seat and slamming the door.

"He seems like a nice guy. Is he new?" asked Dermot, his practised smile fixed firmly on the sergeant before slowly turning to Thomas.

The older officer smiled sheepishly. "Look, Dermot, the situation's pretty bad, and we don't have the manpower to deal with things like this."

"What about support from the army?"

The officer shook his head. "Most of them have been sent to Dublin or other strategic locations."

"Sounds about right. Donegal, the forgotten county," said Dermot.

The Sergent glared out over his steering wheel and tapped the horn.

"Right, I have to go," said Thomas, backing away. "Our shift ends at twelve."

Dermot returned to the car and instructed the driver to pull up outside the shop. He retrieved the sports bag from under the seat and held it in his lap.

"Right, keep these out of sight unless I say otherwise," he said, as he produced three Taurus revolvers and passed them to each of the occupants.

"We'll have a chat with Mr Grinnley and take it from there."

The four men exited the car, taking care to conceal the handguns, and approached the section of fencing which was manned by one of the shopkeeper's sons. A wave of murmurs rippled through the waiting queue as they passed. Most of the crowd recognised Dermot, or at least the Kilpatricks, and thought it best to keep quiet. One man began to voice his displeasure at them jumping the queue, only to be silenced by an elbow to the ribs and a whisper from his friend.

As Dermot and his group approached, the youth manning the temporary fence lifted the foot of one section from the heavy rubber block which held it in place, and let the next customer through. He looked up with tired, angry eyes. "Can you not see the queue?" he said, the sarcasm strengthened by his family's new position of authority.

"Tell your father that Dermot O'Connor is here and wants a word," said Joseph.

The young man's face twisted in defiance, and he shrugged. "He's busy. Join the queue," he said, before moving to slot the section of fencing back into place, but before he did, Joseph lent forward and whispered something in his ear. The young man's demeanour changed in an instant and he reeled back.

"Ah, okay, wait here a minute," he said, as he secured the fence and jogged inside to fetch his father.

Dermot surveyed the queue of desperate people waiting their turn, and the growing crowd of angry bystanders who'd either refused to pay the extortionate prices, or had come to protest at the injustice of the situation. He knew a few of the faces from about the town. One young broad-shouldered lad stood out. He lived on the same street as Dermot, Maria Tobin's lad – he couldn't remember his name. The young lad stared at Dermot, but there was no sign of recognition. His sunken, expressionless eyes seemed to stare right through him.

"Doc!" came a voice from the crowd. "I hope you're gonna do something about this."

Dermot recognised the man. He'd been in school with him fifty-some years previously. He wasn't a friend. In fact, he'd had several drunken run-ins with the man over the years. Dermot didn't react, but took a couple of steps towards the man.

"This fucker's ripping people off, and those useless pricks," he gestured up the street towards the parked police car, "sit there and do nothing."

Dermot followed the man's gaze towards the police car. "Yeah, so I see."

"He took my sister's engagement ring in exchange for baby food," said a red-faced man, the pitch of his voice heightened by fury.

"So, what are you gonna do?" said the first man. Murmurs from those around him echoed the question.

"I'll have a word and see what can be done," said Dermot.

At that, the gatekeeper returned. He held the fence open and beckoned for Dermot and his group to follow him.

"Wait out here," Dermot instructed his driver, the order acknowledged with a nod.

The shop was bigger than your average corner grocery store, the family business having gradually expanded over the years to cater for the growing local population. A handful of camping lanterns partially diluted the gloomy interior, their hum the only thing breaking the eerie silence.

Just inside, the elder of the two Grinnley boys rested against a lifeless chest freezer, a shotgun cradled in his arms. The Kilpatrick brothers hovered near the door as Dermot approached the owner at the far end of the first aisle, where a fold-out table had been positioned in front of the two disused checkouts.

Dermot held back, checking his watch as he waited for the latest shopper to finish settling up with Mr Grinnley. He met the man's eyes as he passed with his small box of provisions.

"I hope you brought the deeds to your fuckin' house," said the man.

Dermot stood with his hands resting in the pockets of his jacket and watched as the man strode from the shop, a wake of curses dropping like confetti behind him.

"Mr O'Connor," said Mr Grinnley, his tone buoyant and unapologetic. "We're running low on most things, but we should be able to get you sorted."

Dermot turned to regard the owner. "Mr Grinnley," he said with a smile. "Business is good, I see."

"Well, the government's food packages haven't made it this far north, so there's a lot of hungry people to feed," said the owner with a shrug, a greedy smile etched on his face. He approached and stood a couple of feet from his visitor.

Dermot smiled, "Yeah, looks like Dublin's forgotten about us." He glanced at the owner, then looked absently around the shop.

"Seems so," said the shopkeeper, all but rubbing his hands. "So, what can I get you?"

"I hear the prices have gone up a bit," said Dermot, with a side-long look and a playfully sarcastic smile.

The shopkeeper laughed, "Well, you know how it is. Supply and demand and all that."

Dermot nodded slowly and turned away again, struggling to maintain the facade of pleasantness.

"But don't worry about it. We'll get you what you need and you can sort me out some other time."

Dermot's fists tightened in his pockets, but he turned and smiled again at the owner.

"That's very kind."

"Well," said the owner, turning his palms up and shrugging in an *it's the least I can do* gesture.

"You know, some people are saying you're taking advantage of the situation."

"Ha, it's called Capitalism."

"Well, the power's gonna come back on at some point, and your customers aren't likely to forget. Or forgive," said Dermot. He continued to glance around the shop at the half empty shelves.

"Well, I have to think of my own family, you know. I'll be able to retire when this is all over."

Dermot registered the smug look on the man's face, then looked at a clock above the tills. It was 12.05. He smiled broadly in agreement, then turned slowly and locked eyes with Joseph for the briefest of moments. The two exchanged near imperceptible nods.

"So, what do you need, Doc?" said the owner, clapping his hands together lightly. "The only milk I've left is that long-life Soya stuff. It isn't great but…"

Dermot withdrew his hands from his pockets and, in a smooth, explosive movement, turned and drove his heavy leather blackjack straight up into Mr Grinnley's jaw. The shop owner's head whipped backwards, a sickening crack echoing through the shop. A follow-up jab to his exposed throat sent the man sprawling backwards, tins and jars clattering and smashing around him as his arms flailed in an attempt to arrest his fall.

Dermot turned to see Grinnley's eldest son look on in horror. The Kilpatricks had reacted as expected, and now had the lad pinned back against the freezer with his own shotgun across his chest, a handgun pressed tight against his temple.

Picking through the broken jars of beetroot and pickles, Dermot moved to where Mr Grinnley was now sprawled, clutching at his throat and fighting for breath. Ignoring the moans and choking gargles, he went down on one knee and grabbed a handful of the man's shirt and overalls. With a frenzy of savage blows, he reduced the man's face to a bloody mess, then wiped the blood from his grandfather's sap on his victim's shirt and placed it back in his pocket.

Dermot stood and closed his eyes, taking long, slow breaths to slow his racing heart. A droplet of sweat, or maybe blood, tickled his temple before being wiped away by his knuckle.

The cries and pleas of the man's eldest son filled the shop and brought his younger brother hurtling through the door, his run halted abruptly by the butt of a pistol to the bridge of his nose. He crumpled to the floor and added his voice to the chorus of moans and cries.

Dermot stepped over the unconscious shopkeeper and approached the counter. Joseph Kilpatrick joined him and waited for his boss to regain his composure.

"What's the plan, boss?"

Ignoring the question, Dermot lifted a small whiteboard which hung on a hook near the tills. With the edge of his hand, he erased the words *NO CREDIT*

GIVEN replacing them, in thick black marker, with the word *THIEF*.

The shopkeeper had begun to stir, and was now moaning through his bloodied and broken face.

"Tie him to the lamppost out front," said Dermot, handing the noticeboard to Joseph. "Put this round his neck."

Joseph nodded unquestioningly.

"And tell the people out there that if anyone touches him, they'll have to answer to me."

Dermot looked past Joseph to the two sons who were cowering in terror at the front of the shop, the younger Kilpatrick's gun sweeping back and forth between them.

"You two fuck off home. If you come back here before it's dark, you'll join your da. Do you understand me?"

The younger son clutched his broken nose and nodded. His older brother's defiance soon fading when prodded roughly with the barrel of a gun. Without a word, the two youths scrambled to their feet and spilled out through the door to run the gauntlet of the angry mob outside.

When Joseph returned to the shop after carrying out his boss's instructions, Dermot handed him a large cardboard box filled with supplies.

"Put this in the car. You and the boys can fill a box too and bring them home to your families."

"Ah, okay boss," said Joseph hesitantly. "The people outside are wondering what's gonna happen now."

Dermot nodded. "I want you to get a couple of volunteers from outside. You and your brother will stay here and let one person in at a time. Each person can fill one carrier bag and no more."

"What about payment?"

"No payment. This fucker's been paid enough."

CHAPTER TWO

Derek savoured his fresh coffee, occasionally wincing when the hot liquid stung his cut lip. He was normally a four or five-cup-a-day man. This was only his fourth cup in nearly a week. He wasn't sure if the tremors in his hands were from caffeine withdrawal, or from the physical and emotional toll that the previous couple of days had taken on him.

He wasn't the only one who was suffering. Simon sat beside him at the Keenan's huge rustic kitchen table, lost in thought and nursing a few bruises of his own. Derek had only known the guy for a couple of days, but he'd certainly shown his character in that short time; taking him and his family in when they'd had nowhere else to go and then putting his life on the line to save him and Lisa.

Yeah, solid guy, thought Derek.

"Who's for some scrambled eggs?" asked Moira, emerging from the larder.

"Yes, that'd be great. Thank you, Mrs Keenan," said Simon. "But are you sure you have enough?"

Moira smiled, "We've over sixty hens, love. So we've more eggs than we know what to do with. And call me Moira."

"Thank you, Moira," said Simon.

"Yes, please," said Derek. "Do you need a hand?"

"Not at all. Sit where you are."

Derek smiled; happy he didn't need to move.

"Jenny still in bed?" asked Moira, placing a large saucepan on the massive Aga stove.

"Yeah, she was up a couple of times with the baby last night."

"Well, we'll let her sleep and I'll get her something later."

The sound of a closing door and removal of boots announced the return of Ray from helping his father with the morning chores.

"What are you making, ma?" asked Ray, as he emerged from the back hall and made a beeline for a plate of freshly baked bread that his mother had just sliced.

"What do you think I'm making?" said Moira, smacking his hand away. "Leave that alone and go wash your hands."

Ray moved towards the kitchen sink.

Moira swiped at him with a tea towel. "Not there."

Ray let out an exaggerated moan and headed to the bathroom to wash up.

His mother rolled her eyes and shook her head at Derek. "Sometimes I think he's still a teenager."

The two men at the table gave polite chuckles.

Within a few minutes, Vinnie Keenan also arrived in from the back porch, and a near-identical scene played out again — a failed attempt to snatch some bread, an order to wash up, followed by a banishment to the bathroom.

Derek and Simon laughed again at the comical scene, however, the brief moment of levity did little to lift the mood at the table.

"Good morning," said Lisa, as she padded into the kitchen, rubbing the sleep from her eyes.

"Afternoon, you mean," said her mother, then tutted when she looked around at her daughter. "Lisa, put some clothes on, will you? We have visitors."

Lisa was in bare feet, pyjama bottoms and a tight white t-shirt which left nothing to the imagination, particularly given the cold floor. She frowned and shook her head, ignoring her mother's request.

Derek greeted her, but made a point to focus his gaze elsewhere. He noticed Simon was less discreet, his mood noticeably lifting with Lisa's arrival.

Despite there being ample space on the other side of the table Lisa chose to take the chair beside Simon. She smiled at him warmly before taking her seat, folding one leg up under herself.

How can that be comfortable? thought Derek.

"Hi Lisa," said Simon, returning her smile.

Derek used his coffee mug to hide a secret smile at the exchange.

Vinnie and Ray returned from cleaning up, each jokingly offering their hands, front and back, to Moira for inspection, before helping to serve their guests and taking their seats at the table.

"So, what the hell's going on in Belfast?" asked Vinnie.

"Vincent! Language," said Moira, with a glare.

Vinnie pulled his chin in and frowned. "What? I didn't curse, did I?" he said, genuinely confused.

"It's not just Belfast, daddy, it's everywhere," said Lisa.

Vinnie gave a shake of his head. "It's only a bloody power cut…"

"Vincent!" admonished Moira again.

Vinnie frowned at her and continued. "It's hardly the end of the world. I don't understand why people are going nuts. We've hardly noticed any difference. Apart from having no TV."

"I think you're an exception here, Vinnie," said Derek. "You've power from the wind turbine and enough food from the farm to get by."

"Ah, now, we've had our fair share of trouble the last couple of nights," said Vinnie, before shovelling a large forkful of scrambled eggs into his mouth.

Derek looked at Ray questioningly.

"Yeah, we've had a few trespassers poking around," said Ray. "That's why we were a bit jumpy last night when Simon here turned up on the doorstep." He tilted his fork at Simon and continued. "We had just chased a few lads away from behind the hen house."

"Who were they?" asked Lisa.

Ray shrugged. "Don't know. Probably after some of the birds."

Vinnie chuffed and took another mouthful from his mug. "I don't see why people can't just hunker down for a few days and wait for it to be sorted out."

Simon placed his fork down, a little more forcefully than maybe he meant to, obviously taking exception with what Vinnie was saying. "I'm sorry, Mr Keenan, but you don't seem to understand what's going on out there."

Vinnie took a sip of coffee and looked over his mug, eyebrows raised.

Derek could see the emotions welling up in Simon.

"You're living in a bit of a bubble here," said Simon. "In the real-world people haven't been able to get food, or even clean water in some cases, for nearly a week."

"Oh wow, a whole week," said Vinnie mockingly.

"Vinnie," said Derek, shaking his head, "seriously, it's not that simple. People can't get money from the ATMs, and even if they could, most shops aren't open. There's little or no communications, so the emergency services and government agencies are in chaos. Public transport is out and most fuel stations can't even pump fuel."

Simon bobbed his head, his face reddening.

"It's true, daddy," said Lisa. "It's a nightmare; I was working with the emergency committee and it was a shambles."

Vinnie didn't respond. Maybe he could see that he was upsetting his daughter and their guests.

"And this isn't just a few days," Lisa added. "This could go on for weeks or months, or even longer."

"That's what Martin was saying," said Simon. "He warned me last Sunday that the power cut was coming and that it would last for months."

"Who's Martin?" asked Vinnie.

"He's..." Simon hesitated, correcting himself. "He was a friend of mine. A physics professor."

Simon's head dropped, his shoulders sagging.

Derek felt his pain. He hadn't known Martin, but he was there when he died, and he saw how Simon had reacted to his friend's murder. He leaned forward to put a reassuring hand on Simon's shoulder but noticed that Lisa had beaten him to it. She placed her hand on top of Simon's under the table and continued for him.

"He was killed by drug addicts in Belfast on Thursday night," said Lisa softly. "Simon and Derek found him."

Vinnie shook his head. "I'm very sorry for your loss, Simon. You know what they say, it's normal in desperate times for normal people to do desperate things."

Simon made eye contact briefly and nodded.

"He'd just left my office," said Lisa.

Vinnie frowned slightly, clearly not yet understanding the relationship between all the parties involved.

"He'd been working with my office from Sunday, advising on the science," continued Lisa. "Not that it made much difference. Too much red tape.

"There just wasn't enough time to do anything," said Simon, re-joining the conversation.

A solemn silence fell across the table.

"So you two knew each other before all this?" asked Moira, directing her question to Lisa and Simon.

Lisa removed her hand from Simon's and lifted her cup.

"No," she said, "we only met once. When was that? Monday? Tuesday?" she asked, turning to Simon.

"Ah, Tuesday night, I think," said Simon.

"Oh. How'd you end up here?" asked Vinnie through a mouthful of eggs.

Derek could see the confusion on the rest of the Keenan family's faces. He couldn't blame them.

"It's a long story," Derek said, offering to take up the narrative.

He recanted the events of the week, occasionally handing the floor over to either Lisa or Simon. He talked about the situation at the prison; Ray quickly coming to his defence when he saw his friend starting to blame himself. He told them about the shopkeeper's murder, and meeting up with Simon. Simon and Lisa told of the chaos at the food distribution point from each of their perspectives, and then of how Martin had been killed for his car-load of supplies. A gambit of emotions played across the faces of the captivated audience; surprise, horror, and sadness.

Moira sat with her hands pressed to her face, her eyes welling up. Ray and Vinnie shook their heads in disbelief, and Lisa openly wept at hearing the full story of how Martin had died.

The table sat uncleared, dirty plates left in place, no one wanting to interrupt the stories being told; one more harrowing than the next. Simon's plate sat mostly untouched, despite his undoubted hunger. The retelling of the events clearly taking its toll on him.

It was when they described what'd happened at George's house, after Lisa had crashed her car, that the gravity of the situation hit home for Vinnie. His frustration and impotent rage boiled over. The realisation of how close his daughter had come to being killed herself, hit him hard. He got up from his chair and rounded the table before enveloping Lisa in a long embrace. When he released her, he held his hand out to Simon and almost pulled him to his feet, embracing him tightly.

"Thank you, Simon," he said, his own eyes now welling. He did the same with Derek, thanking him for saving his daughter.

"When things are back to normal, we'll have to pay this George a visit," said Vinnie, his gratitude and relief palpable.

The entire table sat, mostly in silence, for a time, the odd question coming from one of the Keenans, before Moira rose from her seat to offer more tea or coffee, as if that would help wash away the awful memories.

CHAPTER THREE

Simon sat on the edge of his bed, staring absently at the floor in front of him. He wasn't sure how long he'd been sitting in that same position, but when the sound of a door closing somewhere in the Keenan house shook him from his daze, he noticed a stiffness in his neck.

He was a mentally resilient person — or so he liked to think — but he knew his mental health was now hanging from a cliff by its fingertips. In the past three days, he'd seen six dead bodies. Two of them he'd actually seen die. One of them, his best friend, had bled to death in his arms after being stabbed as he waited for Simon at his locked gate. The paralysing sense of guilt hit him in waves; if only he'd been more vigilant when watching for his friend, or if he'd been fitter, and able to get to the gate sooner.

He took a deep breath and blew it out forcefully, trying again to reset himself. But within seconds, his shoulders had slumped, and again he stared vacantly at the floor, the anxiety welling in his chest as a circus of violent, gruesome scenes consumed him; Janet's crumpled form curled in the corner of a darkened elevator, Seamus' thick white beard soaked red with his own blood as it pooled around his dead body, and the men in George's house, one of which Simon himself had helped to kill. The memory of sickening smells accompanied each image which, even now, made him nearly retch.

A rap on his door pulled him from his latest trance.

"Yes?"

The door opened slightly, and Lisa peered around it.

"Hey, how's it going?" she asked in a gentle, sympathetic tone, as if she knew exactly where his thoughts had been.

He straightened and smiled. "Hey. Yeah, not too bad."

When he'd first moved to Ireland, he'd laughed at how it was such a negative way to answer that question — as if the best people could expect was for things to be not *too* bad. He'd later realised that even if someone was having the worst day of their lives, they'd still answer with *not too bad*.

In this case, it was a lie. Things were too bad. Things were as bad as they could get.

Brave face, and all that, he thought.

"Thought you might fancy a bit of fresh air," said Lisa. "I could give you a tour of the farm if you like."

Simon hesitated for a beat, considering if he'd rather continue to sit and stew in his own thoughts, "Yeah, that sounds good," he finally said, with a smile and a nod.

Lisa looked down at his trainers. "Do you have anything a bit more sturdy than those? It's mucky out there."

"Ah," Simon hesitated again. He wasn't sure what he'd packed, he couldn't even remember doing it.

"I'm not sure," he laughed. "I'll have a look and see what I brought."

"Okay, sure. I'll wait for you downstairs."

When the door closed, Simon stood and took another deep, fuelling breath. His rucksack sat propped against the dresser in the corner. Hefting it onto the bed, he dragged the contents out, roughly segregating the clothes into groups; socks, underwear, tops and jeans. The walking boots, which he half-remembered packing, were wedged together at the bottom.

Pulling off his trainers, keen not to keep Lisa waiting, he donned the first boot, then stopped. He held his palm over his face, not knowing whether to laugh or cry, and given his current state of mind, he felt that crying was never too far away. In his distracted state of mind, he'd packed two odd shoes. Both were walking boots, but one was new, unblemished brown leather, the other an old leather/canvas mix; half tan, half green, which leaked if he remembered correctly. He shook his head and laced the boots up anyway.

You look like a total idiot, he thought, as he pulled the bottom of his jeans as low as they'd go in an attempt to disguise the boots.

It was a pleasant September day, but Simon carried his raincoat over his arm just in case — it was the north-west of Ireland, after all. He followed Lisa down a small set of steps from the back porch into a concrete-surfaced yard which separated the house from a tall conventional looking shed on the right, and a long low-roofed shed on the left, which he assumed was home to the chickens. Directly ahead, making up the fourth side of the square, was an open-sided structure in which various pieces of machinery and tractors were arranged haphazardly, some seemingly used more often than others. Behind the machinery-shed, the blades of a large wind turbine could be seen, silently churning, despite the absence of any noticeable breeze.

Lisa had dressed more appropriately than Simon, experience telling her that Wellington boots would be a wise choice. She carried a long walking stick, which she jokingly raised in the air, the way a tour guide in a big city might do to attract the attention of their party.

She turned and smiled. Simon found comfort in her ability to laugh and joke, despite the fact that the world was falling to pieces around them.

"Today's tour will start in two minutes," she said, in a mockingly formal voice, "Mr..."

She stopped and laughed, returning to her own native accent, "Shit, I forget your last name, Simon."

"Wilson," said Simon, surprised to feel a smile spread across his own face.

"Well, if Mr Wilson would like to follow me, we can begin the tour."

Simon nodded and slid his arms into his jacket, more for convenience than protection from the elements.

"Well, here we have a shed, another shed and on this side... a shed," she said, spinning on the spot and pointing her stick to each of the structures in turn. She led him to the left, past the hen house. The bitter stench became increasingly pungent the closer they got. It caught in his throat and he could feel his eyes begin to water.

"How do you get used to that smell?" asked Simon, before realising how rude that must've sounded.

"Oh, I'm sorry," said Lisa, putting a hand on her stomach. "I've a bit of an upset tummy."

Simon's face flushed red, then he laughed and shook his head.

"Nah, you'll hardly notice it after a couple of days," said Lisa, taking delight in his embarrassment.

The chorus of warbles and clucks, spilling from the row of high windows, rose in intensity as they reached the side of the building.

"So, how many chickens do you keep in there?"

"About sixty or seventy, I think," said Lisa. "And we call them hens, city boy!"

They continued beyond the hen house and along a path which lead past the towering wind turbine.

"Jeez, I never realised how big these things were," said Simon, looking up at the tall white pylon which held the three massive blades. "Does that give enough electricity to power everything?"

"Yeah, more than enough. It's a 25kW, whatever that means," said Lisa. "It's apparently enough to power about three or four properties."

Simon nodded, his eyebrows raised, suitably impressed.

"My dad had it put in about five years ago."

"I'm sure he's glad he did."

"Actually, it was supposed to be shared with the neighbour," said Lisa, extending her stick towards a property a couple of fields over which had an array of antennas reaching up towards the sky. "But the guy pulled out at the last minute."

"What's with all the aerials?"

"He's a ham radio enthusiast," said Lisa. "Breaker breaker, ten-four and all that."

"Ha, he'll be regretting it now."

"I'm sure he is. It caused a bit of a falling out at the time, but the guy had fallen on hard times just when he was supposed to chip in."

"Right?"

"Yeah, they're talking again now. He's a nice enough guy. A wee bit weird, but not a bad guy."

"So, is it connected to the grid too?"

"No, it just charges a stack of batteries in there," said Lisa, pointing to a small shed attached to the back of the machinery shed.

"Right. That's makes sense. I might be wrong, but I think if it was connected to the grid, then it probably wouldn't have worked after the CME."

"Don't know," said Lisa. "And then there's the solar tubes on the roof that heat the water."

"That's optimistic in Donegal."

"Well, there's gas too as a backup. My dad really got into the whole self-sufficiency thing a few years ago."

"We're all lucky he did," said Simon.

They walked on along a small lane, which had been worn down by tractor tracks, a grassy ridge snaking down the centre.

"So, how far does the farm stretch?"

"We used to have about 200 acres, but dad sold a lot off over the years. A couple of developers bought some and built a few holiday homes for you city folk."

"I'm sure that went down well with the locals," said Simon sarcastically.

"Yeah, he took some stick for it. But it let him semi-retire and take life a bit easier. So he put up with it."

"I'm sure."

They veered off the track and Lisa led them to a clearing by a river where a bench sat overlooking a small fishing stand that jutted out from the bank.

"This was always my favourite spot," said Lisa. "I would come down here and read for hours, just to get away from the house. It can be pretty boring for a teenager living on a farm."

"Are there fish in it?"

"Yeah, Ray used to fish a lot. He would bring in the odd salmon now and then."

They sat on the bench and looked out over the water. The gurgling of the river and tweets from the birds in the nearby trees was soothing. It would've been easy to forget the turmoil facing the world.

Simon shook his head. "I thought Martin's place in Fermanagh was the ideal spot for riding this thing out, but this place is perfect."

Simon leaned his elbows on his knees and let out a deep sigh.

"Are you okay?" asked Lisa.

"I was just thinking about Martin's mum and brother," he glanced at Lisa, then away again. "They'll still be waiting for him, expecting him to turn up at any minute."

Simon rested his head in his hands. He was struggling to hold it together. Lisa placed a comforting hand on his shoulder.

"I still can't believe he's gone," he said, with a slow shake of his head.

"I know. It's just not fair. He did everything right, had it all planned out," said Lisa, removing her hand and leaning forward, mirroring Simon. "If I hadn't have convinced him to stay and work with us..."

Simon could see that the joking and fun had left Lisa. He'd dragged her into his pool of depression and despair.

"Hey, you can't think like that," said Simon, mustering whatever positivity he could. "All he wanted was for someone to listen to him. You gave him that."

"For all the good it did," said Lisa.

The pair sat quietly, lost in their thoughts.

"I wonder how George and his wife are getting on?" said Lisa, finally breaking the silence. "I hope he manages to get some help."

"Yeah, I felt bad leaving them there."

"I shudder to think what would've happened to me if he hadn't brought me in," said Lisa, shaking away the possibilities.

"I'll certainly be going back to check on them, when all this is over," said Lisa, after another period of solemn silence. "Whenever that might be."

"Yeah, God knows when things will get back to normal," said Simon.

Lisa stood and tossed a pebble into the river. "Right, let's continue this tour that you've paid for," she said, in her tour guide voice. She seemed to be able to pull herself from the darkness much easier than Simon could. He liked that.

"We'll go back this way," she said, gesturing to a small path running along the river. "I'll show you the Keenan ancestral home."

Simon frowned inquisitively and pushed himself up from the bench to follow.

Within a short distance, they passed through a small apple orchard, and Simon could see what looked like the ruins of an old building.

"This was my great grandfather's house, the original Keenan farmhouse," said Lisa.

"Wow, so your family's been here for a long time," said Simon.

As Lisa disappeared around the corner of the old stone house, Simon heard a brief high-pitched yelp, followed by a string of expletives. When he rounded the corner, he found Lisa lying on her back, looking up at him.

"What happened? Are you alright?" asked Simon, his voice pitched in concern.

"Yeah, just twisted my ankle a bit."

Simon held out his hand to help her up. Lisa rubbed her muddy hands on her jeans and let Simon help her to feet.

She steadied herself, then looked down at the hole that she'd fallen into. It was about a foot deep and a couple of feet wide.

Lisa snatched up the walking stick, her face now red with a mix of rage and embarrassment. "Who the fuck would dig a hole there?"

"There's more," said Simon, pointing to two more similar-sized, freshly dug holes, a spade still protruding from one of them.

Lisa frowned and shook her head, mumbling more curses under her breath.

"Are you okay? Can you walk?" asked Simon.

"Yeah, it's not too bad."

Not too bad. Probably broken then, thought Simon.

He reach down and took her by the elbow. "Here, put some of your weight on me."

"It's okay, I think it's fine," she said, but let him aid her all the same as they headed back towards the main house.

CHAPTER FOUR

Lisa tentatively negotiated the steps to the back porch, and with a sigh of relief, lowered herself onto a wooden storage bench. She leaned back against the jumble of coats which hung from an overloaded coat rack, before easing the boot off her throbbing left foot.

"How is it?" asked Simon.

She peeled off her sock and gently rubbed at her ankle, which was warm to the touch but not yet swelling. "I think it's okay."

"You should get some ice on it to stop the swelling," said Simon, who carefully eased past her into the kitchen.

"Would you have some ice, Moira?"

"Oh, what happened?" asked her mum, rising quickly from the table.

"It's okay," said Lisa, through the open door. "I just turned my ankle." She slid her other boot off and gingerly made her way through to the kitchen – clutching on to the door handle, then the worktop, and then the chair – to keep as much weight off the foot as possible.

Frowning, her mum knelt to examine the injury. "Let me see it. Right, sit there and put your foot up," she ordered, pulling a chair out from the table and sliding another in to place opposite it.

"Simon, will you grab a couple of cushions from that chair, please? So that she can raise it up. I'll get some ice," she said, directing Simon to a small two-seater sofa at the far end of the room, before hurrying off to the freezer.

Lisa shook her head at the fuss being made, but did as she was told.

Simon retrieved the cushions and positioned them under Lisa's foot, which was now starting to redden. Her mum returned with some ice wrapped in a tea towel and gently balanced it across Lisa's ankle, making slight adjustments to get it to sit correctly.

"Okay Simon, can you get me my medical kit from that cupboard, please?" asked Moira, pointing to a long larder-like cupboard behind the kitchen door.

"Sure."

"How did you do that?" said Moira, her tone a mix of concern and admonishment.

"I fell into a hole out by the old house," said Lisa, her brow pinched in anger, partly at herself, and partly at whoever had dug holes and left them uncovered.

"Is this it?" asked Simon, as he slid a large bright-red rucksack from the cupboard and placed it beside Moira. The medical kit was only about the same size as his own camping backpack, which now contained everything he owned. Every surface had a compartment which bulged and strained against the multiple heavy duty straps.

Moira seemed to know exactly where to look for the items she needed and extracted some gel and a thick stretch bandage.

Lisa could see from Simon's expression that he was impressed by her mum's over-the-top first aid kit.

"That's a serious medical kit, Moira," he said, as if on cue.

"Good to be prepared," said Moira, without looking up.

"Mum used to be a trauma nurse," said Lisa, frowning as her mum lifted her foot and began to wrap the swelling ankle. "She stole all this stuff from the hospital."

"Lisa! I *did not*. Don't be saying that. Simon will believe you."

"Careful," hissed Lisa, a stab of pain evaporating all levity as her mum tightened the dressing.

"Do you want to do it yourself?"

"You can't leave holes like that uncovered. Someone'll break a leg," said Lisa, returning to the subject of the excavated ground. "Why are yous digging holes up there for, anyway?"

"What holes?" said her father, as he ambled through from the sitting room, book in hand and reading glasses dangling from a chain around his neck. "What'd you do?"

He looked down at her leg propped up on the chair and shook his head. "Were you not wearing proper boots?"

Lisa's frown deepened. "I *was* wearing proper boots."

"It was a pretty deep hole," said Simon, backing her up.

Vinnie looked at Simon, then down at his footwear. One bushy eyebrow arched, as if pulled by a string, and he nodded at Simon's mismatched boots, a hint of a smile curling the edges of his mouth. "Are you wearing odd shoes lad?"

Simon looked down and let out an embarrassed laugh. "Ha, yeah, the joys of packing in the dark."

Ray eased past his father, catching the tail-end of the conversation, "Nice shoes mate," he said, as he made his way to the sink with a couple of dirty mugs.

Simon's face reddened, and he gave Ray an embarrassed smile.

"What happened to you?" said Ray, seeing Lisa's extended leg.

"Twisted my ankle," sighed Lisa, growing more annoyed with each additional question.

"Idiot," said Ray, with a big-brotherly jibe.

Lisa's face twisted in a sour smirk, which would've been accompanied by a *fuck off,* had her mother not been in earshot.

Two loud knocks on the front door echoed along the hall, distracting the group from Lisa's injury. All heads turned in the direction of the sound.

"Who would that be," said Moira, immediately flustered into visitor-mode. She smoothed her dress and reassembled the medical kit.

Ray exchanged a wordless glance with his dad, then strode off down the hall.

"Hey, Michael. Come on in," said Ray, his voice raised to give those in the kitchen a few seconds warning of their neighbour's arrival.

"That's the neighbour I was telling you about," whispered Lisa to Simon, who'd taken a seat at the table.

"Hello all," said Michael, as he entered the kitchen. "Oh, what happened Lisa?"

Lisa shook her head. "Ah, I just went over on my ankle. Some *idiot* dug a hole and didn't cover it," she said, directing a scowl at her brother.

"Don't look at me," said Ray.

"Have a seat, Michael," said Moira. "Can I get you a cup of tea?"

"Ah now, I wouldn't want to put you out," said Michael, taking a seat anyway. "Well, maybe just a wee cup."

Michael stroked his thick beard, which was greying slightly, slowly catching up with his long, now mostly white hair, which he kept pulled back in a thin ponytail.

"I wouldn't mind a wee cup too, love," said Vinnie, pulling a seat up at the end of the table.

"Well, how's it going Michael? I assume your power's still off?" said Vinnie.

Michael nodded solemnly, the nod turning quickly to a slow shake. "It is, and it's likely to stay off for the foreseeable."

"Are you hearing anything on the radio, Michael?" asked Ray, as he stood at the sink busily drying mugs from the draining board.

"Aye, bits and pieces." He pressed his lips together and shook his head again. "It's not good, not good at all. I've only been able to stay on for a couple of hours a day."

"Right?" said Ray, stepping up to the table and passing the dried mugs out.

Michael turned to Vinnie, a slight apologetic expression playing across his face. "That's the reason I came over. I don't like to ask Vinnie, but would you mind if I charged up a couple of batteries? My solar panels are barely giving me enough to keep the receiver going."

"Not at all, whatever you need. We're not even running the turbine at full capacity," said Vinnie.

Lisa wondered if Michael would take that as a bit of dig at him, for not joining in on the wind turbine venture. She knew her dad hadn't meant it that way at all though. He wasn't one to hold a grudge and certainly wasn't the type to rub someone's nose in it.

"Thank you, Vinnie. That's very kind."

"Ray will sort you out."

"Yes, not a problem. I'll get you a few of our backups, they're fully charged and sure you can give me your empty ones and we'll put them on the charge," said Ray.

"That's great Ray, thank you."

"So, are you getting through to anyone?" asked Vinnie.

Michael bobbed his head, his brow creasing.

"Sorry, Michael. This is Simon. Lisa's… friend," said Vinnie, gesturing to Simon who sat across from his neighbour.

Lisa could feel her cheeks flush slightly, and she fidgeted and adjusted the ice pack on her foot. *Nice one daddy. He probably thinks Simon's my boyfriend or something,* she thought. She stole a glance at Simon to see if he'd picked up on it. He hadn't, it would seem.

"Nice to meet you, Michael," said Simon, rising and reaching across to shake Michael's hand.

"Oh, here he is," said Moira, in a cheerful sing-song voice, as Derek appeared carrying a baby carrier, followed closely by Jenny with the subject of Moira's delight cradled in her arms. Moira instructed Ray to take over the tea making duties and immediately started to fuss over the infant.

"And you've met Derek and Jenny before, I think?" said Vinnie.

"Ah, yes, I think I have," said Michael, craning his neck.

"Yeah, a couple of years ago, at Vinnie's birthday," said Derek.

"Oh my God, daddy I completely forgot, it's your birthday today," said Lisa.

"Aye, don't worry about it love, people have more important things on their minds at the minute."

A chorus of birthday salutations followed and when Ray arrived with a huge pot of tea, the mood soon settled to a more sombre tone.

"It's bad everywhere," said Michael. "Everywhere!"

"Even in Dublin?" asked Vinnie.

"I don't just mean across Ireland, I mean *everywhere*!" said Michael, drawing out the word for emphasis.

"Where have you been in contact with?" asked Lisa.

"I've personally spoken to people in a few countries in Europe, but some friends of mine, who've more powerful setups than mine, have spoken to people in America and Asia. It's the same all over. All power networks are down and the governments are in tatters."

Vinnie used a sip from his cup to hide a slight cringe of scepticism. Lisa could see that her father still didn't believe the true extent of the problem.

"How can things just fall apart so quickly?" asked Moira. "Surely the authorities have plans for this kind of thing?"

"I'm telling you, mum, there were no plans for this kind of thing."

"Lisa was part of an emergency committee thing in Belfast last week," Vinnie explained to Michael.

"Oh right? You must have firsthand knowledge then?" said Michael, keen to get some hard facts, which he would undoubtedly relay to his ham radio buddies.

"Well, the speed that it hit, and the sheer scope," Lisa directed her statement more to her parents than to Michael, "meant that there was no time to react."

"Yeah, that's what I'm hearing from all over," said Michael, bobbing his head between sips of tea.

"Yip, I can confirm that too," said Derek from the sofa by the window, where he and Jenny sat with their son.

"That's a fucking understatement," said Ray.

"Raymond! Watch your language," said Moira, accompanied by a prolonged glare.

Vinnie still didn't seem to be convinced. "Hold on," he said, setting his mug on the table. "Every country has had power cuts before. They always get it up and running again. Alright, sometimes it might take a few days, but they always get it sorted."

"This is different, daddy," said Lisa, the irritation clear in her voice.

"Lisa's right, Vinnie," said Michael. "I'm hearing it from all over. If the problem were confined to a specific area, like in a normal power cut, then help would come from the outside. They'd bring in whatever people and equipment they needed to fix the problem, and that would be it."

Lisa nodded in agreement, but allowed Michael to continue; more chance of her parents listening to a stranger.

"The problem here is that it's not limited to a single area, or even country, and when you add the lack of communications; it's a perfect storm," said Michael.

"So, we can't just call someone for help, daddy," added Lisa. "And even if we could, they're in the same situation. If they have the replacement parts, like transformers and things like that, they need them themselves."

"So, what are you saying? The power could be off for weeks?" asked Vinnie.

"At least," said Lisa. "God only knows when things will get fully back to normal."

"Fuel is gonna become a serious problem," said Ray, from his position by the sink.

"It already is," said Michael. "I'm hearing reports of people rioting at petrol stations. Those that can pump their fuel at all, are being taken over by the authorities, or in some cases armed gangs."

"Ah come on, that's ridiculous," spat Vinnie. "The power's been off for less than a week. Do you think people would just go crazy over night? I think it's all exaggerated."

"It's not exaggerated!" said Simon, anger that had been building in him erupted. "I'm sorry, Mr Keenan, but you've no clue what's going on out there. People have reached breaking point. They woke up one day and had no lights, no heating, and very little food, and no way to get more."

Vinnie sat back in his chair, obviously surprised by this quiet Englishman's outburst.

"I've been in the middle of angry crowds, fighting over food packages. I've witnessed shops being looted and their owners murdered." Simon stood and pushed his chair back. "I held my best friend's head in my hands as he bled to death," Simon's voice was now breaking, his breath hitching. "Stabbed repeatedly for a few boxes of food."

"Alright mate, take it easy," said Ray, hands extended.

"No, I won't take it easy." Simon pushed past Ray on his way to the door. "You people need to wake up to what's going on."

A stunned silence filled the room. Lisa moved to follow Simon, but Derek had already risen from the sofa and gestured for her to stay where she was. "I'll see if he's okay."

The rest sat wide-eyed with eyebrows raised, not sure what to say.

"Well, anyone want a refill?" asked Moira, rising from her chair as if nothing had happened.

"He's right, daddy, things are out of control," said Lisa, more calmly than her racing heart should've allowed.

Vinnie sat forward. "Well, I suppose you've all been through a lot in the last few days," he said, a air of contrition in his voice. "Maybe we have been a bit sheltered from it here."

"Well, you're in the ideal situation here, Vinnie," said Michael. "You've your own power, enough food to feed an army, and you even have the river in case the water goes off."

"Yeah, I suppose we're lucky."

"People in town aren't getting it so easy," said Michael. "You know Grinnley's shop?"

Vinnie nodded. "Yeah, I went to school with him."

"He's taking the piss," said Michael, passing his cup to Moira for a refill. "He's jacked up his prices, like tenfold, and is even taking jewellery from people as payment."

"He always was a prick," said Vinnie, before looking to Moira for the expected rebuke.

"Can the Guards not do something about that, or the army?" asked Moira.

"From what I hear, the Guards are stretched to breaking point, and the army has mostly been redeployed to Dublin or other important locations."

"As usual, the North West is left to fend for itself," said Vinnie, with a huff.

"There's a public meeting tomorrow in the community centre at two. Might be worth checking it out to see what they're saying."

"Ray, maybe you could bring some food over to your auntie Maria and Conor?" said Moira. "Oh, Lisa, I didn't get to tell you about Conor's poor wee friend."

Lisa frowned and tilted her head inquisitively.

"He was killed out on the lake last Saturday when he was out with Conor," said Moira.

"Oh my God, what happened?"

"Some freak accident. He hit his head on something, diving off the jetty," said Moira. "Poor family, they haven't even been able to have the funeral or anything."

"Yes, I'll bring them something over," said Ray, coming back to his mum's initial request.

"Michael, do you need anything other than the batteries?" asked Moira. "You'll take some eggs, and maybe some potatoes, will you?"

"I wouldn't say no, Moira. As long as you can spare them."

CHAPTER FIVE

Dermot O'Connor didn't hear the driver's question, he was lost in his thoughts, feelings of anger and remorse consuming him. He'd snapped at his father again, for not understanding what was going on, and of course, for throwing his dinner across the room. The bowl of Weetabix and cold soya milk, which Dermot had gone out of his way to procure and prepare, now stained the wall and curtains. The old man was infuriating. Dermot told himself it was the dementia, but he knew his dad had always been a sour, angry bully, who was rarely pleasant to be around.

Dermot had more important things to deal with. He shook his head and tried to release the tension that had tightened his core. Looking out the window, he realised they had yet to start moving.

"What are you waiting on?" he shot the driver an icy glare, locking eyes with him in the rear-view mirror.

"I need to know where we're going Boss," said the driver. A tinge of attitude in his voice forced Dermot's fists to tighten into balls.

"Are you being a fuckin' smartass? Where do you think we're going?" Dermot's rage had found an outlet.

I should split this useless prick's skull. He pictured himself launching through the space between the seats and ripping the arrogant fucker's face off. *If he looks at me again in that mirror, I fuckin' will,* Dermot told himself. Then he stared, waiting, willing the driver's smug eyes to look at him again in the long, dirt-covered mirror. He could feel the heat rising around his neck, his pulse racing.

"Sorry boss, I just wanted to make sure," said the driver, twisting in his seat to face Dermot, careful not to let his gaze rest too long on his boss. "Mac's? Right?"

"Yes!"

"The Killpatricks and a few of the others are already there waiting for you," said the driver, turning to face the road again and pulling away from the curb.

Dermot didn't reply. He knew his actions against the insubordinate volunteer would've been fully justified, but he forced himself to relax and to think of the problems at hand.

Mac's Bar, if you could call it a bar, was no more than a couple of small rooms off an alleyway between two shops. Access was granted through a hatch-like door in a set of thick wooden gates, which were likely only ever opened to allow the delivery of crates and kegs of beer. There was no name above the gates, nor drinks company logos advertising the presence of the establishment. If you didn't know exactly where it was, you'd walk straight by, and if you did manage to accidentally stumble inside, you'd likely be met with the silent, suspicious, and questioning eyes of the handful of regular patrons.

As the car eased to stop, Dermot could see Joseph and his brother standing by the gates, awaiting his arrival. The younger Kilpatrick stepped forward and opened Dermot's door, for which he received a curt nod.

"Boss," said Joseph.

"What's the situation at Grinnley's?" asked Dermot as he approached the door to the run-down pub, which acted as their unofficial headquarters.

"I left Maguire in charge. He's coordinating things," said Joseph. "But he'll not need to be there much longer, the place is nearly cleared out."

Dermot nodded and ducked in through the small door in the middle of the gates.

"We picked up a few more volunteers today," said Joseph, as he followed Dermot through the gate. "A lot of people are pissed off with what's going on and want to do something."

"Who are they?" asked Dermot. "We don't want any strangers."

"They're known to us, or at least their families are," said Joseph.

"Okay. Good," said Dermot, as he entered the front room of the bar. The place was dreary and depressing at the best of times. Now it was cold and dark, and stank of stale beer and body odour. The wooden shutters had been pulled back from the front window, years of grime half-heartedly wiped away to let some light through. With the aid of a few candles, Dermot could see his ragtag group of volunteers huddled in groups around the handful of tables.

He strode to the small counter in the corner, which acted as the bar.

"Guinness?" asked the barman.

"Yes please, Tommy."

When his Guinness had settled, he took a generous mouthful, then turned to address his expectant audience.

"Okay then, let's get down to business," he said, surveying the room. "I see we've a few new faces. It's good to see that when the establishment fails, we can still rely on good men and women to step up."

"So, what'll we be doing?" said a new face from the corner of the room. All eyes turned to the newcomer, a young lad in his late teens or early twenties.

Dermot squinted through the gloom to see who'd spoken. "Who's that now? What's your name?"

"Oisín Gallagher," said the young man, taking a tentative step forward. "I was just wondering what we'd be needed for."

"Anything to Paddy Gallagher?" asked Dermot.

"Aye, he was me ol' man."

"Yeah, I can see it. You're the spitting image of him. He was a good man," said Dermot. "Well, good to have you here, Oisín. As for your question. Well, you've all seen how the authorities have handled this crisis so far." He turned to address the rest of the room. "The guards are useless and Dublin seem to have forgotten about us, as usual. There's been looting and break-ins, and people generally taking advantage of the situation, and all of it going unanswered."

"That scumbag Grinnley got what was coming to him," said a voice from the end of the bar.

"Aye, but what about the joyriders? My ol' man got his car stole the other night and the fuckers just raked up and down the street without a care in the world," said someone else.

Dermot nodded, "Well, it's clear that it's up to us to protect the community."

"What about food, Dermot?" said the only woman in the room. "The packages the army gave out were a joke, and by the time most of us even heard about them, they were all gone."

"Yes, Fiona," said Dermot. "That's something we have to sort out."

"My brother works for Lidl, and he says that they've tons of food that's just rotting away," said another of the younger men.

"Does he have access to the store?" asked Dermot.

"No, they locked the place up at the start of the week, and now there's an army patrol out the front. It's a fuckin' joke."

"Okay, well, it's up to us then. We're gonna have to look after our own community. We have to take control."

Murmurs of agreement rolled around the room.

"I'll warn you, though, things might have to get ugly if we're gonna do what needs to be done," said Dermot sternly.

"What happens when the electric comes back on though, Doc?" asked Oisín.

Dermot locked eyes with the young man. "We've no idea when that'll be, Oisín, but what we do know is that something has to be done now."

"To start with, we're gonna put a stop to the joyriding and the burglaries. Joseph here will split you up into groups," said Dermot, looking to his right-hand man. "We'll organise some checkpoints and patrols to keep the streets safe."

Joseph stepped up beside Dermot and nodded in agreement.

"We'll work on the details and let you know. For now, we'll be operating from here," said Dermot, turning and receiving the expected nod from the owner behind the bar.

He lifted his pint from the counter and gestured to the Kilpatricks and a couple of his other long-term followers, and headed through to their usual spot in the back room.

The barman brought some candles and positioned them around the table beside the well-worn dart board, and the small group huddled in close.

"Okay, Joseph," said Dermot, once the door had been closed. "What's the situation with the Keenans'?"

Joseph shifted uncomfortably in his seat. He clearly didn't have good news. "We were out there again last night, but we still haven't been able to find the exact spot."

Dermot glared at his second in command and shook his head, "How fuckin' difficult can it be? I've drawn you a map."

"I think we were close, but then Ray Keenan and his ol' fella came out with shotguns and we had to leg it."

Dermot clenched his jaw and narrowed his eyes at Joseph.

"You said you wanted us to do it quietly, so I thought it was better for us to leave. We can go back tonight," said Joseph defensively.

"So, Raymond's back, is he?" asked Dermot, rubbing his chin. "Right, I want you to go out there and talk to him."

Joseph frowned. "I thought you said he doesn't know anything about them?"

"He doesn't," said Dermot with a sigh. "Just tell him I need to speak to him."

"Will do."

"Right, I want you to go and check out the situation at the supermarket," said Dermot, to another of his inner circle. "I want to know how many soldiers are there?"

He turned back to Joesph, "We'll need a van, the bigger the better. And you'll need to go and see Barry about diesel for it."

"That might be difficult with the army patrol there too," said Joseph.

"Well, we'll just have to reason with them," said Dermot with a smile. "Although that might be a bit easier when we're properly armed."

A waft of air blew across the table as the barman pushed the door open, carrying a tray of fresh pints. The candle in the middle of the table strained against the breeze, then blinked out, leaving a thin trail of smoke.

"For fuck's sake, this is ridiculous," said Dermot, sitting back in his chair.

"Sorry Doc, let me get that for you," said the barman, setting the tray down and relighting the candle before retreating again.

"We can't run this operation from here, this is crazy," said Dermot, folding his arms across his chest.

"You know what?" said Dermot, as if a solution had just occurred to him. "The Keenan's have a great set up out there. They have power from a wind turbine and grow their own food."

"They've hens too," said Anthony Kilpatrick.

Dermot pinched his lower lip between his fingers and looked down at the table, then back to Joseph. "Get Ray Keenan here asap."

CHAPTER SIX

Derek stepped out into the afternoon sun, its rays poking through the clouds for what was likely to be only a brief visit. Darker skies in the distance promised a colder, wetter evening to come. The harsh, unmistakable ring-ding clatter of a two-stroke engine immediately told him where he would find Ray.

As he approached the machinery shed, he saw his friend squatting behind his beloved, and much talked about, Yamaha scrambler, one hand reaching up to twist the throttle and send another chorus of deafening coughs echoing through the enclosed yard. The immaculately clean blue and yellow dirt bike rested on a T-frame stand, the back wheel spinning furiously.

"Have you ever actually ridden that thing?" shouted Derek, picking a beat between revs.

Ray raised his head, then reached across to kill the engine. "What ya say?"

"That thing looks like it's just out of the showroom," said Derek. "You just like to stare at it and polish it don't you?"

"Yeah, yeah. I'd like to see you try to handle it," said Ray with a smirk.

"Wouldn't want to get it dirty on you."

Derek leaned against a bench just inside the shed, looking round him at the various tools and bits of equipment.

"How's Jenny holding up?" asked Ray, as he approached, trying in vain to rub a smudge of oil from his hand with an old rag.

"Surprisingly well, to be honest," said Derek. "She freaked out a bit after the incident at the old man's house, but hey, who wouldn't?"

"Are *you* okay mate?" asked Ray.

Derek held his gaze for a moment, then lowered his head. "I'm hanging in there. A lot going through my head at the minute, you know."

"I can imagine."

"Never shot anyone before," said Derek, glancing briefly at his friend again, half expecting his actions to be judged, but knowing that Ray wouldn't be the one to do it. The scene played out for an instant in his mind — the cracks of his shots, the violent shudders through his arm as the bullets left his gun, and the look on the man's face before he slumped to the ground clutching his chest and expelling his final breath — Derek blinked the image away, feeling a nauseous tightening in his gut.

Ray put a hand on Derek's shoulder and gave him a single, firm shake. "You know you had no choice, Derek. If you hadn't have taken the shot, my sister would be dead."

Derek met his friend's eyes but said nothing.

"God knows who else would've died if you hadn't stopped those fuckers," said Ray, his eyes demanding affirmation.

Derek obliged with a slow blink and a sharp nod. "I know. When I think about it logically, I know it was the only option in the moment."

Ray bobbed his head in agreement.

"But then that makes me think, what other options were there back at the prison? We were the ones… I was the one who let them get out in the first place," said Derek, looking out into the yard and blowing out a long, calming breath.

"Mate, you know there was nothing else we could've done, and it wasn't all on you. I helped make that decision. It was the only option we had," said Ray. "Plus, we were working on the assumption that the army would be there within a day or two."

"They better be there now."

"I'm sure they are."

"If they're not, then all the prisoners will be out," said Derek, with a shake of his head. "There're some sick fuckers in there, too."

"Well, there's nothing anyone can do about it until the power comes back on," said Ray, reaching past Derek to hang a spanner on the wall beside its siblings.

"What do you think will happen when this is all over?" asked Derek. "I'll probably end up on the wrong side of those bars, mate."

"It'll not come to that. There'll be an enquiry and we'll all have your back," said Ray, putting a reassuring hand on Derek's shoulder again.

Derek lifted an adjustable spanner from the bench and turned it over aimlessly in his hands.

"And don't worry, if it does come to that, I'll make sure you've first pick of the new books, and might even get you extra ice-cream on a Sunday," said Ray with a smile.

Derek faked a swipe at him with the spanner, coming closer to hitting him than he meant to.

"Here, give me a hand with this, will you?" asked Ray, moving to the back of the bike and gesturing for Derek to help him lift it off the stand.

"So, what do you think about what your neighbour was saying?" asked Derek, as he took a grip of the handlebars.

"I really didn't think things were gonna be as bad as he's saying," said Ray with a grunt, as he lifted the back end of the bike off its stand and set it to the side. "Don't get me wrong, I know we had to abandon a prison and all, but I didn't think it'd last more than a few days or a couple of weeks at most."

"Yeah, it's worrying."

"Sound's like it's anarchy in the cities," said Ray, rocking the bike back onto its kickstand.

"Yeah. Mate, we're so grateful that you and your folks have taken us in," said Derek. "I don't know where we would've gone."

"We wouldn't have it any other way. You know that."

Derek smiled and nodded. "To think we were nearly heading to Fermanagh with Simon, to the professor's place."

Ray crouched and lifted the heavy stand that the bike had been resting on and crab-walked it over to a space by the wall. "Who is this Simon guy, anyway? Is he alright?"

"I really don't know much about him. Seems to be a good guy, though," said Derek, a mischievous smile spreading across his face. "Lisa seems to have taken a shine to him. Future brother-in-law, maybe?"

"What? Fuck off!"

Derek raised his eyebrows and shrugged, the smile now seeming to irritate Ray.

"Fucker better not try to take advantage of the situation," said Ray sternly.

"Knowing your Lisa, he'll not be the one taking advantage," laughed Derek.

"Fuck off, you prick," snapped Ray.

A clink of bottles sounded from behind them and they both spun to see Simon standing a few feet away with three bottles of Budweiser in his hands. Derek wasn't sure if he'd heard them talking about him, but an awkward silence settled, eased only by a round of nods.

"Vinnie told me to bring you guys out a beer," said Simon, handing a bottle to each of them. "He said we better enjoy them. They're the last three."

"Sláinte," said Ray, tapping the neck of his bottle on the other two.

"Cheers," said Derek, doing the same. "Fuck, you know what that means?"

"What? No more alcohol to get through the apocalypse?" asked Simon.

"No. Worse!" said Ray dryly, as he lifted a fold-up chair from a shelf and handed it to Derek.

"Vinnie's homemade wine," said Derek, feigning a shudder.

"Ha, excellent. Can't be that bad," said Simon.

Ray went to hand Simon a similar chair, then paused. "Have you ever drank your own piss?"

Simon took the chair, looking at each of the men in turn, trying to determine if they were winding him up.

"Well, you'll wish you had a fresh glass of warm urine when you taste this stuff," said Derek. "And you'll have to be the polite guest and pretend to like it."

Derek and Ray laughed, and Simon joined in with a chuckle.

Ray got his own chair and the three unfolded them, arranging them in a loose semi-circle facing out into the yard.

"So, is that a London accent, Simon?" asked Ray.

"Southampton. South coast of England."

Ray nodded slowly and took a sip of his beer.

"What has you over here?" asked Derek.

"Came over for university, met my wife, never went back."

"Ah, you're married? Where is she?" asked Ray, with a quick glance towards Derek.

"She passed away a couple of years ago," said Simon, before putting his bottle to his lips.

Ray grimaced and gave a slow shake of his head. "I'm very sorry to hear that, mate."

"Sorry for your loss, Simon," added Derek quietly.

"Yeah, car crash," said Simon, in a practised way to prevent more questions. "I was actually supposed to be moving back home in a couple of months."

"Have you other family back there?" asked Derek.

"Yeah, my mother and a sister."

"I'm sure you're worried about them," said Ray.

"Yeah, I spoke to them on Sunday to warn them, so they were able to prepare a little, at least."

"That's good," said Ray, before retreating back to his beer.

An awkward silence circulated again as the three bobbed their heads aimlessly and sipped at their beers.

Ray slipped his bottle into the little net pocket on the arm of his deckchair and rotated it with his fingers. "So what is it that you do, Simon?" he asked.

Simon rolled his eyes. "I'm a financial analyst. A stock trader," he said, almost apologetically. "Not much use for people like me at the end of the world."

Derek laughed. "It's hardly the end of the world now."

"Well, financially it may as well be," said Simon, with a tight-lipped frown. "I work for myself, and everything I have is tied up in cryptocurrency and stocks. Mostly high-tech companies, but I had a safety net, in what was supposed to be, low-risk insurance stocks as well. Both of which will be totally fucked when the power comes back on. I'll be left with the clothes on my back."

"Jeez, mate, you really think it'll be that bad?" asked Ray.

Simon nodded solemnly.

"Well, at least you'll still have your shoes," said Derek, nodding at Simon's odd boots.

Simon looked down at his mismatched walking boots and laughed. Ray and Derek joining him.

"Sorry, mate, I shouldn't laugh," said Derek.

"Well, I probably wouldn't laugh if I were you," said Simon. "I'm sorry to say, but your prison pension fund is probably gonna go the same way."

"Seriously?" said Ray, the levity suddenly gone. "I hadn't thought of that."

"Afraid so."

"Fuck, thanks mate, way to kick a guy when he's down," said Derek, before draining the end of his beer.

The mood darkened and three men sat in silence. Derek noticing that both Ray and Simon were lost in thought. He relaxed back into his canvas chair and looked around at the various bits of machinery and benches of tools and equipment. The place smelt of a mix of engine oil and chicken shit. He could almost taste it in his beer.

"That's a serious collection of fishing rods," said Simon, spying a rack of poles perched above one of the benches.

"Do you fish?" asked Ray.

"Me? No, never tried it," said Simon.

"You wanna give it a go?" asked Ray, rising from the chair and lifting one of the rods.

Simon shook his head, stifling a yawn. "No, I think I'll leave you guys to it. Didn't sleep great last night."

"I'm not surprised," said Derek.

"What about you?" Ray said, raising his brow and tilting one of the rods towards Derek.

"When? Now?" asked Derek.

"Yeah, why not?" said Ray.

"Okay, but let me go and check how the wee man is doing," said Derek.

"I might go and lie down for a while," said Simon. He rose from the chair and folded it up, looking for where he should put it.

"Here, I'll take it," said Ray, taking the camp chair and sliding it into a shelf under the workbench.

"Thanks, I'll see you guys later," said Simon, before turning to head back to the house.

Ray called after him. "I'll tell the ol' fella you're a big fan of homemade wine."

Simon turned and smiled. "Yeah, I'll give it a try later," he said with a smile.

"You'll regret it," said Derek, laughing.

CHAPTER SEVEN

"Are we gonna be out that long that we'll need flasks?" asked Derek, as he entered the kitchen and saw Ray finishing filling the second of two thermos flasks with hot tea.

A chorus of laughs came from Jenny and Vinnie, who sat at the kitchen table.

"I told you Ray, he'll last ten minutes and then start moaning," said Jenny with a laugh. "He has no patience at all."

"Shut up, you," said Derek with a smile, knowing his wife was probably right.

"You'll see," said Ray, turning to his mum, who'd just entered. "Mum, we'll be having fresh fish for dinner tonight."

Moira nodded and rolled her eyes. "You haven't caught a fish in about ten years."

"Derek's gonna be my lucky charm, you'll see."

Lisa ambled in from the hall, favouring her injured foot.

"How's the ankle?" asked Derek.

"Yeah, it's not too bad. The ice helped. It should be okay. Did I hear you saying you're going fishing?"

"Yip," said Ray curtly, expecting further jabs from his sister.

"Omelette it is for dinner then tonight, mum," said Lisa.

"Ha ha," replied Ray, with a sibling smirk.

"Why don't you see if Simon wants to go too?" asked Lisa.

"We already asked him," said Derek.

"Yeah, your boyfriend's too tired," Ray added, with a revengeful grin which left Lisa red-faced and stuttering.

"What? What are you talking about? He's not my boyfriend. I hardly know him," she said, glaring at her brother. "Prick!"

"Lisa!" scolded her mum.

"Well, he is," said Lisa, as she hobbled to the settee. "And cover those bloody holes while you're down there, will ya?" she called after Ray as he headed out through the back door.

"That was cruel," said Derek, as they crossed the yard.

"Ah, she's always winding me up," laughed Ray. "Right, let's get some gear together."

They approached the bench where the fishing rods were hanging and Ray selected one for Derek before taking his own down from its hook.

"This one should do you."

"Why do you need so many?" asked Derek, staring at the rows of rods. "Are they not all the same?"

"These are all old ones. Most of them were my grandad's."

"Is that you and him there?" asked Derek, pointing to a faded photo pinned to the wall above the bench. It showed an older man with his arm around a very young-looking Ray. Between them, they held a huge fish, which they proudly showed off to the camera.

"Yeah."

"Jeez, that's some mullet you had," said Derek, leaning in for a better look at Ray's haircut. "You really were a fucking hillbilly, weren't you?"

"Fuck you," said Ray, pushing Derek to the side. "Move your ass. I need in there."

Ray pulled at a heavy drawer built into the bench, which had obviously not been opened in quite a while. It finally came free with a jolt, the contents rattling inside.

"What are these for?" asked Derek, leaning in and poking at the rows of colourful objects in the drawer. Each looked like an exotic dragon fly, with multi-coloured wings and long, elaborate tails.

"Careful, there's a hook on each of them," said Ray. "You'll know it if you get one stuck in your finger."

Derek pulled his hand back, heeding the warning.

"They're the lures. The fish think they're insects. Each one is designed to attract a different type of fish."

"Cool."

"Most of these are made from dyed feathers," said Ray, lifting one out and holding it up for Derek to get a better look. "But we should probably use the marabou jig if we're gonna try for a salmon."

"Salmon? Can you really get salmon in that river?"

"Absolutely, although it might be a little late in the season," said Ray with a proud smile. "That's a fifteen-pounder that we caught that day." He nodded to the photo.

Ray placed a selection of the jigs into a small pouch and gathered a few other required items before packing them into a old canvas bag. He then lifted a pair of PVC waders down from a hook and handed them to Derek.

"Here, put these on."

"Are you serious? They're the biggest pair of wellies I've ever seen."

"They're waders. Jeez, have you ever been out of the city?"

"I'm not wearing *them*," said Derek, handing them back to Ray. "My boots will be alright."

"Well, you're gonna be pretty wet and cold standing in the middle of the river."

"Standing in the river? I thought we'd be sitting on the bank," said Derek, face scrunched in horror.

"Nope, the best chance is if we fish from the centre of the river," said Ray, stepping into a similar pair of his own.

Derek hesitated, perhaps thinking his mate was winding him up, then kicked his walking boots off and worked his way into the waders, pulling the thick PVC overalls up to chest height and clicking the belt-like faster closed as he'd seen Ray do.

"These feel horrible," said Derek. "I look like something out of the Texas Chainsaw Massacre."

"Jenny was right. You're fucking moaning already and we're not even at the river yet."

Derek looked down at the waders like a teenager forced to wear his brother's hand-me-downs.

"Come on, let's go," said Ray, handing Derek a waterproof jacket to complement his new look.

###

As they approached the fishing stand at the river, a light drizzle began to fall. Ray saw Derek look up at the sky and he readied himself for more complaints.

Ray prepared the lines and, after a few minutes of basic instruction on how to use the rod and cast the line, he led Derek out into the river. He rolled his eyes and smiled as he heard his friend mutter curses to himself from behind him.

"Fuck, this water's freezing," said Derek, as he gradually made his way out into the river until it was just above knee height.

Ray stayed close beside him for the first few minutes, instructing him and correcting his casting technique. When he was confident that Derek wasn't going to put his own or Ray's eye out with a hook, he moved further out to give him a bit of space.

"How long does it usually take to catch one?" called Derek after a few minutes.

"Fuck me!" Ray muttered to himself. "It could take a while, if we catch anything at all," he said, just loud enough for Derek to hear him. "But we have to be quiet,"

He shook his head. *What was I thinking?* he thought, but he smiled as he looked over at his friend and saw his mixed look of concentration and total confusion.

The tuts and sighs from Derek soon subsided as he seemed to embrace the tranquillity and the rhythm of the repeated casting and recalling of the line, although Ray didn't feel confident that they'd have any luck and wasn't looking forward to the abuse he would surely get from Lisa when they landed back empty-handed.

"Oh, oh," shouted Derek excitedly. "I think I've got something."

Ray looked over to see Derek bouncing on the spot and pulling back on his rod.

"Start reeling quickly, but keep the rod low," shouted Ray. *The bastard's got something alright,* he thought, making his way towards him while reeling his own line in.

"Reel it in, quickly. As fast as you can," called Ray.

The look on Derek's face was priceless, a sudden adrenaline rush had wiped away the boredom in an instant. He was now giddy with excitement and frantically spinning the reel and pulling back on the rod.

"Keep it low, keep it low," shouted Ray.

"It's bloody heavy."

"Keep reeling," said Ray, a little more calmly.

"I'm trying."

"Okay, you need to tire it out," said Ray.

"I need to tire *it* out?" shouted Derek, with an excited laugh. "It's tiring me out."

"Start edging your way to the bank."

Derek stopped reeling and started slowly side-stepping towards the river bank where they'd left their gear.

"I'll get the net," said Ray, as he moved past Derek, taking large steps to power through the water.

Ray's heart was racing now, too. *Fuck, this'll be worse than coming back with nothing,* he cursed to himself. *Fuckin' city-boy lands a salmon on his first try.*

"Hurry up, this thing's pulling the arms off me," shouted Derek, as he alternated between reeling fanatically and back-stepping towards the bank, stumbling slightly on the occasional slippery rock.

Ray dropped his rod beside their gear and grabbed the large net, then took a couple of steps out into the river again towards Derek, who was shouting and laughing like a lunatic. Before Ray could get to him, Derek took another blind step. He let out a yelp and a string of curses as he tumbled backwards, landing on his ass, the water now sloshing up to his chest. To Ray's surprise, he didn't let go of the rod and continued to pull and reel even as he fell further onto his back, barely keeping his head above the water.

"Help me Ray, I'm filling up. I'm gonna drown," he screamed, between laughs. "I can't get up. I can't get up."

"Get up, get up!" Ray wanted to help, but the laughter paralysed him, and so he stood for a moment, bent over with his elbows on his knees, watching Derek writhe about on his back but still reeling furiously.

"I can't get up!" shouted Derek, trying desperately to keep his head above the water.

"It's gonna get away, keep reeling," shouted Ray, grabbing his friend under the arms and straining to haul him to his feet, all the while laughing hysterically.

"There it is. I saw it!" shouted Derek. "It's a fuckin' shark. Get me up, get me up!"

Ray pulled Derek to his feet and bear-hugged him, trying to get his arms around him to get a grip of the rod.

"Get the net!"

"Keep reeling!"

The fish broke the surface again a few feet from them. It thrashed and bucked, darting back and forth in a desperate fight for life.

Derek's wet hands lost their grip on the reel, and it started to spin in the opposite direction as the fish made a final dash for freedom. Ray caught the reel again and for another five minutes, the two men wrestled with the fish, gradually edging it closer to the waiting net.

"Jesus, it's big," shouted Ray, as he manoeuvred the net under the monster salmon.

The short pole on the end of the net strained as Ray hauled their catch out on to dry land. "Bloody hell, that's a big fish," he said, looking back at Derek, who was struggling to make it back to the bank, his waders now filled with water and bulging. The sight sent Ray into another laughing convulsion, and he fell backwards, landing beside the netted fish, laughing uncontrollably as Derek waddled heavily from the water.

"These bloody things are full of water," he shouted, as he sloshed up beside Ray.

As he collapsed beside Ray, a wave of river water erupted from the top of the waders, catching him full in the face and resulting in a series of coughing laughs.

Ray pushed himself to his feet, tears of laughter streaming down his face.

"Lie back and put your legs up," said Ray, grabbing Derek's feet and lifting them up, like an athlete helping a colleague with cramp. Another torrent of water forced its way up through the chest-high waders and hit Derek on the face, causing another fit of laughter from Ray.

Derek tried to protect himself with his hand but still received a mouthful of the cold, murky water. He spluttered and coughed, then rolled on to his front before sitting back into a kneeling position.

"Holy shit, look at the size of that thing," he said, looking down at the wriggling mass which was now gasping for breath. "Is that a salmon?"

"Yip, it's a salmon alright," said Ray, moving to his angling bag. He pulled out a pair of pliers and a bright red rod with a string attached to the end, then knelt beside the net and grabbed the writhing fish just under its head.

"What's that?"

"A fishing priest," said Ray. "Do you want to do it?"

"Do what?"

"Kill it," said Ray, holding the priest out to Derek.

"Ah, no, it's okay. You do it, please."

Ray turned back to the fish and like a carpenter lining up his hammer, held the small club close to where he intended to strike, then lifted his hand and brought it down with a hard swift blow, and then another to make sure the fish died as painlessly as possible.

He worked with the pliers to remove the hook from the fish's mouth, then untangled its tail from the net and raised it up, visibly straining to hold his arm out straight. With its tail fin at head height, it stretched down to Ray's waist. "That's got to be twenty pounds at least," he said, handing Derek his prize.

"Ha ha. We'll eat well tonight," exclaimed Derek, taking the enormous fish and cradling it in his arms.

"I have never seen a salmon that size in this river," said Ray, genuinely delighted for his friend, but trying to hide the stab of jealousy he felt.

"I'm fucking freezing," said Derek, shifting uncomfortably from one foot to the other, his rubber waders squeaking with every movement. He set the heavy fish down beside Ray's bag and unscrewed the top from one of the flasks of tea.

"Right, let's head back," said Ray, gathering their gear. He paused for a second, then burst out laughing again. "I'm filling up. I'm gonna drown!" he shouted, imitating Derek's excited screams.

Derek shrugged and laughed. "I didn't want to let go, and you weren't being much help."

Between fits of laughter, they packed up their gear and headed back towards the house. Ray carried the bag and the rods and Derek followed behind, proudly cradling his monster catch, his sodden waders squelching and sloshing with every step.

###

Ray led Derek along the path and through the orchard, laughing to himself at some of the things Derek had said during his epic fight with the salmon.

"It's a shark, it's a shark. Help me, help me," he called over his shoulder in a mockingly high-pitched voice, before bursting out laughing again.

"I didn't say that, ya dick," said Derek.

"You bloody did," said Ray, turning to see the comical sight of his friend waddling along in his rubber dungarees.

As he rounded the corner of the old farmhouse, he stopped abruptly. "What the hell's going on here?" he said, looking down at the three holes that'd been dug close to the side wall of the house.

Derek squeaked to a halt beside him, readjusting the slippery fish in his arms. "Is this what Lisa was talking about?"

"Must be," said Ray, setting the fishing gear down and lifting the spade that protruded from the nearest hole.

"Maybe your da is planting something?"

Ray looked at Derek, a deep frown pinching his forehead. "No. He knew nothing about it when Lisa mentioned it. I assumed it would've just been a badger or something."

"Who else could it be and what would they be doing?"

Ray examined the spade. "This isn't ours either."

"Could it have been the ones you chased off last night?" asked Derek.

"Maybe, but why the hell would they be digging holes in someone else's land in the dark?"

Derek shrugged and shifted back and forth between feet, obviously cold from his soaking.

Ray looked at him and smiled again at the thought of his waders filling up. "You must be freezing. You head on back. I'm gonna cover these or fill them in or something. I can't leave them like this."

"Are you sure?" said Derek, in weak protest. "If you want to leave it, I'll come up and help you when I get changed."

"No, it's fine. You go and get out of those waders. There's probably leeches in them. You need to get them off."

"What? Leeches?" said Derek, his eyes wide and his dance becoming suddenly frantic. "You didn't say anything about leeches."

"Could be," said Ray, with a quirked eyebrow and a sly smile.

"You're winding me up, you prick," said Derek, skipping away towards the main house.

Ray listened to him trudge away, then turned to survey the holes again, his confused frown returning. The line of holes was parallel to the wall and about three feet out. Two of them were about two foot square and about the same in depth, the removed soil piled in a small mound to the side. *Lisa was lucky she didn't break her leg,* he thought.

The third hole, the one that the spade had been sticking out of, was a similar shape but wasn't as deep as the others. It was clearly unfinished. *Looks like we did disturb them,* thought Ray, looking around for any other signs of the trespassers he and his father had chased off the night before. He shook his head in frustration, a reasonable explanation escaping him, then began to refill the holes.

He shovelled the loose contents back into the first two holes, stomping down the sectioned sods of grass that he found under the loose soil. There was still a slight dip, but it was no longer dangerous. He then moved to the third, more shallow, hole.

The first shovel-full of soil contained some small rocks, and as he tossed it into the hole, he heard the dull thud of a rock hitting wood. He looked down but wasn't able to see what the rock had hit. With the tip of the spade, he prodded and scrapped at the bottom of the hole. There was definitely a piece of wood.

Probably just some rotting plank or piece of timber from the old house, he thought, but his curiosity was now piqued. He scrapped at the wood, moving in increasing circles to try to expose the edges. Each time he prodded with the tip of the spade, expecting to hit soil and thus the outer extent of the wood, he would strike more wood. It seemed to extend even beyond the edge of the hole into the undisturbed soil.

He let out a sigh and considered just filling the hole in and returning to the house to join in the celebration of Derek's catch, and to face the undoubted abuse, but something told him that he needed to uncover this plank or board, or whatever it was. He placed the spade six inches to the side of the hole and stomped down with his heel. The spade sank into the soil easily under his weight; the earth crumbling away like a landslide into the hole. He scooped it out and added it to the small mound, then repeated the exercise until he'd doubled the area of the hole.

He scrapped again with the tip of the spade and finally found the edge of the wood. A little more scrapping and scooping exposed the whole thing. It seemed to be the top of some kind of crate, about two foot wide and four foot long. Two rusted metal clasps were visible on one side, with two similarly rusted hinges opposite them.

"What the fuck is this?" muttered Ray, staring down into the hole.

He flicked at the edge of the lid with the tip of the spade but couldn't get purchase and so set about widening the hole even further to give him access to the crate. After about fifteen minutes, he was out of breath and sweating — the PVC waders weren't helping — but he'd managed to widen the space around the crate to give him access. Two padlocks secured the latches and after a moment of hesitation, he decided he had the right to force entry.

A couple of well-placed heavy blows with the spade were enough to compromise the ageing latches and the metal stripped away from the moistened wood with ease. Ray set the spade to the side and knelt beside the hole. With an equal mix of trepidation and excitement — childhood thoughts of buried treasure fleeting through his mind — he reached down and pulled at the lid.

The rusted hinges groaned but gave little resistance. Inside there was no yellow glow of gold coins or sparkling jewels, just a dark-green, thick plastic sheet. He pulled at the sheet and it came away easily. Ray's eyes widened, his breath stopping for a moment. He couldn't believe what he was seeing. This made no sense. He sat back, looking around nervously, as if expecting hidden observers to pounce. A million thoughts raced through him, none of them making any sense.

CHAPTER EIGHT

Conor Tobin was barely aware of the crowd around him. He just shuffled along, waiting his turn. He'd been queueing now for a couple of hours, desperate to get something that'd keep him and his mother going until the power came back on. Their cupboards weren't exactly bare, but for the past couple of days, they'd been less successful in finding ways to combine the random ingredients into something that would pass for a meal, particularly when they'd no way to even boil a pan. Dry pasta may as well be sand when you can't cook it.

The tension in the crowd had eased considerably since Dermot O'Connor and his men had turned up. Emotions had reached fever pitch when the semi-conscious form of the owner had been dragged out and tied to the lamppost, his face a bloody and swollen mess. It was a warning to others who'd seek to take advantage of the situation. Angry bystanders jeered and cursed at him, some wanting to add to the beating he'd obviously received in the shop, only backing down when a stark warning was issued to all in attendance. Conor felt nothing; not anger at the greedy shopkeeper, not elation at his dethroning, and not relief that he would now hopefully return home with something for them to eat.

Ten minutes passed without anyone else being admitted to the shop. The shopkeeper's two sons had emerged — one of them clutching a bust nose — and with their heads held low, they pushed through the crowd. They stopped briefly at their father tied to the lamppost, but thought better of trying to untie him when a shout from one of O'Connor's men ordered them to leave him and go.

Reluctantly, they backed away from their father, the older of the two dragging his younger brother back. As they pushed through the group of aggrieved customers, they were jostled and cursed, and received more than a few punches and kicks to help them on their way.

When one of O'Connor's men emerged from the shop carrying a large cardboard box full of groceries and placed it in their car, muted objections arose from the crowd.

"What about the rest of us?" asked one woman.

"Yeah, sort yourselves out, sure!" shouted a man behind Conor boldly, but not so bold as to step forward and identify himself.

O'Connor's henchman returned to the shop without answering, which caused the agitation of the crowd to grow further.

"Fuckin' great, these guys are just gonna clear the place out for themselves," protested a curly-haired man in a Donegal football top.

The anger was rising; the queue becoming less orderly as people started to press forward. Conor could feel that things were about to get nasty.

The same man appeared in the doorway again.

"Right, listen up." He held his hand up to hush the crowd. "What was happening here was unacceptable and will not be tolerated."

"What's gonna happen now?" shouted the man who'd initially spoken to Dermot.

"We're gonna be letting one person in at a time," continued the man at the shop door. "Now, the only fair way we can do this is to limit the amount that each person can take. Each person will only be allowed to take one plastic bag-full of items. No exceptions!"

"Yeah, but what are the prices gonna be?"

"There'll be no charge. You fill one bag, and you leave."

At this revelation, the mood in the crowd changed immediately, anger turning to praise for O'Connor and his men.

"I knew Doc would sort this out. He's a good man, so he is," said the man in the football top, who'd suddenly changed his opinion.

Others around Conor joined in the buoyant praise, seemingly making peace with the brutal treatment of the shop owner.

"I need two volunteers to help keep things orderly," said the man, as he stepped towards the crowd.

He made eye contract with Conor and raised a questioning eyebrow. Conor lowered his head, making it clear that he wasn't interested. Yes, it might mean that he would be in a better position to get some decent groceries, but he wasn't in the mood to talk to people or interact with them in any way. The man passed him by and called on two other men who'd raised their hands to volunteer.

It took another hour before Conor's turn came to enter the shop. By the time he stepped through into the gloomy interior, the shelves were almost bare. He managed to find some items that he thought might be eatable; some packets of crackers, a tin which had lost its label, but which he was fairly certain from the shape contained processed ham — the little key used to open it was also missing but that shouldn't be a problem — and a couple of tins of minestrone soup, which he didn't look forward to eating cold, but it'd be better than nothing.

He packed the items into the bag provided and nodded to the guy manning the door. The sky had darkened and a light drizzle was starting to fall. He felt sorry for those still queueing. They'd now have to stand in the rain, and would likely be disappointed by the meagre pickings left in the shop.

As he passed by the lamppost, the shopkeeper lifted his head. He was sitting with his back against the metal post, his arms tied together behind it. Blood from his nose had dried over this mouth and stained the front of this shirt. He looked up at Conor through his one working eye, the other now pressed shut by his swelling cheek. He didn't try to speak, he just stared pitifully, then lowered his head again, allowing his chin to rest on his chest.

Conor paused for a moment. Under normal circumstances, he would be overcome with compassion for a person in this position and would likely try to help him in some way, but not today. He stared down at him and felt nothing.

CHAPTER NINE

Ray reached into the crate and lifted one of the individually wrapped rifles. Even without the ubiquitous curved magazine being in place, he was certain that the gun was an AK47 assault rifle. He tore the clear light-plastic bag away from the gun and turned it in his hands. It was covered in grease, which probably explained why it was in such good condition despite being buried in the ground. *How long had it been here? Who put it here? He had some suspicions, but how did he not know about this?* The questions tumbled through his head, but the absence of answers was numbing.

Ray stood and paced in a small circle, checking around the corner of the old house and back down towards the orchard. When he was sure he was alone, he crouched by the hole again and reached into the crate. There were a least ten AK47s — the banana-shaped magazines stacked underneath — two or three other rifles that he couldn't immediately identify through the plastic covering, and about five or six handguns, at least two of them Beretta 92's, from what he could make out from the lettering on the slide. Tightly packed at the foot of the crate were a number of canvas bags. He lifted one out; the weight strengthening his suspicion as to its contents. He untied the drawstring top and spread the neck of the bag wide. Inside, within another clear plastic bag, were hundreds of loose bullets.

"What are you doing?"

Ray's heart leaped. He dropped the bag into the crate and kicked the lid closed – like a toddler caught playing with something he knew he shouldn't – he spun to face the source of the question.

"What's that?" asked Derek, now dried and dressed in fresh clothes.

Ray scrambled to his feet, unable to find words. He just stared at his friend, then back at the crate, his mouth moving wordlessly.

Derek frowned at him. "What'd you find?"

Still without a word, Ray crouched again beside the crate, and waited for Derek to approach, before swinging the lid open. Derek frowned inquisitively, his eyes taking a couple of seconds to focus on and then identify the contents. He reeled backwards, shifting his focus back and forth between the weapons and Ray.

"Holy fuck!"

"I know," said Ray, staring intently at his friend.

"What? Who… fuck," said Derek, drawing his palm across his face. He turned in a slow circle as if, like Ray, expecting someone to appear from the trees.

"I was filling the holes in and I felt something wooden," said Ray, tailing off, no further explanation needed.

"IRA?" asked Derek, a grave stare fixed on Ray.

Ray shrugged, "I don't know. Probably."

"Who else could it be?"

Derek approached the crate and carefully inspected the contents. "Holy shit. There's a lot of guns here, and ammo," he said, looking into one of the bags. "There must be hundreds of rounds, maybe thousands."

Ray nodded.

"Shit!" said Derek, jumping to his feet and grabbing Ray by the shoulder, pulling him away. "There might be explosives in it."

"There's not. I checked."

"What about under the other bags?"

"It's okay. I checked."

"What do we do? Go to the cops?" asked Derek.

"We can't."

"Why not?" asked Derek, turning to his friend, confused.

"Are you forgetting the bag of British-issue weapons you brought over the border, which are now stuffed under your bed in my parents' house?"

Derek cradled the back of his neck, then drew his hand slowly up and over his head, bringing it to rest over his mouth.

"Fuck!" he said, the obvious assumption only dawning on him.

"What?"

"Whoever you chased off last night must've been looking for these. And the fact that they knew, more or less exactly where to look, means that they put them there."

"Yeah, I thought of that."

"So, they're gonna come back," said Derek.

Ray nodded slowly.

"So?" asked Derek.

"So, what?"

"So what the fuck are we gonna do with them, Ray?"

"I don't fuckin' know, Derek."

"Well, we can't just hand them over to them," said Derek.

"I'm not suggesting we do," said Ray, crouching down beside the hole again.

The two men fell silent, Derek pacing back and forth, and Ray on his hunkers staring wide-eyed into the crate.

"How long do you think they've been there?" asked Derek, returning and crouching beside Ray.

"A long time, by the looks of the crate."

"We have to get them out of this hole and fill it in," said Derek.

Ray wasn't listening, his mind was filled with possible scenarios, faces from the past, thoughts of an older time, though not that long ago, when the Provisional IRA was rumoured to have arms caches buried all over the country, the locations of which being known to only a few trusted quartermasters.

"Ray!"

"What?"

"We have to move them and fill in the hole before whoever buried them comes back for them," said Derek, his tone betraying his agitation.

"Right."

"We can't lift the crate," said Derek. "The thing would likely fall apart if we tried to move it."

"Stay here. I'll go and get something to carry it all in," said Ray, before hurrying off towards the machinery shed.

When he returned, Derek had already removed the contents of the crate and closed the lid, and had started to refill the hole.

"We'll put them in these," said Ray, holding up two large burlap potato sacks.

Derek frowned.

"What? It's the best I could find," said Ray defensively. "They'll do in the meantime."

They packed the weapons and ammunition into the sacks and finished filling the hole. On the way back to the shed, Ray grabbed Derek by the arm. "We can't tell anyone about this," he said. "Not even my da. Okay?"

"Fuck sake Ray, someone is gonna come looking for these."

"I'll take care of it."

Derek stopped and narrowed his eyes. "What do you mean, you'll take care of it?"

"Just leave it with me, okay?"

"Tell me what you mean."

"I'll talk to someone."

"Hold on, what the fuck does that mean? Talk to who?"

"Just trust me Derek, okay?"

Ray walked on towards the shed.

"Ray," Derek said sternly.

Ray turned and looked at him.

"Did you know these were here?"

"No, I didn't know they were here!" shouted Ray, taking a couple of steps towards Derek and locking eyes with him.

Derek held his friend's stare. "Okay. But Ray, whatever you're planning to do, do not keep me in the dark. I've my family to think about here as well," said Derek.

Ray nodded. "Okay, I will. Let's put these somewhere safe."

CHAPTER TEN

Ray couldn't help feeling a twinge of jealousy when he saw the fuss that was being made over Derek's salmon, which was now making up the main course for the evening meal, but the joy of helping his friend land such a huge fish and the memory of Derek's comical attempts to reel it in, outweighed any envy.

They'd both told the story of the epic fight with the monster fish more than once, each of them exaggerating various aspects which had their audience in fits of laughter. Ray imitated Derek's cries for help when he thought he was going to drown, whilst Derek continually wound Ray up about how easy fishing was, and how bad at it Ray must be, to have never caught a fish like that.

Ray took the ribbing in good humour, even when the abuse came from Lisa. It was good to see everyone enjoying themselves after what they'd been through. It would've been easy to forget about what was going on in the world.

As jovial as the evening had been, though, Ray would occasionally lock eyes with Derek and the two would share an unspoken concern over their secret find, which was now hidden away among the tools and machinery parts in the shed. More than once, he'd glimpsed a look of anxiety on his friend's face when all those around him were laughing and joking. Ray was feeling it too. There was a tightness in his gut that he couldn't shake. He tried to push it away.

"Oh, I meant to say," said Ray, turning to his father and raising his voice loud enough to get the attention of the rest of the table. "Simon here's a bit of a wine buff. I was telling him that you make your own."

Ray turned to Simon, a broad conspiratorial grin on his face. Moira rolled her eyes and the rest of the table smirked behind their mugs or napkins, or anything else that they could hide behind. Vinnie jumped from his seat and rushed off to retrieve a bottle of his latest batch.

"You're cruel," said Lisa to her brother, careful not to appear to be too defensive of Simon.

Ray smiled and shrugged. "I think I'll hide in the bathroom for a while."

"Damn you," whispered Derek. "I was gonna do that."

"It can't be that bad," said Simon, looking round the table. Every head bobbed, eyebrows raised in mocking seriousness, including Moira's.

"Good luck," said Ray, as he patted Simon on the shoulder and scurried from the room before his father could return.

Ray laughed to himself as he made his way along the hall to the small bathroom beside the front door. Just as he was about to enter, a bright light shone through the small stained glass panel in the door. He opened it cautiously and peered out. The light was coming from a vehicle's headlights. It was stopped at the gate at the bottom of the lane. He watched for a moment, hoping that the driver was merely using his entrance as a place to do a three-point turn, and the car would soon reverse and drive away. It did not.

Looking back towards the kitchen, where he could still hear the jovial voices of his family and friends, he considered getting Derek or his dad to come with him to investigate. Deciding against that, he opened the door to the closet beside the bathroom and withdrew one of his dad's shotguns from the gun safe bolted to the wall. He loaded two cartridges into the gun and stepped out on to the front steps, quietly closing the door behind him.

As he slowly descended the driveway towards the gate, he could just make out a figure silhouetted in the beam from the headlamps.

"Who's that? What do you want?"

"Rayso?"

There was only one person that called him Rayso. Someone whom he hadn't spoken to in years. Anytime Ray had been back in Donegal, he'd gone out of his way to avoid the kind of places where their paths might cross.

"It's Joe."

Shit. A handful of names had been running through Ray's mind since finding the crate. Joseph Kilpatrick's had been one of them.

He considered returning to the house. He shouldn't be out here alone.

"We need a word Ray."

"Don't have anything to say, Joe. Just get back in your car and fuck off."

"Now Rayso, what way's that to talk to an old friend?"

"You and your boys stay off our land, Joe, or someone's gonna get hurt."

"We just want to talk, Ray. Come down so that I don't have to keep shouting. I wouldn't want to disturb your family."

Ray's jaw was clenched so tight at the mention of his family that he thought his teeth might break, but he also didn't want those in the house to hear the conversation. He approached the gate slowly; the shotgun held firm but low. The shapes of three men resolved through the blinding car headlights.

"Turn the fuckin' full beams off," said Ray, lifting his hand to shade his eyes.

Joseph turned and nodded to the driver, who immediately switched from full headlights to sidelights. When Ray's eyes adjusted, he saw Joseph leaning on the gate, and two others further back by the car.

"So how are you keeping Ray? Haven't seen you in a long time," said Joseph.

"Were you on our land last night?" asked Ray, ignoring Joseph's attempt at civility.

Joseph frowned and shook his head. "Wasn't us."

"What do you want?"

"Dermot wants to talk to you."

"I've nothing to say to him."

Joseph raised an eyebrow and smiled. "These are crazy times Ray, we all need to pull together."

Ray held Joseph's stare but didn't respond.

"We're trying to help the community, Ray. Dermot just wants to talk to you about that."

"That's not my concern. I've my own family to think about."

Joseph glanced casually behind him, then lowered his voice. "Ray, you know what Doc can be like. It's best if you just come down and talk to him, hear him out."

"I told you Joe, I've nothing to say to you or him." Ray took a step back and adjusted his grip on the shotgun, but was careful not to raise it. "Right, now it's time for you to be on your way, Joe. And don't come back."

Joseph stared at Ray for a long moment, then smiled and removed his hands from the top of the gate, raising them slightly in mock surrender. "Okay, Ray. Sure, you have a think about it. You know where we'll be."

The three men returned to the car and the full light snapped on again, washing over Ray and illuminating the driveway. Ray turned back towards the house and looked beyond his elongated shadow, which stretched up to the front steps. No one else had come out. He was thankful for that. Less explaining to do.

Ray's shadow twisted, distorted and then disappeared, as the car at the gate reversed and swung out on to the road. He resisted the urge to look back as it pulled away.

CHAPTER ELEVEN

"Is this everything?" asked Lisa, looking through the box that her mum had packed for Aunt Maria.

"Yes. I've a couple of fresh loaves in there and a container with some of Derek's salmon," said her mum.

Lisa smirked at Ray when her mum referred to it as *Derek's* salmon, but he didn't react. He seemed distracted and distant.

"Oh here, don't forget the flasks," added her mum, reaching for two large thermos flasks on the counter. "Tell her that's vegetable soup, made fresh this morning. But it'll not stay hot long, so they should have it for lunch."

"Okay."

"And the eggs," she said, lifting a cardboard egg carton and wrapping it in a tea towel.

"I thought you were gonna hard boil those for them?"

"I did."

"So why are you wrapping them in a cloth?" asked Lisa, turning to Simon and rolling her eyes.

"Oh, umm, well, it'll stop them from falling out," said her mum, fussing with the contents of the box and wedging the eggs in tight. She covered her mouth with her hand and looked to the ground, wrecking her brain for anything else that she could send. "Okay, that's it I think. Ray, will you carry the box, please?"

Ray sat at the kitchen table in a vacant daze.

"Ray!" said Lisa.

"It's okay. I'll take it," said Simon, when Ray didn't respond.

"Planet earth to Raymond Keenan," said Lisa.

"What?" said Ray, snapping from his daydream. "Right. Are we ready?"

Ray stood and lifted his coat from the back of the chair.

"Now, remember to tell your aunt Maria that her and Conor are very welcome to come and stay here."

"And where would they sleep?" asked Ray, as he shrugged into his jacket.

"We'll find somewhere for them."

Lisa could see Simon squirm. He must've taken that as a dig at him for taking up one of the beds. *Nice one Ray.*

"You know what Maria's like, mum," said Lisa. "There's no way she'd come over." She glanced at Simon again, hoping that would put him at ease a little.

"Well, make sure you offer anyway."

Ray led the way down the hall, followed by Simon and Lisa.

"Did you remember the logs for the fire, Ray?" his mum called after them.

"Yes, they're in the car, mum," said Ray. "See you in a couple of hours. Make sure you keep some of that soup for us. Don't let Henderson eat it all."

"Okay, be careful on the roads now."

As the car rolled down the driveway, crunching over the loose gravel, Ray turned to Simon. "Would you mind getting the gate, Simon?" He held out a bunch of keys. "It's the one with the blue tape on it."

"Sure," said Simon, taking the keys and singling out the key for the padlock. He jumped from the car as soon as Ray had stopped, and started working at the lock and chain. He fumbled with the keys, dropping them twice in the progress.

Lisa could see Ray silently judging, an eyebrow raised in derision.

"So, has he made his move yet?" asked Ray with a smirk.

"Shut up you, will ye!" snapped Lisa.

Simon swung the gate open and waved them through.

"Poor guy doesn't know what he's getting himself into."

"Stop it!" said Lisa, her irritation growing, which was exactly what Ray was going for. Lisa had had a lifetime of being wound up by her older brother. It seemed to be his favourite source of amusement.

Ray looked out the side window while they waited for Simon to close the gate again. Lisa couldn't see it, but she knew her brother had a huge grin plastered across his face. *Prick!* She could feel the heat rising on her own face. She wasn't usually like this, and the more she tried to ignore it, the worse it got.

Simon climbed into the back, leaning forward slightly through the space between the seats. "What's your fuel situation like Ray?" he asked, lifting his head to try to see the fuel gauge through the steering wheel.

"Full," said Ray, confidently.

"Yeah?" said Simon, a surprised inflection in his voice.

"We've a diesel bowser for the farm machinery," said Ray.

"And you can use that same stuff in your car?"

Ray cast the slightest of glances at Lisa. "Yeah. Well, you're not supposed to for tax reasons, but I can't see us getting stopped and tested today."

Simon sat back and looked out at the passing Donegal scenery. It'd been dark when they'd made their tired hike along this same road on Friday night, but today the valley stretched out towards the hills in the distance, a patchwork of varying shades of green.

Lisa fiddled with the radio for a while, but soon gave up when she couldn't find a station.

"Look!" said Lisa, nodding at the road ahead. A white van, with the letters ESB stencilled on the back, was parked beside a small electrical substation. A man in a hi-vis jacket could be seen at the side door.

"What is it?" asked Simon, sitting forward.

"An ESB engineer."

"What's ESB?"

"It's the main electricity company," said Lisa. "Slow down, Ray."

"Maybe he'll know something about when the power will be back on," said Simon excitedly.

Ray slowed and pulled to a stop behind the van. The engineer raised his head at the sound of their car pulling into the lay-by. He paused for a moment before returning to his task of loading his equipment. He lifted the final piece of gear into the van and pulled the sliding door closed.

"We probably shouldn't all just bounce out and run up to him," said Ray.

"I wanna hear what he has to say," said Lisa, ignoring Ray's advice. She opened her door, placed the two thermos flasks on the seat and strode over to the engineer, wincing slightly when she momentarily forgot about her still-weak ankle.

"Hello there," she called as she approached.

The engineer opened the driver's door of the van, then paused, probably wishing he'd been thirty seconds faster. He looked tired, and didn't seem in the mood to answer questions; likely the same questions that he'd been asked by every person he'd come into contact with in the past few days.

"How's it going?" said Lisa, with a friendly smile.

The man sighed and put his hands on his hips. "Before you ask. No, I don't know when the power will be back on."

Lisa heard Ray and Simon's doors close behind her, curiosity obviously getting the better of them.

"There's no word then, of when it'll be fixed?" asked Lisa, careful not to appear pissed off.

"Afraid not."

"I suppose you've never seen anything like this before?" said Simon, stepping up beside Lisa.

"Nothing to this extent, no."

"Were these things damaged by the CME too?" asked Simon, pointing to the cluster of grey units enclosed behind a small square of green security fencing, a familiar yellow sign warning *Danger of Death - Keep Out*.

The man tilted his head at Simon, maybe surprised at his use of the term.

"No, not really," he said. "I've checked quite a few in the last week, and there's only been a couple of minor issues. The problem's further up the chain."

"The transformers?" asked Simon.

"That's right."

"I assume that's not good," said Simon.

"Ha. You could say that," said the engineer, with a humourless laugh. "It's been hard to get a clear picture of exactly what's going on. I'm just going round making sure we're good to go locally for when they do get it sorted."

"And they've no idea when it'll be back to normal?" asked Ray.

The man shook his head and huffed. "God knows when it'll be *back to normal*," he emphasised the last three words. "Depends when they can get replacement transformers. If that's what the problem is. We haven't heard for sure. But even when they do start to get things going again, it'll not be like flicking the switch."

Ray frowned. "Why's that?"

"We'll probably see some areas come on before others, depending on where they are in relation to the power stations and wind farms."

"The wind turbine at our place is working fine," said Ray.

"Yeah, the wind farms themselves are probably fine. The problem is getting that electricity to where it needs to be. And I'm sorry to say once they do start to get things connected, I'd expect them to be directing that power to major cities. Can't see Donegal getting back online anytime soon."

"What are you thinking? Weeks?" asked Simon.

"No idea."

"If you were to guess?" said Lisa, again with a disarming smile.

"Yeah, weeks, at least. If your wind turbine is working, you're in much better shape than most," said the engineer, as he started to edge towards his door. "Must get on."

"Thanks for talking to us. I'm sure you're sick of answering the same questions," said Lisa.

The engineer rolled his eyes and nodded in agreement. "Well, good luck to you," he said, before climbing into his van to resume his rounds of the substations.

###

"So it looks like Michael Foy was right," said Lisa, as Ray pulled out on to the road again.

"And Martin called it from the start," said Simon quietly from the back seat.

Conversation was sparse for the rest of the journey to Maria's house, as each of them contemplated the information that the engineer had given them. Until now it'd been guesses and hearsay, but there wasn't much better confirmation of what they'd feared than hearing it from an actual engineer who worked for the electricity company.

The roads remained quiet for most of the journey. The only people they'd seen on the way had been a couple of small army patrols; one at a petrol station and another manning the gate at the main supermarket on the edge of the town. In the town itself, there was a little more life; a few small groups of people congregated outside one of the churches and at a community centre, and they passed a handful of cars on the road.

As they pulled up outside Maria's house, a few of her neighbours, who'd been gathered in conversation, paused their discussions to watch as Lisa, Ray and Simon unloaded the car and approached the door. They were likely questioning the source of the supplies that the three of them carried. Lisa felt a little guilty, envious eyes watching as they waited for Maria to answer.

"Ah Lisa, Ray, it's good to see you," said Maria, as she ushered them inside.

"My mum sent over a few things to keep you going," said Lisa, stepping past Maria into the living room of the small terrace house. "This is my friend Simon."

A broad smile stretched across Maria's face. She looked thin and pale. Lisa had only been back home a handful of times for the weekend so she hadn't seen her aunt in a few months. Sometimes the closer you live to someone the less effort you make to visit. There's always tomorrow or next week. She was surprised, though, at how much Maria seemed to have aged in that short time. Maybe it was her diabetes or one of her other many ailments. Ray would visit a lot more often though, he and Maria had always been close.

"Hello, Simon. Nice to meet you. Please excuse the mess," said Maria, lifting a loosely folded blanket which had been tossed over the back of an armchair. She looked to Lisa again, lingering just long enough in the hope of receiving a little more explanation of who this Simon was. Lisa didn't bite.

"So how have you been? Have you had enough to keep you going?" asked Lisa, glancing towards the adjoining kitchen.

"The first couple days were fine," said Maria, perching on the edge of the single chair and gesturing for Lisa and Simon to take the small two-seater settee. Ray had gone straight through and out into the backyard with the sack of chopped firewood. "We had enough bread and milk and stuff. It was a real pain not being able to heat anything, though."

"You've an electric cooker, don't you?" asked Lisa.

"Yeah. Thought about getting the gas in a couple of years ago. Wish I had've. The neighbour has one of those barbecues with a little gas ring on it. He let me use it to cook some tinned stuff that we had. But I didn't want to ask too often or use too much of his gas, you know."

"I think we might have a gas bottle at the house. We could bring it over," said Lisa.

"Yeah, that'd be great, would be useful for boiling some rice and pasta. I've a cupboard full of that."

"How's Conor doing?" asked Lisa in a hushed tone.

"He's barely come out of his room all week," said Maria, matching Lisa's volume.

Lisa leaned forward slightly, her brow furrowed. "It must be awful for him."

Maria turned to Simon. "My son's best friend died in an accident last weekend, when they were out on the lake," she said, by way of explanation.

"Yes, Lisa's mum had mentioned it. It must've been terrible," said Simon.

Maria cupped her cheek with her hand and rocked her head back and forth. "They haven't even got the body back from the morgue. The poor family. And then all this going on. God knows when they'll be able to bury him. Ah, it's terrible." She let out a deep sigh and closed her eyes, pressing her hand to her chest. "And Conor blames himself."

"Why does he blame himself?" asked Lisa, careful again to keep her voice hushed.

Maria leaned forward, her voice barely above a whisper. "They were fooling around and Conor threw Eamon's paddle off the end of the jetty. When Eamon dived in to get it he hit his head. Died instantly."

"Jeez, that would be awful to try to deal with," said Simon.

"He's barely spoken, or even left his room. He went to the shop for me yesterday. That's the only time he's left the house."

"I didn't think any of the shops were open," said Ray, appearing in the kitchen doorway.

"Did you not hear what was going on at Grinnley's in the town?" asked Maria. "Well, let me tell you," she settled back into her chair and began to recant the events at the grocery shop. Lisa and Simon voiced their shock and horror as the story progressed; first at the greed of the owner, then at the brutal vigilante justice doled out by the armed gang. Ray remained quiet at the door, a stern expression etched on his face.

When Maria had finished her retelling of the events at the shop, Ray tilted his head to her and motioned to the kitchen. "Here Maria, let me show you what my mum sent over."

"Oh, okay."

Lisa stood to follow them, but Ray stopped her. "It's okay, I'll show her," he said, a little abruptly.

Lisa frowned at her brother's strange behaviour, but a noise on the stairs distracted her and she turned to see Conor enter from the hallway. "Hi Conor, how are you holding up?" she asked in a gentle tone.

Conor stood by the door, his head held low. "Alright," he said, unconvincingly. He looked at Simon quizzically.

"This is my friend, Simon," she said, nodding to Simon, who'd twisted in his seat to greet Conor. "He came up from Belfast with me and Derek Henderson. You remember Derek, don't you? Ray's friend."

"Yeah, I've meet him."

"Nice to meet you, Conor," said Simon, standing and turning to offer his hand.

Conor looked down at Simon's extended hand, then awkwardly meet it with his own. "Alright. Nice to meet you," he said quietly, almost a mumble.

"I'm sorry for your loss. I lost a close friend last week too," said Simon, with a grimaced, sympathetic smile.

Conor looked around, seemingly unsure where he should go in his own home. He rounded the settee and took the chair that his mother had been using. He looked dreadful, his eyes dark and sunken, like he hadn't slept in a week – which was probably about right.

"How are things in Belfast?" he asked, directing his question towards Lisa.

"Not good," said Lisa.

"We barely got out with our lives," added Simon, before catching a glare from Lisa and dropping his eyes to the floor.

"What? What happened?"

Nice one, Simon, thought Lisa. She hadn't planned on telling the whole story during the visit. Her cousin had his own trauma to deal with.

"It's a long story," said Lisa. "I'll tell you some other time. How's your mum doing, Conor? She looks very pale."

"It's her diabetes. Her blood sugar's been all over the place."

"Okay, well, you'll both have to come home with us," said Lisa, rising and striding towards the kitchen.

With pursed lips, Conor shook his head. "Good luck convincing her of that."

Ray and Maria stood by the counter where the box of supplies sat untouched. Their hushed conversation stopping abruptly as Lisa entered. Lisa noticed Maria's stern expression, which was quickly disguised with another broad smile. "Lisa, thank your mum for me. This is great," she said, picking a loaf of bread out of the box.

"What are you two whispering about?" asked Lisa.

"Just talking about the situation with Conor," Maria whispered.

Ray looked away, reluctant to meet his sister's eyes. "I'll get the rest of the wood from the car," he said, then hurried from the kitchen.

Lisa glared at him as he slipped past her. She'd long since given up trying to understand her brother's moods.

"So how's your blood sugar, Maria?"

"Ah, you know, up and down."

"The food situation can't be helping," said Lisa, starting to unpack the items from the box.

"Yeah. This is good though," said Maria, taking a genuine interest in the box.

"My mum said you should come over and stay with us until the power's back on."

"That's kind, but can you really see me and your mum under the same roof for more than a few hours?" said Maria with a laugh.

Maria was ten years younger than her sister, and although they were usually amicable, old sibling tensions had been known to resurface at family gatherings, particularly with the aid of a few drinks.

"I'll be fine," she added, lifting a zip-lock bag of blueberries and another of strawberries from the box. "These are perfect."

Lisa's brow furrowed in disapproval. Not that she was surprised that Maria hadn't taken up her mum's offer.

"Well, you need to be very careful. You're looking very run down," she said.

"Oh, thank you very much, young lady," said Maria, feigning offence. "You're not looking great yourself. What happened to your head?"

Lisa sighed. "Long story."

CHAPTER TWELVE

Ray opened the front door and scanned the street as he waited for Lisa and Simon to say their goodbyes to Maria and Conor. On the way into the small council estate, he'd been cautious and on-edge, but somewhat hidden behind a pair of dark sunglasses. Now he was much more exposed and identifiable. He knew that Dermot O'Connor lived in the same estate, but he wasn't sure exactly which house was his. He'd meant to ask Maria, but Lisa had interrupted their conversation.

He was glad he had his aunt Maria to confide in. She'd always been supportive and encouraging, and when he was a teenager, she treated him like an adult. He didn't want to cause her any further stress. She looked like she was struggling as it was, but he needed to talk to someone, someone who'd understand the background.

He stepped to the side as Simon exited the living room, having said his goodbyes to Maria and Conor. Ray was impressed. He hadn't heard everything that was said, but Simon and Conor seemed to be getting on well and it looked like Simon sharing the story of losing his own friend had helped Conor open up a little.

"I'll be out in a second," said Ray, as Simon slipped past him into the front path. Ray pointed his keys at the car and it unlocked with a beep. He wanted to spend as little time in the open as possible, so he stepped back inside and waited for Lisa and Maria to finish their hug.

"Okay, so we'll be back tomorrow with a few more things and I'll see if we can get a gas bottle for you," said Lisa. "Ray, we've a gas canister that'd fit a barbecue, don't we?"

"Yeah, I'm sure we do. I'll check when we get back."

"That'd be fantastic," said Maria, her arms folded tightly across her chest as protection from the slight breeze from the open door.

"Now don't forget to take that soup before it gets cold," said Lisa, looking back as she sidestepped past Ray.

"Jeez, you're sounding more and more like your mother, Lisa," laughed Maria, rolling her eyes at Ray before pulling him in for a tight hug.

Lisa gave an exaggerated frown. "No, I am not!" She smiled and headed up the path after Simon.

"Right, now you be careful around O'Connor and his ones," said Maria, when Lisa was out of earshot.

"Yeah, I will."

"I mean it, Ray. He's not to be messed with."

"I know. I'll be careful," Ray said with a nod. "I'll see you later, Conor," he added, looking past Maria into the living room.

Ray hurried up the path and scanned the area again, before climbing into the car and pulling away, giving a quick nod to Maria, who waved from the door.

The roads through town were just as quiet as during their journey in. Ray had never seen the main street so desolate.

"Conor seemed to come out of his shell a bit," said Lisa, twisting in her seat to look back at Simon. "You two seemed to hit it off."

"Yeah, he seems like a good kid. He's really struggling, though. He blames himself for his friend's death," said Simon, looking down at his hands to break eye contact with Lisa. "I told him about what happened to Martin."

"Okay," said Lisa, with a sympathetic nod.

"I think he sensed that I felt where he was coming from."

"Fuck!" spat Ray, interrupting the conversation.

"What's wrong?" asked Lisa, turning to face forward again.

Ray eased his foot off the accelerator and nodded towards a group of men on the road a few hundred yards ahead. One of the men had just finished talking to a driver whom they'd stopped. He stepped back from the car as it moved off and was now focusing his attention on them as they approached.

"Are they cops?" asked Simon, squinting through the gap in the seats.

"Nope," said Ray dryly.

"What are they doing?" asked Lisa. Ray could feel Lisa's stare, but didn't answer.

The car kept moving, although noticeably slower. They were now within fifty yards of the makeshift road block and it was clear that the men weren't police or army. They were dressed mostly in black and wore ski masks over their faces.

"Okay, just let me do the talking," said Ray. He took a deep breath and let it out slowly. His heart was racing and his hands felt slick on the steering wheel. He thought about flooring it, it wasn't as if they were actually blocking the road and he couldn't see any weapons.

"Who are they?" asked Simon, the sight of the masks clearly spooking him.

"Ray?" said Lisa, anxiety creeping into her voice too.

Ray placed his hand on the gear stick, ready to slide it into first and hit the accelerator, if needed.

They were now twenty feet from the man standing in the road. Ray scanned each of the four men. Two stood beside a small hatchback car parked at the side of the road, another was positioned on the opposite side and the last was standing in the middle of the road. They stared at the approaching car.

Ten feet. Ray had a decision to make. Stop, or hit the accelerator.

The guy in the road raised his hand, gesturing for Ray to stop. He dipped his head slightly, looking under the sun visor, then his hand went to his chin and peeled his mask up. He smiled, an ugly, unmistakable grin revealing a wide space where two teeth should've been.

Ray's decision was made. He shifted from third gear into first and was just about to press on the accelerator when Joseph Kirkpatrick waved his hand, signalling for Ray to carry on. As the car glided past, Joseph brought his hand to his forehead in a mock salute, then extended his thumb and pinkie finger and held it to his ear.

Ray glared at Joseph as he applied controlled force to the pedal, moving off gently rather than powering away.

"What was that?" asked Lisa, twisting again to watch the men through the back window.

"What does he mean? Call me?" said Simon from the back seat.

Ray fixed his eyes straight ahead, stealing nervous glances in the side mirror.

"That was Joe Kilpatrick, wasn't it?" said Lisa. "Is he still involved? Have you been talking to him?"

Ray didn't respond, but could feel Lisa's stare burning into him from the passenger seat.

"What do you mean, *involved*?" asked Simon, flicking an involuntary glance at Lisa while trying to temper the anxiety in his voice. "Like IRA involved?"

"No," said Ray, irritated.

"Yes," snapped Lisa. "IRA involved."

"He was in the old IRA before the ceasefire. They're not active anymore," said Ray.

"Looked pretty active to me," said Simon, receiving the briefest of eye contact from Ray through the rear-view mirror.

"Probably just some of the local community making sure looters and burglars aren't making the most of things," said Ray, returning his eyes to the road.

Lisa and Simon continued to stare out the back window until the men drifted out of view as Ray increased speed and rounded a bend.

Ray blinked slowly, and quietly let out a long breath. This wasn't gonna go away. He couldn't just ignore these guys.

CHAPTER THIRTEEN

Derek sat on the front steps, his elbows resting on his knees, enjoying the midday sun on his face. He didn't smoke very often, a pack of twenty usually lasting him at least a couple of weeks, but as he rattled the solitary cigarette in its packet, he regretted not buying another box the last time he was in a shop.

He extracted the last cigarette and the cheap plastic lighter, which he kept wedged in the packet, and ran through his usual ritual; he rolled the cigarette back and forth between his finger and thumb, then stubbed the end a couple of times on the packet. He wasn't really sure what the purpose of this was, maybe it was to loosen the tobacco, but he'd seen it done in a movie once and it just kinda became a thing that he did.

Lighting his cigarette — probably his last for a while — he took a long draw and leaned back to rest on one elbow. He'd a perfect view of the hills sweeping down across the valley, and if he were to stand, he would just be able to see the edge of a small lake in the distance. A picnic area for sightseers ironically spoiled his view — a neglected old-style phone box, with at least one window smashed, sat beside two wooden picnic tables on a small, usually tended, square of grass opposite the Keenans' front gate. He doubted if it got much use in the age of the mobile phone, but he did remember that it'd still been in operation the last time he'd visited. Its lights had been on, and for him it helped identify the turn for their house, on the otherwise dark country road.

It was a beautiful day, with the sun sitting high in the unblemished cobalt sky. He thought of how rare it was to not see a plane in the sky or even the high-level contrail of at least one that'd passed by earlier. The sound of an approaching car brought his gaze back down to the gate to see Ray's car pull up and Simon emerge to tend to the lock.

Simon swung the gate open and the car pulled in. Ray didn't stop, instead he continued up the drive to the side of the house, leaving Simon to secure the gate and cover the thirty or so yards of driveway on foot. Derek shook his head and smiled. *Jeez, you can be a prick sometimes, Ray,* he thought.

Derek flicked a hand in greeting as the car passed by. He took a final drag on his cigarette, then looked around for somewhere to stub it out. With nowhere else to discard of it, he popped it into a small drain at the bottom of the gutter running from the roof. A faint sizzle confirmed its fate as it hit the water below.

"Hey," said Simon as he approached, seemingly unperturbed by having to walk up from the gate.

"How'd you get on?" asked Derek, pushing himself up from the steps.

"Yeah good. Well, actually not sure if good is the right word."

Derek tilted his head and fixed Simon with a quizzical frown.

"Well, we had an interesting journey over, and a scary moment on the way back," said Simon. "On the road over to Maria's, we came across an ESB engineer. That's the electric company."

"I know what ESB is," said Derek, impatient for Simon to get to the point.

"We stopped and chatted to him. He basically confirmed what the neighbour was saying," said Simon, flicking his head towards the neighbouring property. As he continued to relay what the engineer had said, Lisa and Ray rounded the corner of the house and made their way over. Lisa lagging behind slightly.

"And what was the scary moment on the way back?" asked Derek, glancing from Simon to Ray to include him in the question.

"An IRA roadblock," said Simon, eyebrows raised, emphasising the drama.

Derek shot Ray a look of concern.

"Ha, you're overreacting, big man," said Ray, with a laugh and pat on Simon's shoulder, before continuing up the steps towards the front door. "They were only local community members."

"Ray!" said Derek, irritated at his blasé attitude.

Ray looked back but didn't stop. "It was nothing, seriously," he said, with a dismissive wave of his hand.

"Sorry, I'm bursting for the loo," he added and disappeared inside.

Derek turned back to Simon and Lisa, who now sat on the bottom step massaging her ankle. "So what happened?"

"There were masked men stopping traffic," said Simon.

"And what'd they say?"

"They didn't stop us. They just waved us through."

"What makes you think they were IRA? Apart from the masks?"

Simon turned to Lisa. "You and Ray recognised the guy, right?"

"Yeah, Joseph Kilpatrick. Ray was at school with him," said Lisa. "He was in prison for IRA membership back in the nineties."

"How'd you know it was him if he was wearing a mask?"

"He lifted it up when we pulled alongside," said Simon. "Then he did this," he added, screwing his face in confusion and copying the *call me* gesture that Kilpatrick had used.

"And he directed that at Ray?" asked Derek, turning to Lisa.

Lisa shrugged, "Must have."

Derek's mind began to race. *Was this the guy Ray said he would talk to? Why didn't he mention him? Was he the one who was looking for the weapons?*

Derek smiled and shrugged. "Yeah, strange one," he said, making a conscious effort to remove the scowl that was now etched on his face. "I wonder if your mum has any of that soup left."

"Hope so. I'm starving," said Lisa, holding out her hand so that Simon would help her to her feet.

###

Derek dipped the edge of his freshly baked bread roll into the steaming bowl of vegetable broth. Questions still swirled in his mind as he regarded Ray across the table.

"This is fantastic, Moira. Thank you," he said.

"Well, you may get used to it. Looks like we're gonna be having it for a while," said Moira, with a smile. "Unless you can catch another one of those salmon."

"I could do. Although I think it's Ray's turn," said Derek.

Ray didn't respond.

"Isn't that right Ray?" asked Derek.

Ray looked up, suddenly aware that he was the topic of conversation. "What's that?"

"It's your turn to catch a fish."

"Ah yeah, right. No problem," said Ray with an unconvincing smile. "I'll go out a little later."

"Actually Ray, would you mind taking me to pick up my car?" asked Derek. "We left some of the baby's stuff that we couldn't carry."

"Ah, yeah, okay," said Ray, as he took his empty soup bowl and began to wash it at the sink. "When do you wanna go?"

"Now, if you don't mind."

"Okay, give me ten minutes and I'll get some diesel and a funnel."

"Right, sure I'll see you out front," said Derek.

Derek was intentionally quiet as they drove along the deserted country road. He wanted to see if Ray would elaborate on what Simon and Lisa had told him. Ray, however, seemed in no mood to talk.

"You alright?" asked Derek, finally breaking the silence.

"Yeah," said Ray, flashing another unconvincing smile.

Derek let out an irritated sigh. "Do you not think I've known you long enough to know when something is wrong?"

"What? I'm fine."

"Ray!"

Ray kept his eyes straight ahead.

"So what about this Kilpatrick guy? Lisa says you went to school with him?"

"Yeah, I knew him when I was a kid."

"Ray!" Derek was losing patience. "I told you not to keep me in the dark. We've always dealt with things together, mate. What is going on?"

Ray's shoulders dropped and he closed his eyes for a long moment, longer than he should've, considering he was driving. "He came to the house last night."

"What? When? Where was I? For fuck's sake Ray!"

"Just to the gate. I saw the car when I went to the bathroom," said Ray defensively.

"And what'd he want?"

"I don't know," said Ray, glancing at Derek.

"So is he IRA?"

"He used to be. Years ago. Before the ceasefire."

"So, what did he want?"

"He just asked me to go and talk to his boss."

"His boss?" Derek loosened his seatbelt with his thumb and shifted in his seat to face Ray. "So he's still connected?"

"He must be."

"Do you think he was the one looking for the weapons?"

"Don't know."

"It'd be a hell of a fucking coincidence for someone to be searching for a stash of IRA weapons, then for an IRA man to turn up at your gate asking for a chat, and for the two things not to be related. Don't you think?"

"Maybe."

"Maybe? What the fuck, Ray?" Derek stared at the side of Ray's face as his friend kept his focus on the road. *This was ridiculous. What was Ray not telling him? He needed to know what was going on.* "Okay, that's enough. Stop the fucking car. Now!"

Ray looked at Derek and, seeing the fire in his friend's eyes, he slowed and pulled off onto the hard shoulder. The car vibrated as it coasted across the rough surface. When it'd finally come to a stop, Derek turned fully in his seat to face Ray.

"Okay Ray, enough of these fucking *maybes* and *don't knows*," said Derek, his brow pinched. "What the hell's going on?"

Ray sat stony-faced, both hands still gripping the steering wheel.

"Ray! What are you not telling me?

"Okay. I had my suspicions when we found the crate," said Ray, turning and looking sheepishly at his friend. "Joseph Kilpatrick was one of the names that sprang to mind. And then when he turned up last night, that confirmed it."

"Did he mention the weapons?"

"No. I asked him if he'd been on our land and he denied it."

"Ah well, that's alright then. If he said it wasn't him, then nothing to worry about," said Derek, the sarcasm dripping from every word. "For fuck's sake, I told you not to keep me in the dark. It's not just your family back there, you know."

"I'm sorry. I thought I could go and see a guy and sort it out."

"No more fucking secrets, Ray. What guy?"

"Kilpatrick's boss. Dermot O'Connor."

Derek waited.

"He used to be the IRA's Quartermaster before the ceasefire. He would've been one of the guys responsible for the decommissioning of their weapons. I was hoping that maybe they'd just forgotten that one cache."

"And what? You thought he would just say *Oh yeah, I forgot about those ones, sure you just hold on to them*?"

Ray flashed a look of anger, as if tired of being talked down to. "I don't fucking know, Derek. I was gonna suss it out."

"Jesus Ray. Why the hell didn't you just tell me?"

Ray shook his head apologetically.

"Right, let's get this car and get back to the farm. I don't like the thought of us not being there."

CHAPTER FOURTEEN

Simon mumbled a curse and tried to rub away the pain from his forehead. He'd forgotten to duck, *again,* when exiting the small toilet which had been shoehorned in under the staircase.

"I don't think that was designed with tall people in mind," laughed Lisa, as she rounded the bottom of the stairs.

Simon smiled, red-faced. "Yeah, you're probably right. Is your ankle still sore?" he asked, seeing that Lisa was still hobbling.

"Nah, it's not too bad. Just a bit sore on the stairs."

"You should try to keep your weight off it for a while and maybe get more ice on it."

"Thank you, Doctor Wilson," Lisa said with a cheeky grin.

A solid rap on the front door directly behind Lisa made her jump.

"I think it's your neighbour," said Simon, spying the neighbour's unmistakable white hair through the small window.

"Hello Michael," said Lisa, when she swung the door open. "Come on in."

"No, it's fine, thanks. I was just wondering if anyone was planning to go to the meeting in town? I was hoping to grab a lift if possible. I can make my own way back," said Michael, patting the seat of the ageing bicycle that rested against his hip. "Just don't want to miss the start."

"I'd actually forgotten all about it," said Lisa, apologetically.

"Starts at two," said Michael, peeling the cuff of his coat back to glance at his watch.

"Do you fancy going?" asked Lisa, looking towards Simon, who'd joined her at the door. "We could drop that gas bottle over to Maria afterwards."

"Yeah, okay. But what about the roadblocks? You think it'll be okay?"

"Yeah, it'll be fine."

"Road blocks?" asked Michael.

"Yeah, there were masked men stopping cars earlier."

Michael laughed, "Ah, I wouldn't worry about that. It's just the local boys. As long as you're not planning to do any looting, you'll be grand."

"Okay Micheal, give me a minute and I'll get my coat, and make sure my dad's okay with me taking his car."

Simon, Lisa and Michael joined the steady stream of people filing in through the double doors, which led to the main hall of the community centre. The lines on the floor suggested that it was used for badminton and basketball, and probably a multitude of other activities. Today it was bare of all apparatus apart from two foldout tables in front of a row of plastic chairs at the far end of the hall. The attendees were expected to stand, so Simon and Lisa weaved their way towards the front and stood off to the side against the wall. Micheal had been lost to a conversation with a friend somewhere near the back.

Two construction site spotlights on yellow-legged tripods had been positioned at either side of the speakers' table, a cable running out through another set of double doors, presumably to a generator. The rest of the hall relied on the light from the open doors and from a row of small windows which ran along one side, high up near the ceiling.

As the organisers started to file in and take their seats, Simon scanned the crowd, trying to estimate the numbers. The hall looked like it would hold about two hundred people standing, but at a guess, he'd say there was only about half that number.

"Thought there would've been more people," he said, leaning in close to Lisa to be heard over the din of chatter from the expectant crowd.

"Yeah, me too."

As the crowd began to hush in anticipation of the organisers starting to deliver what everyone hoped would be good news, Simon felt Lisa's hand on his elbow. She pulled him down slightly and leaned in to whisper in his ear. She was so close that he could feel her warm breath on his skin. The sensation sent a ripple of electricity up the back of his neck to behind his ears. He couldn't help but smile.

"See over there, in the blue cap, beside the fire extinguisher?" she whispered. "That's Joseph Kilpatrick."

"Right, okay," said Simon, looking over but not quite registering who she was talking about or the significance. He was still distracted by the intimacy of her touch.

"From the roadblock today. The guy that went to school with Ray," she pulled him in even closer — to the point where the tip of her nose brushed lightly against his ear — and whispered even quieter. "The IRA man."

"Oh," said Simon, straightening and taking a more keen interest. He wasn't subtle either in his attempt to identify who she was referring to. Thankfully, Joseph Kilpatrick wasn't looking in their direction.

Simon saw who she was talking about. The man stood directly opposite them in a small group of similarly aged men with one much older man in the center, his arms folded across his barrel chest.

"See the older guy?"

"Yeah."

"That's Dermot O'Connor. Apparently, he was very high up in the IRA back in the 80s and 90s."

Simon turned to acknowledge Lisa with raised eyebrows. Their faces were so close that they must've looked like they were about to kiss. Simon, suddenly self-conscious, jerked back and looked away. He immediately regretted the abrupt movement as it caused Lisa to release her hold on his arm. *Maybe she realised how it looked, too?* He glanced back at her and caught her doing the same. They both smiled.

"Okay, everyone, thank you for coming," said the man in the middle chair behind the table.

The hum from the crowd quietened slightly, but some conversations continued further towards the back of the hall. The man raised his hands. "Can we have some quiet please and we will start? Thank you," he all but shouted.

The call for quiet passed like a wave through the crowd and the background noise dropped to a manageable level.

"I'm sorry, but we don't have a microphone this afternoon, but we will do our best to ensure that everyone can hear us," the man announced. "Can you hear me okay at the back?"

After a couple of confirmations from the back of the hall, he continued. "I am sure most of you know everyone at the table here, but just in case you don't, I will do a quick introduction, then we will make some announcements, and finally take some questions."

"Just tell us when the electric's coming back on," came a shout from the center of the room, followed by a flurry of murmured affirmations.

"Okay, okay, thank you. Yes, I know that's the question on everyone's lips, but if we can please keep the questions until the end, that would be very helpful."

The room quietened again.

"My name is Councillor Thomas Mallon. I am a member of the town council, although I have to point out that this is not an official council meeting. With me here is Chief Superintendent Trevor Kennedy of the Garda Síochána, Father Desmond Rice from St Anthony's, Captain Leon McGrath of the Defence Forces and a representative from the hospital, Doctor Sheetal Gupta."

Each representative acknowledged their introduction with a nod and a brief smile. None of them looked particularly happy to be there, and all wore stern or solemn expressions, except for the priest who had that universal priestly-look — a cross between optimism and sympathy.

"As you all know, we are currently experiencing an unprecedented and widespread power outage..."

The committee member went on to summarise the extent of the disruption, before handing over to the Chief Superintendent, who stood and addressed the crowd in a forceful and commanding voice.

"For the past number of nights, we have seen an increase in instances of antisocial behaviour, theft and vandalism. We in the Garda Síochána are taking this very seriously and, although we are currently experiencing shortages in manpower, we will be investigating every incident fully as soon as the power is restored. Make no mistake, anyone who engages in any form of unlawful activity will be held to account and will be prosecuted to the fullest extent of the law."

Next up was the doctor from the local hospital. She was a short Asian woman who, given by her accent, had lived in Ireland for many years. The hint of a Donegal lilt on top of her native accent was unusual, but endearing. She began quietly, then when informed by someone near the back that she couldn't be heard, her somewhat shy, unassuming voice transformed into a roar, which immediately demanded the attention of the crowd.

"I am here to give a brief update on the status of the hospital," she bellowed. "The hospital is open, but at a greatly reduced capacity. Due to issues with transport, and due to the fact that the schools and childcare establishments are closed, we too are experiencing staffing issues," she turned and nodded to the Chief Superintendent. "In addition to this, we are running off generators, therefore we have had to postpone all elective surgeries and procedures for the foreseeable future. We would ask the public to only attend the hospital in cases of emergency. Thank you."

Murmurs of decent started to hum through the crowd. They were obviously not impressed with what they'd heard so far.

A man at the front of the audience spoke up, clear and polite, but loud enough to cut through the rising noise of the crowd. "Excuse me."

The Councillor held up his hand. "I'm sorry we have a couple more announcements and then we will take questions."

"No, I'm sorry, this can't wait," said the man forcefully. "All we've heard so far is what we can't or mustn't do, and what the consequences will be if we step out of line."

The man's words emboldened the crowd, with multiple people now jeering and venting their frustration.

The man continued, encouraged by the support from behind him. "When are you gonna address the main issues? When will the power be back on? And why has the army stopped distributing food packages?"

A chorus of similar questions followed from the crowd. The organisers were close to losing control.

"Okay, let me answer the first question," said the Councillor, hushing the crowd again with raised hands. "ESB are working hard to make repairs, so the power is likely to be back on in a couple of days."

Lisa and Simon exchanged frowns at this comment, then Simon noticed a man making his way through the crowd with his hand raised. It was Michael; he seemed anxious to be heard. "Excuse me, Mr Mallon," more than a hint of derision in his voice. "Where are you getting this information from? Have you spoken directly to ESB? Have they provided you with that estimate?"

"Ah, no. I haven't spoken directly to them. As you can imagine, they are extremely busy, and with the telephone network down, it has been hard to get through. But, going by past experience, it is likely that the issues will be resolved very soon."

"I'd say you've just pulled that estimate out of your arse, Councillor," shouted Michael. "I'm part of an amateur radio network, and I've been talking to people all over the country, and in other countries, too. There is no evidence that this situation is anywhere near being fixed."

The crowd erupted again, the hostility in their voices growing.

Lisa leaned in to Simon again. "We should maybe tell them what the ESB guy said."

Simon nodded, then took a couple of tentative steps forward and stood beside Michael. "Excuse me. We spoke to an ESB engineer today," he said, waving his hand to get the attention of the Councillor. The Councillor looked at him and Simon repeated himself a little louder. "We spoke to an ESB engineer today, and he said it'd be weeks at the earliest before the power was back on."

"There you go," shouted Michael, as he put his hand on Simon's shoulder. "Even visitors know more about what's going on in our own country than you do. Or maybe you do know and you're keeping it from us. Is that it?"

The Councillor looked sheepishly towards the panel behind him for support. The army captain got to his feet.

"Okay, okay, everyone, please settle down," he said. His uniform and commanding tone gaining him a little sway.

Simon returned to stand beside Lisa and was met with a beaming smile.

"As you know, we distributed ration packs to the public last Thursday and Friday," the Captain continued.

"Yeah, but by the time most of us even heard about it, they were all gone. When are we getting more?" shouted someone in the crowd.

"We are having some logistical issues at the minute, but as soon as that is resolved, we will work with Father Rice and other clergy in the area to distribute ration packs as fast as possible."

"Why don't you just open the supermarket and give out that food?" asked a woman standing beside Michael.

"We do not have the authority to do that," said the Captain. "The supermarket is a privately owned company, and they have taken the decision to remain closed."

"Ah, hold on. You are the Army! Take control and do the right thing," said the woman, all deference for the Captain's position now gone.

"I'm sorry, but that is not something we have either the legal authority nor the resources to do at this time."

"So we're left to starve, or be at the mercy of scumbags like Rory Grinnley?"

The army captain looked blankly at the woman as a chorus of shouts backed up her question.

"Or are you gonna pretend that you know nothing about what he's been up to?"

The Chief Superintendent stood again. "We are well aware of the incident in question and the brutal attack on Mr Grinnley," he said.

"I'm not talking about him getting beat up," shouted the woman, the veins on her forehead and neck now bulging.

"He got what was coming to him!" shouted another man.

"I'm talking about him charging €10 for a tin of beans or taking people's jewellery and valuables as payment," continued the woman.

The man who Lisa had pointed out stepped forward. "Mr Kennedy," said Dermot O'Connor.

The furious woman turned to look at him, then yielded the floor, happy that he would take up the fight.

"As someone said earlier, you all seem to be doing a lot of talking, but all we've heard are warnings about us behaving ourselves, and what we shouldn't do. What we need to hear is what you're gonna start doing for the people of this town. Other than sit by in your cars and let people get ripped off. People need food, they need leadership, they need someone to take control."

"I am quite aware of what is needed, Mr O'Connor," said the red-faced police officer. "And I certainly know that the community does not need a bunch of vigilantes roaming the streets, intimidating people and attacking business men."

"You've no clue what's going on out on the streets, do you?"

"You can be sure, Mr O'Connor, that we know very well what is going on and who the perpetrators are. And I can guarantee you, when this crisis is over, we will be knocking on doors."

Dermot O'Connor laughed and turned to his group and then to the wider crowd. "You see, this is the mentality of the people responsible for keeping you safe. The people who're supposed to be managing this crisis." He turned back to the police officer. "You're a disgrace, Mr Kennedy. You have lost control of the situation."

The hostility of the crowd reached a new high, and Dermot O'Connor had to shout to be heard.

"Father Rice and Dr Gupta, I don't aim this point at you, but the rest of you up there, you're either totally uninformed as to the reality of the situation, or you're just blatantly lying to the people because you don't know what to do. Either way, we're not gonna accept it anymore."

The organisers looked at each other, faces flushed with embarrassment or anger. The priest stood and attempted to placate the crowd. It was too late, emotions were now running at fever pitch and his words were smothered by the cacophony of angry shouts.

Dermot O'Connor turned and spoke to his group of followers. Simon couldn't hear what was said, but the group immediately turned and made their way through the crowd towards the doors at the back of the hall. Some joined them, others remained and continued to shout questions and demands at the bemused organisers.

Simon looked at Lisa with raised eyebrows. "Wasn't exactly what I expected."

"No. I think it's time to go," said Lisa.

CHAPTER FIFTEEN

Dermot strode from the hall with purpose. He'd heard exactly what he'd expected to from the authorities; nothing. They were clueless, and now the people knew it too. As he made his way through the crowd, he could see that they were expecting him to do something, to take control of the situation and help them; where the council, the police, and even the army were unable or unwilling to. People shouted words of encouragement, some shaking his hand and patting him on the back as he passed. Many of them filed out through the doors behind him, angry and determined.

"Right. Start spreading the word. I want as many people as possible outside the gates of Lidl at 4pm," Dermot said, as he huddled with the Kilpatricks and a couple of others.

"What about the army patrol?" asked Joseph. "We don't have the guns yet."

"Yes, Joseph, I know we don't," snapped Dermot, leaving Joseph in no doubt that he blamed *him* for that fact. "We won't need them, not for this. We'll make the numbers work for us. Just make sure you spread the word. I want at least one hundred people there."

Joseph peeled off and drew a handful of their already recruited volunteers around him, instructing them to spread the word.

Dermot stood with his back against the car, watching as the excitement grew amongst the angered attendees of the pointless public meeting. There wouldn't be enough people in this group alone, but he knew word would spread quickly through the community. People were already frustrated by the lack of action from those in charge, and when the news spread that the electricity was likely to be off for an extended period, they would respond to his call to action.

With a wave of his hand, he beckoned Joseph over. "What's the situation with the truck?"

"It's ready to go. Barry was able to get us a couple of jerrycans of diesel," said Joseph. "It's all he could get past the patrol, but it'll do for a few runs."

"Right, we'll make do for now until we get properly equipped."

Dermot looked over Joseph's shoulder. "That's Ray Keenan's wee sister, isn't it?" he asked, flicking his head towards a small group who'd emerged from the hall.

Joseph turned to see who Dermot was referring to. "Yes, Lisa. And the one with the ponytail is their neighbour, Micky Foy."

"The other guy, the English one. Who's he?"

"I don't know, boyfriend maybe."

"Well, find out. And this guy, Foy. What do you know about him?"

"Not much, keeps himself to himself. A bit of a tech geek, I think."

"He said he was into amateur radio."

"Yeah."

Dermot turned back to Joseph. "If he's got walkie-talkies, they'd be very useful."

"I'll see if I can get a word with him."

"Let's sort out this Lidl thing first," said Dermot, before opening the back door of the car and climbing in.

As the car slowed to pick its way through the throng of people who'd spilled out onto the road, Dermot bobbed his head, satisfied that the numbers would work. There were easily over one hundred people making their way towards the supermarket at the bottom of the hill, more than enough to ensure that the small army patrol stationed at the gates would be powerless to stop them. He wanted to get there before the crowd became too unruly.

"Use the horn," he ordered the driver. "I want to get there before this crowd."

The driver did as instructed and forced his way through, encouraging those on the road to clear a path with a few blasts on his horn. Some shouted and gestured at his impatience, the fired up crowd easily angered by the aggressive driving.

"Pull up behind their jeep."

Dermot climbed from the car and looked back up the hill at the eager citizens who had answered his call. A small number had already begun to gather near the gates, some already in angry discussion with the two young soldiers who stood defiantly in front of the gates that they'd been tasked with securing.

"Alright folks, step away please," said Dermot as he approached the gates. "The lads are just doing their job. Back away please and give them some space now, will you?". The small group, recognising Dermot and encouraged by Joseph Kilpatrick and his men, backed away and stood expectantly on the other side of the road.

"Alright boys, how're you doing?" asked Dermot, approaching the two sentries with a disarming smile.

The two soldiers glanced at each other, uncertainty and worry etched on their faces. They nodded a weary thanks to Dermot for defusing the situation, but remained stoic.

"Looks like things are getting a bit heated," said Dermot, making a show of looking around at the gathering crowd.

"Yeah," said one of the soldiers, looking across at the group who'd been giving them a hard time. "I told them that we've been ordered to keep these gates closed."

"I think people are just hungry. Maybe they feel it's time to take matters into their own hands," said Dermot.

"There's nothing we can do, we've been ordered not to let any looters near the store."

"Looks like you might need to call in some reinforcements then," said Dermot with a sympathetic smile.

"I wish we could," said one of the soldiers, glancing nervously to Dermot, then up the hill at the people starting to fill the street as they made their way towards the supermarket.

"Are you locals, boys?"

"I am," said the smaller of the two soldiers.

"Do you know who I am?" asked Dermot, still wearing a politician-like smile.

"Yeah," said the soldier, uncertain if he should be admitting it or not. His partner frowned at him questioningly.

"Well, I'm here to make sure things don't get out of hand, and that no one gets hurt," said Dermot.

The local soldier shuffled on the spot, the other fidgeted with the strap of his assault rifle. He seemed unsure whether he should remove it from where it rested against his back.

Dermot nodded to the rifle. "I think it's safe to assume that you are not the only ones who are armed here, son."

The soldier looked wide-eyed at Dermot and slipped his thumb under the strap.

Dermot raised a calming hand. "It's important that everyone keeps a cool head here now, lad," he said. "We wouldn't want to incite the mob, now would we?"

The soldier kept his hand on the strap but left the rifle where it was.

"I was just at a public meeting with your commanding officer, Captain McGrath."

The two soldiers frowned, eyes still fleeting back and forth between Dermot and the growing crowd.

"Stay back there now, please," commanded the taller soldier as two of Dermot's men approached.

"It's okay, son, they're with me," said Dermot. "I told you, we're here to make sure things don't get out of hand."

The smaller soldier stepped in close and whispered in his buddy's ear, causing him to turn sharply and look at Dermot and then at his men, who now stood on either side. He looked them up and down, seemingly wrestling again with whether to unsling his rifle.

"Your Captain told the meeting, which I'm sure most of these good people attended," said Dermot, sweeping his hand in an arc towards the crowd, "that there're no more food rations to distribute."

Dermot stepped closer to the two wary soldiers. "So the reality of the situation here, boys, is that these people, your fellow Irish citizens, have been left with no option but to take matters into their own hands to feed their families. I'm sure you understand that."

"We can't let them do that," said the taller soldier defiantly, his raised pitch giving away his heightened anxiety.

"Okay, son, let me be very clear," said Dermot, the cordial facade suddenly replaced by a menacing tone.

"Unless you do as I say, this mob *will* get out of control and someone, maybe even yourselves, *will* get hurt. I'm sure you don't want to be the soldier who's remembered for firing on his own people because they were hungry?"

Dermot fixed the soldiers with an icy stare, waiting for his comments to sink in.

"Me and my associates here," he continued, "are gonna make sure that things are done in a controlled and orderly fashion. We're gonna access the store, doing as little damage as possible, and we're gonna load up a van and take the food to St. Anthony's church, where Father Rice will distribute it to the community."

As if choreographed perfectly, a large white van, with McNamee Furniture Removals stencilled on the side, turned the corner at the top of the hill and made its way towards them.

"Don't worry," said Dermot. "I'll make sure that we keep a record of everything that's taken and you can observe. I have to insist that you stay in your jeep, though, for everyone's safety. I'll make sure that your commanding officer is made aware of your sensible decision not to intervene, and that you were left with no other option, given the situation."

The young soldiers huddled again to confer, a brief whispered argument ensuing before being interrupted by Dermot.

"Okay lads, we need to do this now while we can still control this mob," said Dermot, a stern tone of finality helping to make the decision for the young soldiers. "Open the gates and bring your jeep down to the corner of the carpark."

The two soldiers conferred again briefly before the smaller of the two produced a set of keys and moved to unlock the gates.

Dermot smiled to himself. *Maybe I should've been a politician,* he thought.

CHAPTER SIXTEEN

The tension and anxiety, that usually companied Ray on his trips back to Donegal, had been multiplied tenfold since he'd found the crate, and since Joseph Kilpatrick had come to his home. He always feared that his past associations might come back to bite him at some point. That tension, although eased slightly since he'd told Derek about Kilpatrick and O'Connor, still knotted his brow and left a dull, unshakable headache. He was angry at himself for the lies he'd been telling his friend. Maybe he should've told him sooner. Surely Derek would understand and have his back. He was also angry at Joseph Kilpatrick and Dermot O'Connor and maybe just at the world in general.

"For fuck's sake, this is all we need," said Derek, as they rounded a bend and the lay-by, where he'd abandoned his car on Friday night, came into view.

A pickup truck was parked behind Derek's Nissan Primera Estate. Three men stalked around the stranded car, peering in through its windows and checking the doors. One of the men had something in his hand.

"Fucker!" spat Derek. "He just smashed the fucking window."

Ray's grip on the steering wheel tightened and his jaw clenched, as he accelerated hard and swerved into the small picnic area off the main road. He blasted the horn, which got the attention of the three men, then slammed on the brakes, coming to a skidding stop in front of Derek's car.

Ray exchanged a look with Derek, the rage in his friend's eyes burning as hot as his own. They flung their doors open and bounded from the car, fists clenched.

"That's my fuckin' car, you prick," screamed Derek, as he stalked towards the guy who'd just smashed the side window of the Nissan with a claw hammer, which he now held low at his side.

"What the fuck are you doing, asshole?" shouted Ray.

Derek's pace slowed when he spotted the hammer. "Careful Ray, he's got a hammer," he said under his breath.

"I see it," said Ray, as he powered past Derek and made his way directly towards the man.

The guy was big, even taller than Derek, with broad muscular shoulders. He wore a farmer's uniform of checked shirt, mud-caked jeans and heavy work boots. The man on the other side of the car was of similar appearance, albeit with a different-coloured checked shirt. He started to make his way around the front of Derek's car to join his mate. The third guy, who'd been peering through the back window, was shorter and much thinner than the other two and seemed happy to hang back.

The man with the hammer smirked and shrugged his shoulders. "Thought it was abandoned."

"Well, it's not fucking abandoned, it's ours," shouted Derek.

"Aye, so you say."

"Yes, we do fucking say," snapped Ray.

The big guy took a step back, surprised by the fact that Ray hadn't slowed. He raised the hammer and swiped it in an arc as Ray stalked towards him. Ray anticipated the move and halted abruptly, letting the heavy weapon slice through the air inches from his chest. As the farmer tried to reverse his swipe, Ray stepped in close and caught the man's wrist with his right hand, rotating it slightly to line up the huge man's elbow. In a near simultaneous move, he drove the palm of his left hand into the man's elbow, causing a jarring hyper-extension. It wasn't enough to break the muscular arm but did cause the guy to screech in pain. The hammer dropped to the ground and Ray flicked it away with his foot.

As part of their job, Ray and Derek were sent on self-defence and hand-to-hand combat courses every couple of years. Ray took every chance he could to get to the various conferences even more frequently. He'd even attended one where the guest instructor was an ex-special forces trainer who'd then gone on to work in the private sector as a bodyguard for celebrities like Madonna, Britney, and even Michael Jackson. That instructor's speciality was how to take down a much larger opponent, techniques that Ray now hoped would work in real life.

When the second man saw things kicking off between his mate and Ray, he launched into his own attack on Derek. He lunged forward, swinging a wild right hook, followed by a left, as he barrelled towards Derek. The man's bulk made him slow, which allowed Derek to retreat just enough with each swing that he managed to avoid the sledgehammer fists. Derek anticipated the next wide right hook, and instead of stepping backwards, he held his ground. He ducked under the blow, feeling the fabric of the checked shirtsleeve brush against his hair, and stepped to the left. The right side of the man's ribcage was now fully exposed. Derek remained low and drove off his left foot, channelling all the power he could muster through a left hook to the man's side, just below his armpit. A less-padded opponent would've crumpled from the pain of broken ribs, but this guy, likely hardened by many years of manual labour, managed to stay on his feet. The air left his lungs with a groan and his right arm folded in to protect his damaged side.

A few feet away, Ray tried to use the split second advantage he'd gained from the elbow strike. He slid his left hand down to meet his right, gripping the guy's wrist, both his thumbs pressed into the back of his assailant's hand. Ray stepped back, drawing his hands in a wide upward arc as he applied pressure to the wrist lock and attempted to execute a wrist throw. A normal sized opponent would've succumbed to the pressure and been brought crashing to the floor, but not this guy. The farmer stumbled slightly, but managed to yank his hand from Ray's grip. Ray had to rethink. Getting this monster of a man on the ground wasn't gonna be easy. *If in doubt, go for the knees,* he remembered the special forces instructor telling the class. The guy stumbled forward, swiping at Ray with a balled fist. Ray curled his right arm up to protect the side of his head just in time to absorb the blow. At the same time, he rotated and landed a sweeping kick to the inside of the man's right knee before spinning away and stepping out of reach. The pain registered on the big man's face, but he stayed on his feet. It'd take more than one kick. Ray glanced quickly in Derek's direction and saw that he too was now in a tussle with one of the other men. The third guy hadn't moved from behind Derek's car.

With his opponent cradling his bruised ribs, Derek stepped in and clotheslined him across the throat. The blow stunned the farmer and he reflexively dropped his chin, but not before Derek had wrapped him in a choke-hold. He tightened his forearm across the man's throat, angling it up across his jugular vein and clamping it in place with his other hand. Derek pressed himself into the man's back, leaving no wriggle room. As he rotated his arm, so that his radius bone all but closed off the farmer's blood supply, the man writhed and squirmed. He desperately twisted one way, then the other, trying in vain to shake Derek loose. In desperation he threw himself backwards, slamming Derek on to the front of his car, knocking the wind from his lungs as he bucked violently in a last-ditch attempt to free himself. Derek gritted his teeth and held the choke tight, every muscle and tendon straining. Derek could hear the choking groans growing weaker. The man clawed at Derek's vice-like grip, fighting to gain purchase, until finally, starved of oxygen, his limbs went limp.

Ray, meanwhile, used his superior speed and agility to evade the lumbering attacks of the first man. He ducked and weaved, frustrating his opponent and staying mostly out of reach of his scything swings. Ray kept his arms curled up tight to the sides of his head, elbows pointing forward. Even with his defences in place, the blows that did land rattled his brain. He continued to target the farmer's right knee with kicks. The accumulative effect was taking a toll. With each kick, the grimace on the man's crimson, sweat-covered face intensified. His lunging attacks had slowed, allowing Ray to target the knee with greater veracity, to the point where he felt one more solid connection would bring the bigger man down. The farmer knew it too. His attempts to land one of his hay-maker punches ceased. He stood, fists still balled and face twisted in pain and rage, but no longer chasing Ray in circles.

The farmer looked past Ray to where Derek was now placing his unconscious friend in a recovery position, his demeanour changing in an instant as he opened his fists admitting defeat, or at least stalemate.

"Alright, alright. Take your fucking piece of shit car."

Ray was a little disappointed. He wanted to beat this fucker to a pulp, and he knew with Derek's guy now out of action, they could easily take this one down between them. He glared at the man and tried to bring his heavy breathing under control before speaking.

"Take your fat friend and get the fuck out of here."

The third man approached tentatively like a nervous cat, ready to bolt at the slightest flinch from either Derek or Ray. He approached the unconscious man, who was slowly starting to stir.

"Is he alright?" he asked, timidly.

"He'll be fine. He'll have a serious headache for a while, though," said Derek.

Ray's guy glanced to where his hammer lay a few feet away, then back to Ray. Ray shook his head.

"Leave it. Just help your mate and get in your fucking car."

The big man glowered at Ray, but did as he was told. He moved slowly towards his two companions, trying and failing to hide the pain in his knee as he limped past Ray.

Derek joined Ray, and they watched as the three would-be car thieves hobbled to their car and bundled their semi-conscious friend into the back seat before pulling away, spinning their wheels and throwing up dust and stones in a final show of defiance.

Derek looked at Ray. "So you don't think we could've just talked them down?"

"Doubt it. Not pricks like them," said Ray. He turned to Derek, a slight smile curling the side of his mouth. "I think I needed a good fight, anyway."

Derek shook his head and blew out a long breath. "Fuck me Ray. That could've easily gone the wrong way."

Ray shrugged and turned to get the fuel and funnel from his car. "Right, let's get this car back home."

CHAPTER SEVENTEEN

As Lisa pulled to a stop outside her aunt's house, she could see Maria standing at the door with yard brush in hand. She, like a number of other neighbours, had been roused by a commotion in the street. Some pretended to water their hanging baskets, others swept their paths, and some just stood with arms folded and watched as a small cluster of people argued intensely a few doors up from Maria's.

Lisa wasn't the rubber-necking type but she couldn't help overhearing some of the dispute as she and Simon retrieved a small two ring camping stove and a bottle of barbecue gas from the car.

"They're my kids!" screamed a blond-haired woman, trying in vain to escape the embrace of her male companion, presumably to launch an attack on the man on the other side of the small garden gate.

"They're staying with me till this is over," shouted the man. An ex-partner, Lisa assumed.

"You can't fucking do this. I was supposed to have them this week." The woman thrashed wildly, trying to get free.

Another woman stood on the front doorstep, arms folded defiantly across her chest. "Get the fuck away from my house, you psychopath."

"What did you call me? You fat, ugly bastard," screamed the restrained mother.

"Hey, shut your fuckin' mouth, bitch," shouted the man behind the gate.

By the time Lisa and Simon had made it up the path to join Maria and Conor, the argument had kicked into high gear. The two men, ex-partner and new partner, were now in each other's faces in the front garden, spitting insults and defending their respective partner's honour. In a flash, the two men were entangled. They wrestled back and forth, before tumbling in a heap over the small brick wall and into the street.

Lisa and Maria exchanged *oh dear* expressions of wide eyes, raised eyebrows and a hint of a smile. They watched on in guilty fascination. Just as Lisa began to feel that panicky urge – that she, or someone, should intervene – two other local men jumped in and tugged the two broiling rivals apart.

To Lisa, it seemed like an appropriate time to move inside, which they all agreed on wordlessly.

"We brought over a gas bottle," said Lisa. "Now, it's probably only half-full, but it should do for a while. And we found this camping stove."

"Oh, that's brilliant, thank you love," said Maria, as she made her way through to the living room. She moved slowly and a little paddedly, as if carefully stumbling in after a night on the town. With a steadying hand on the arm of the chair, she folded into it with a sigh.

"Are you feeling okay, Maria? You're looking a bit unsteady there," said Lisa, perching herself on the edge of the chair opposite. "Have you tested your levels?"

"Aye, I'm probably a bit low. I'm feeling a bit off, a wee bit dizzy."

"I'll get you something, and I'll make you a cup of tea," said Lisa, hurrying through to the kitchen to find something to bring Maria's sugar levels up.

"Thank you, Moira," said Maria sleepily. Lisa twitched a frown, then headed through to the kitchen.

When she returned with one of her mum's fresh plums, Simon was finishing adjusting a blanket around Maria's shoulders. Before he could retreat to his chair, Maria grabbed him by the wrist and pulled him close.

"Ray, you have to give him the guns," said Maria, in a weak but urgent rasp. "He'll come for them. Listen to me Ray. He's dangerous."

Simon's polite smile faltered and he flashed a look of concern at Lisa. Maria gripped his arm tighter, the whites of her knuckles beginning to show, and continued to speak with urgency, although most of what she said was incoherent.

And she's mistaking Simon for Ray, thought Lisa. *This is not good.*

"Promise me Ray."

"Maria, that's Simon, not Ray. Here you need to eat this," said Lisa, taking Simon's place and going down on one knee in front of Maria. She could feel her aunt trembling uncontrollably.

Maria's head began to lull. The babbling now replaced with a barely audible groan. Lisa steadied Maria's head with her left hand and held the plum against her lips.

"This isn't gonna work," she said sharply to Simon. "She's having a full hypo."

"What do you need me to do?"

"Get Conor. Tell him to get the Glucagon."

"The what?"

"He'll know. Just tell him his mum's having a hypo."

Simon moved to the foot of the stairs and called Conor's name. Not waiting for a response, he bounded up the stairs to fetch him.

Lisa continued to try to rouse Maria, but she was barely conscious. Hearing voices, and the clattering of the contents of a drawer, Lisa folded back the blanket and worked the sleeve of Maria's blouse up to expose her arm.

Conor strode through from the kitchen, a small bright-red plastic box, already open, in his hand. He withdrew a small vial and a syringe, and let the red box fall to the floor.

"Mum, we need you to open your eyes. Mum!" said Conor, firm and loud. He took her by the arm and shook her forcefully. There was little response.

Pulling the protective cap from the end of the needle with his teeth, Conor pierced the vial and injected the liquid from the syringe into the Glucagon powder. He withdrew the syringe again and began to rotate his wrist to swirl and mix the contents of the vial.

Lisa wasn't aware of Maria having had many diabetic hypos in the past, but with the way Conor moved so confidently and without a moment's hesitation, it looked like he was well practised.

He held the vial up and inspected it before inserting the needle again and extracting the required amount of dissolved solution. Lisa held the top of Maria's sleeve up and Conor administered the medication.

Conor put the protective cap back on the syringe and placed it on the sideboard, then pushed a small coffee table to the side to clear a space on the floor.

"Can you help me move her to the floor, please?"

Lisa and Simon helped to ease the unconscious Maria onto the floor and into the recovery position.

"How long before it takes effect?" asked Simon.

"Probably about ten minutes or so," said Conor, as he shook the blanket out and draped it over his mother. "Would you mind grabbing a basin from the cupboard under the sink please, Simon?"

"Sure."

"She might feel sick when she wakes up."

Lisa was amazed at how Conor had sprung into action. Before this, he'd been barely functioning — consumed by grief and wallowing in self-pity. Now he was calm and focused, and fully in charge of the situation.

"Do you think we should take her to the hospital?" asked Lisa.

"We'll see how she is when she wakes, but yes, I think we probably should," said Conor, from where he knelt beside his mother's head. "Would you mind taking us?"

"Of course. But when they check her out, the two of you are coming back to our house until the power is back on. No arguments! You don't have the right foods here to keep your mum's sugar levels stable."

Conor kept his attention on his mother, but bobbed his head in agreement. "Okay, thank you Lisa."

CHAPTER EIGHTEEN

Ray parked his car tight behind Derek's at the side of the house and sat for a moment, collecting his thoughts. He watched as his friend proceeded to unload the gear from his car, shaking little beads of safety glass from the items that'd been stacked on the back seat.

The adrenaline in Ray's system had now subsided. The fight with the farmers having proven a welcome, if temporary, distraction from his current worries. A less than friendly look from Derek reminded him of his dilemma. Doing nothing, and hoping the problem would go away, was no longer an option. He couldn't put off talking to Dermot O'Connor for much longer. How the meeting would go, he didn't know. He hadn't spoken to the man in nearly twenty years, but he was in no doubt that things would get a lot worse if he didn't go to see him.

Ray took a deep, recharging breath before getting out to help Derek carry the rest of their belongings into the house.

"I'll get that," said Ray, reaching for a suitcase.

"Thank you," Derek replied dryly.

The house was strangely quiet. For the last couple of days it'd been alive with people and activity and awash with the peculiar aromatic cocktail of baking bread infused with baby's nappy — a welcoming slap in the face. The only sound came from the kitchen, and as they entered they found Moira busy, as usual, at the counter kneading doe.

"Hi mum."

"Hi boys, I didn't think you'd be so long," said Moira, as she placed a tray into the oven and turned to see Ray and Derek. "Oh my God! What happened to your head, Ray?"

Ray's hand went to his forehead and he turned to examine it in the mirror. A lump had developed around an angry-looking scrape above his right eyebrow. He hadn't noticed it until now.

"Ah, it's nothing. We had a little tussle with a couple of guys who were trying to break into Derek's car."

"What? Who were they?"

"Just a couple of local lads."

"They thought it was abandoned," said Derek. "We were just lucky to arrive at the same time."

"My God, what's the world coming to?" said Moira. "Sit down, Ray, and let me look at it."

Like a five-year-old with a scraped knee, Ray sat and allowed his mother to apply a liberal smearing of antiseptic cream to his forehead, a scene which would normally have been accompanied by amused ribbing from his friend. But Derek's mood seemed too dark for such teasing.

"Is Jenny upstairs, Moira?" asked Derek.

"Yes, she went up to put the wee man down for his nap."

"I'll see how she's getting on," he said, as he lifted an armful of their rescued belongings.

Ray winced as the antiseptic cream went to work on his wound. "Where's everyone else?"

"Your Dad's out with the birds. Lisa and Simon took Micheal down to the public meeting in town. Then they were going to call over to Maria's again."

"I forgot all about that."

"I'm sure they won't be long," said Moira, giving a final stinging dab with a ball of cotton wool.

A sudden noise in the hall snatched both their attention. A scuffling at the front door, followed by a series of loud thumps.

Ray rose quickly and went to the hall. An intense fear gripped him, and his pulse quickened. He hadn't locked the door – they never did during the day – but he also wasn't armed. He suddenly felt naked, defenceless. At any second, armed men could burst through the door, and he wasn't carrying his gun.

Another set of thumps bounced off the door.

As Ray advanced, he caught a glimpse of a foot in his periphery. His head snapped around to see Derek crouching near the top of the stairs. He nodded to Ray, then lifted the towel that he held to reveal his Glock 26, before returning it to its casual concealment. Ray nodded solemnly and reached for the door handle.

Just as he closed his grip around the handle, it turned and the door swung in quickly, bringing with it a stumbling body.

Ray recoiled, then immediately sprang forward again when he recognised the man in front of him.

"Jesus, Michael, what happened?" shouted Ray, as he grabbed hold of his neighbour, who was using the swinging door as an aid to remain standing. Blood dripped from a wound on his head and ran down his bruised and swollen face.

"Oh my God, Michael, what happened?" asked Moira, as she pushed past Ray and helped him escort Michael into the kitchen.

Other than a few groans, Michael didn't reply.

"Michael, what happened? Where's Lisa?" Ray asked, with frantic urgency.

"Men came to the house," said Michael, as they helped him into a chair.

"I left Lisa and the other guy in town."

A wave of relief washed over Ray.

Moira lifted the first aid kit, which still sat on the table beside them, and began to tend to the cut above Michael's eye.

"I was just back from town when they came to the door," said Michael, in a weak, shaking voice. "As soon as I opened the door, they forced their way in."

"Who were they? What did they want?" asked Derek, who'd followed them into the kitchen.

"They wanted portable radios," said Michael. He looked down at his trembling, blood-covered hands in a daze.

"Did you recognise any of them?" asked Ray.

Michael looked up at him, interrupting Moira's cleanup job. "Yeah, they didn't even bother covering their faces. It was one of them Kilpatrick brothers. And two other fuckers who I've seen about the town."

Moira gently repositioned his head so that she could continue. Ray and Derek exchanged worried looks at the mention of Kilpatrick.

"Joseph Kilpatrick?" asked Ray.

"No, the other one. They were at the town meeting with Dermot O'Connor."

Ray could feel Derek's eyes burning into him.

"O'Connor made a big scene at the meeting, saying that the authorities were useless and that people needed to take matters into their own hands. Then him and his followers stormed out."

Michael raised his hand to the cut on his forehead, only to have it brushed away by Moira.

"They must've followed me home."

"What did they take?" asked Ray.

"I told them they weren't getting a fuckin' thing," said Michael, his voice starting to break. "Then they threatened to shoot my dog, so I gave them two old Motorolas that I had."

"They had guns?" asked Derek.

"At least one of them did."

Moira tended to the wound and cleaned the blood from Michael's face. "It doesn't look too bad, Michael, now that the blood's been cleaned," she said.

"Thank you, Moira."

"You shouldn't need stitches. But you should maybe get it checked anyway, and go to the police."

"There's no point going to the police," said Michael, as he gently inspected Moira's dressing with his fingertips. "The police said themselves that they're totally over-stretched. I'll report it when the power comes back on."

"Ray, will you put the kettle on the stove please and we'll get Michael a cup of tea?"

"Yip."

When Ray finished filling the kettle, he finally allowed himself to meet Derek's persistent glare. Derek gestured with a nod for Ray to join him in the hall.

"Okay, Ray, this is getting out of hand," said Derek, when Ray stepped out into the hall and closed the kitchen door behind him.

"I know," said Ray, rubbing the back of his neck.

"We need to let everyone know," said Derek, "about the guns, the Kilpatricks, everything."

"Okay, but we have to wait until Michael leaves."

Derek held Ray's stare, then nodded, "Okay, but as soon as he's gone we tell them everything, right?"

"Okay."

"And we need to get the police involved."

Ray paced back and forth by the front door. He could feel the knot in his chest tighten. His whole world was about to change and he could think of no way to prevent it.

"It's not gonna be easy, Derek. There's gonna be questions asked about why we brought our own British-issued firearms over the border."

"I think we're beyond that now, Ray, don't you?"

"Not to mention the prison's weapons that you have upstairs."

"Well, we're just gonna have to explain the situation and hope they understand that we'd no choice."

"Yeah, well, I don't think it's gonna be that simple," said Ray with a deep sigh.

A silence hung between them for a moment as Ray, and likely Derek too, considered the consequences of their next step.

"Where's your PPW?" asked Derek, referring to Ray's personal protection weapon.

"In the gun safe," replied Ray, nodding towards the cloakroom.

"I think you need to have it with you. At least in your ankle holster."

Ray ran both hands slowly through his hair, then bobbed his head in agreement.

"We'll deal with this together, mate, okay?" said Derek, placing a supportive hand on his friend's shoulder.

"Derek!" called Jenny from the top of the stairs. "What's going on?"

"It's Micheal, from next door. He's had a break-in. I'll be up in a second," replied Derek. He turned back to Ray. "It's gonna be okay, Ray. I've got your back. We just need to be honest with everyone and take it from there."

"Yeah," said Ray, taking a deep breath to steady himself. "You're right. We need to deal with this."

Ray watched as Derek climbed the stairs and ushered Jenny into their room. For what would likely be a difficult conversation about what had been going on.

Following Derek's suggestion, Ray retrieved his sidearm from the safe and strapped his holster to his ankle before returning to the kitchen. His father had returned from his chores, and after hearing of Michael's ordeal, he was trying to persuade Michael to let him take him to the police. Michael continued to resist.

"There's no point at the minute, Vinnie," said Michael. "Thanks for patching me up, Moira. I think I'll just head back over home. The dog's pretty agitated. I don't want to leave her alone."

"Don't mention it Michael. But at least stay and have a cup of tea first and calm yourself," said Moira.

"And then I'll go over with you," added Vinnie.

Ray joined them at the table, although barely contributed to the conversation. His mind was elsewhere, consumed by the search for a solution that might result in him not having to tell his parents about the weapons cache, or at the very least, not having to involve the police. *Maybe there was a way.*

As soon as his dad and Michael had left, Ray made his way to the shed. He'd have to work quickly though. As soon as his dad and Lisa were back, he'd have to come clean about the weapons, and about the Kilpatricks coming to the house.

Closing the shed's heavy sliding door behind him, he retrieved the weapons from their hiding place and cleared a section of the workbench. The thick wooden surface of the bench had seen some action over the years, with stains and chips and even burn marks, showing its age. He looked down at the ancient vice bolted to the edge of the bench, remembering how he helped his grandad paint it a metallic-silver when he was a boy. The silver paint was now mostly gone, chipped off by tools and time.

When Ray caught his grandfather's judging stare from the photo above the bench, his eyes fell. He wondered what his grandfather would think of him now. He thought his past association with the Kilpatricks would've remained a benign secret, although a small voice often liked to remind him how dangerous secrets could be.

One by one, he began to disassemble and clean each of the guns, using a liberal amount of gun oil from his father's cleaning kit. The distinctive smell of the gun oil, like turpentine-soaked bananas, filled his nostrils and he remembered how his father had first shown him how to clean and care for the farm's rifles and shotgun. Ray cradled his head in his hands, his elbows resting on the bench. *Would his father even look at him again when he heard the truth?* He shook away the thought and continued with his task.

It took him nearly an hour to clean and reassemble the weapons and pack them into an over-sized canvas holdall. He jostled and adjusted it on his back, then kicked his bike free from its stand and pushed it out of the shed and around the side of the house. He wouldn't start the deafening engine until he was clear of the house, and clear of Derek, who'd undoubtedly try to stop him.

He hoped he was making the right decision.

CHAPTER NINETEEN

Dermot unlocked his front door and stepped inside, holding it wide for Joseph to enter with another large box of supplies, courtesy of Lidl.

"Put it in the kitchen please, Joseph," said Dermot.

"Hello Mr O'Connor," said Joseph, as he passed through the living room, startling a dozing Dermot Senior.

"What?" said Dermot Senior, jolting awake. "Who are you?"

"It's okay Da. He's with me."

"I'm Joseph, Mr O'Connor," said Joseph loudly.

"You don't have to shout boy, I'm not fuckin' deaf," said Dermot's father while rubbing an eye with the heel of his palm. "Joseph what? Where you from? Who's your Da?"

"Leave him alone Da, will ye? Go on, Joseph, put that in the kitchen, and get out before he interrogates you."

Joseph did as ordered as Dermot waited by the door. When they'd confirmed the arrangements for later that evening, Dermot closed and locked the door behind him.

"What's that?" asked Dermot Senior, tipping his head towards the box in Dermot's arms.

"It's a camping stove. We can heat some soup now, and make a cup of tea."

Dermot Senior looked unimpressed as he rolled his eyes and made a series of grunted tuts. "Sure, the tea's stinkin' with that fake milk stuff, anyway."

Dermot gritted his teeth, but held his tongue.

"And are you stupid or something? You need a gas bottle for those."

"It comes with two mini bottles," said Dermot, as he made his way through to the kitchen. He knew there was no pleasing the man. You could buy him a new car, and his first response would be that he didn't like the colour. It wasn't just his age, he'd always been a cantankerous ol' git. But at least he seemed to be having a good day. He knew who Dermot was, which wasn't always the case these days.

Dermot got the camping stove going and made tea, albeit with Soya milk. As expected, when he handed his father a mug, it was received with a grunt.

"That's that fake milk again," said his father, after a less than pleasing sip.

"It's all there is," replied Dermot, rolling his eyes.

"So, tell me what's been happening, son."

Dermot was a little taken aback, his father hadn't called him *son* in a long time. He remembered a time, before his father's faculties had started to fade, when they'd sit for hours talking about politics, history, and the struggle against the British, and tactics for defeating them.

"Well, it's a shambles. The authorities are useless. They're doing nothing to help the people."

Dermot relayed the events since the power had gone off; the emergency supplies given out by the army — which dried up after just one day — the shopkeeper who was jacking up his prices, the antisocial behaviour in the streets, and the events of that day.

His father listened quietly, taking in every word, which was strange in itself, as he would usually butt-in to tell Dermot what he should've done differently.

"I think there's more to this blackout than we're being told," said Dermot.

His father nodded slowly as he sipped on his tea. "You're finally starting to understand, son."

"What'd you mean?"

"Of course, there's more behind this. It's the British. They're finally implementing Operation Darkness."

Dermot frowned and shook his head in confusion.

"In the seventies, we uncovered details about an invasion plan by the British, backed up by the French."

"The French?"

"Yeah, we were surprised too," said his father, grunting with effort as he adjusted his seating position. "It sounded stupid at the time, but the intel was there. I saw it myself. And now, here we are, it's happening."

Instead of dismissing the idea as the ramblings of a senile, bitter pensioner, Dermot settled back in his seat and listened to his father's theory, which began to make sense.

Dermot's family had been involved in *the struggle* for nearly one hundred years, starting with his grandfather. Dermot's grandfather, at seventeen, was due to join a cousin in America and start a new life. That dream ended the night before he was due to leave, when he was dragged from his bed by the Black and Tans, a branch of the Royal Irish Constabulary made up of mostly unemployed ex-British soldiers who'd served in the First World War. The Black and Tans were notoriously brutal, as his grandfather would later attest. They tortured him for three days, trying to get the names of his IRA comrades. Seeing as he was not involved in the IRA, nor knew anyone who was, he couldn't tell them anything — so the torture continued. On the third day, they took him to a remote location on the back of a horse-drawn cart and told him he was free to go. They told him to run, which he struggled to do due to his injuries, and when he was about twenty yards away, they shot him in the back, leaving him for dead. Luckily, a farmer heard the shot and found him. After he'd recovered, he set his dream of America aside, and did indeed join the IRA, quickly rising through the ranks.

Anti-British sentiment was in the air that they breathed when Dermot was growing up, and also when his father was young. Hatred for the British had a hand in every decision the family made, and was discussed daily, but he'd never heard of a British plot to invade. He felt stupid for not seeing it sooner.

His father went on to tell him how they'd intercepted a British agent and learned of the invasion plot. The British, with help from the French, had a plan to simultaneously attack power stations throughout Ireland. That's where the French came in, their saboteurs would pose as tourists in camper vans and begin the invasion with a country-wide blackout, allowing the British to invade and take the rest of the country.

Rather than reacting, like any reasonably minded person, to the absurd idea of the British and French wanting to invade Ireland, Dermot listened intently — not just because he was happy to be having a lucid conversation with his father, but because he believed every word. Everything was starting to make sense. The British must've infiltrated the Irish government, the army, and the Guards. That's why they were leaving the people to fend for themselves.

"They've infiltrated the government, Da," said Dermot, when he'd fitted all the pieces together in his head.

"I'd say you're probably right, son."

"Fuckin' traitors."

His father nodded solemnly. "So what you gonna do about it?"

CHAPTER TWENTY

Ray parked his bike in an alleyway a couple of streets from the dingy little bar. He was confident that his hiding place for the weapons was secure, at least for a few hours.

Before stepping out of the alley, he considered whether to move his pistol from his ankle holster to his waistband, but decided against it. He wasn't expecting there to be trouble at this meeting.

The main street was eerily quiet as Ray approached the heavy wooden gates. The small hatch door in the center of the gates was closed, as it normally was. He banged on the door with his fist, and almost immediately heard the clatter and slide of a bolt. The door inched open and a sliver of face and suspicious eye filled the gap.

"What do you want?"

"I'm here to see Doc."

After a slight delay, the door swung inward. Ray stepped over the lip of the hatch, ducking at the same time to avoid the top of the frame.

In addition to the young gatekeeper, two other men – neither of which he recognised – stood and eyed him suspiciously. The older of the three, a man in his fifties with a crooked nose and a rapidly receding hairline, stepped forward.

"What do you want with Doc?" he asked, a stern, unwelcoming scowl fixed on his face.

"That's between him and me," replied Ray, holding the man's stare.

A flash of amusement appeared on the man's face as he came within inches of Ray's, expecting his intimidating stance to unnerve him. It didn't. Ray was used to dealing with people who thought they were hard, and he knew that showing any kind of weakness was like waving a red rag at a bull.

"We need to search you," the man finally said, nodding to the wall behind Ray. "Put your hands against that wall."

"How about you go fuck yourself?"

The balding man stopped short, surprised by Ray's show of defiance. He turned to his two comrades.

"Thinks he's a tough guy," he said with a sneer.

"Get up against the fuckin' wall, tough guy," the man shouted, as he stepped in and tried to shove Ray towards the wall.

Ray knew the man would expect him to resist the push, but Ray did the opposite. He trapped the man's hand against his chest with his own and stepped back, absorbing the force and pulling the man off balance. As the man took an involuntary step forward, Ray peeled the offending hand away and rotated. With the intense pain from Ray's wrist-lock, the man could do nothing but follow Ray's lead. In a swift, fluid action, Ray had him bent over and pinned in place by an agonising wrist and shoulder lock. The two other men moved to intervene.

"One more step and I'll snap his wrist," said Ray, in a calm but commanding tone. A scream of pain from their friend stopped the two men in their tracks. They looked at each other, neither wanting to decide their next move. When they looked back to Ray, he applied a little more pressure to the wrist lock, inciting another painful groan from the man bent double in front of him.

"Ray!"

Ray glanced briefly towards the source of the voice, not wanting to take his eyes of the other men for too long.

"Let him go, Ray," said Joseph Kilpatrick.

Ray stared at the man he used to call a friend, then relaxed his grip on the balding man's wrist and gave him a nudge, sending him stumbling into his two comrades. The man straightened and spun to face Ray, pain still squinting his eyes as he rubbed at his strained wrist. His cheeks flushed with rage and embarrassment as he set himself to take his revenge.

"I'm gonna fuckin' kill you, you prick."

"That's enough, Barney," shouted Joseph, stepping into the space between Ray and the three men. "Go inside, please."

The older man glared at Joseph, contemplating whether to obey the order, or follow his primal rage and reclaim his pride. Joseph stared at the man and raised an eyebrow, challenging him to defy him.

The two younger men began to move towards the door. Barney reluctantly followed, nursing his wounded pride and wrist, his eyes burning into Ray's.

When he passed Joseph, he leaned in towards Ray. "If I see you out in the street, you're a fuckin' dead man," he said, barely above a whisper.

Ray stood his ground and smiled defiantly. "An icepack should help your wrist," he said, with a smile, then waited until the man had turned away. "There's fuck all you can do about that hairline, though."

The man snapped and spun back to lunge at Ray, only to be wrestled away by Joseph.

When he'd bundled his men through the door into the bar, Joseph turned to Ray. "Was that really necessary?" he asked, a hint of a smile in his eyes.

Ray shrugged but gave no reply.

"I'm glad you decided to come, Ray."

"You didn't give me much choice, did you?"

"Well, Doc is starting to lose his patience," said Joseph, all trace of a smile gone. "He wants the guns, Ray."

"The guns you knew nothing about?"

"What do you want me to say, Ray?" said Joseph, with a shrug.

The two men glared at each other for a long moment, then both looked away.

"Seriously, Ray," said Joseph, after checking that the door to the pub was closed properly. "You need to be careful."

Joseph stepped closer to Ray and lowered his volume.

"Doc isn't fuckin' around. He's already taken on the Guards, and the Army."

"And beat the fuck out of a defenceless man in his home?" Ray could feel his veil of calmness slipping as he stared questioningly at Joseph.

"I don't know what you're talking about, Ray."

"So that's not one of Micheal Foy's radios clipped to your belt?"

Joseph looked down at the radio, a look of confusion quickly turning to realisation.

"I didn't know anyone got hurt," said Joseph, in a tone tinted with regret, but he wasn't going to apologise for it.

"Well, someone did."

"I don't know anything about that."

"Maybe you should ask your brother," said Ray.

Joseph looked away for a moment, then back to meet Ray's icy stare.

"You know Ray, when your country's in crisis and the authorities are doing nothing, then it's time for the people to step up. Step up and take control. And in the process of taking control, there may be civilian casualties."

"Civilian casualties? Will you listen to yourself?" Ray snapped.

"You know what I mean, Ray."

Ray turned away — it was either that or let his anger draw him nose to nose with Joseph.

"But Ray," Joseph lowered his voice again. "Doc's taking this very seriously." He paused, searching for the right words. "He's starting to believe there's more to this whole power cut than we're being told."

Ray turned back to face Joseph.

"What do you mean?"

Joseph looked at the ground briefly.

"He says it's the Brits."

Ray's face creased, like he'd smelt rotten meat.

"Are you fuckin' serious, Joe? Have you any idea how fuckin' stupid that is?"

"I know," said Joseph, a little defensively.

"You know?" snapped Ray. "You know he's fuckin' insane and you're still doing his bidding? Being his fuckin' lapdog?"

"Fuck you Ray. I'm helping the people, my community. I don't know what's behind this. All I know is that people are going hungry while warehouses full of food are allowed to sit and rot."

"Well, I *do* know what's behind this. It's nature, not the British," said Ray, shaking his head in disbelief. "So why are you still taking orders from him when you know he's nuts?"

Joseph looked away.

"Just take over and send him on his way," said Ray.

"It's not that simple, Ray."

"It *is* that simple."

A brief silence marked the stalemate.

"Look Ray, I'm just telling you not to piss him off. Just give him what he wants. I'm telling you as a friend."

"Friend?"

"Well, we used to be friends."

"Is that right? Friends don't bury weapons in another friend's land."

"I knew nothing about that until this week."

"Bullshit! Who was it then if it wasn't you?"

Joseph shrugged and moved towards the door. "Maybe you should ask your aunt."

Ray opened his mouth to reply, then stopped. He knew his aunt Maria had been a supporter of the Republican movement during the troubles, but he never thought she was actively involved. Or did he? A thousand snippets of memories flashed by him; it was through Maria that he'd first met Dermot O'Connor, and Maria *did* have pretty militant views, and she *had* been the most supportive of him applying for the Prison Service — even encouraging it.

"You coming?" asked Joseph, interrupting Ray's thoughts.

Ray shelved his musing and followed Joseph into the gloomy bar. Ten or so patrons inside eyed him suspiciously, word of the fracas in the alley obviously having spread.

Ray's wrist-lock victim stood by the door to the backroom glaring at Ray menacingly as he approached.

"You calm the fuck down, Barney," whispered Joseph to the enraged hard man.

Barney wrenched his eyes from Ray just long enough to acknowledge Joesph's comment.

Joseph opened the door to the back room and beckoned Ray to enter. As Ray passed the aggressive door man, he smiled and gave a provoking wink. The man's jaw clenched, nostrils flaring, but he didn't react. Ray knew he'd be in trouble if this guy did react, particularly with his ten mates behind him, but he was just in that kind of mood; angry and confrontational.

"Ray Keenan. It's been a long time, son. We've been wanting to speak to your for a while now."

"Well, I'm here now," Ray said, curtly.

Dermot rose from the small rectangular table he was perched behind. As he stood, he put both hands in the pockets of his jacket and relaxed into it.

Ray glanced at Dermot's right jacket pocket. He knew what was likely gripped within. He'd heard the many stories, and had even seen the man in action once with his infamous Blackjack, albeit from a distance. During a rare night out, while on a trip home, Ray had witnessed Dermot's rumoured temper. The image of a man's face, or what was left of it when Dermot had lost his temper, was something that he would never forget. The speed at which he could turn from calm and reasonable, to vicious and psychotic, was frightening.

Dermot smiled warmly. "It's good to see you, Ray. Take a seat," he said, gesturing to the padded bench behind the table.

Ray didn't like being boxed into a corner, but he guessed he already was. He slid into the seat, Dermot taking the chair opposite. Joseph remained standing just inside the door.

"Okay, Ray, let's get down to business," said Dermot, leaning back in his chair. "I know you're not happy with where we buried them, but I need you to get over that and hand over the weapons, today."

"What are you gonna use them for?"

Dermot's cordial demeanour faded. "What are we gonna use them for?" he said, leaning forward. "We're going to use them to protect the people of this town and this country. You've no clue of what is going on here. British forces are preparing, as we speak, to invade and to enslave the rest of our country."

Ray's poker-face must've slipped when he heard this. Dermot slammed his fist on the table, causing half-empty beer glasses to bounce and rattle.

"Do you not believe me, Ray?"

Ray thought for a moment. *What's the smart thing to say here?*

"No, I don't Dermot. It was a solar flare."

"That's what they want you to think," said Dermot, tapping his temple with his finger. "Anyway, I don't care what you think. You'll hand over the weapons, and that's an order."

"I don't take orders from you," said Ray defiantly.

Dermot tilted his head. "I think you're forgetting, Mr Keenan, that you are a soldier of the Irish Republican

Army, and you'll follow my orders or you'll be shot as a traitor."

Ray glanced at Joseph and registered the look of shock and confusion on his face. Ray had assumed that Joseph had known, but obviously not.

"I am not a member of the IRA and you know it," said Ray.

"I know that we asked you to take on a covert mission, and you said yes," said Dermot.

Ray could see Joseph in this periphery. He stood, arms folded, listening intently.

"I know that we arranged for you to go into the Prison Service training programme," continued Dermot.

"I never did a single thing for you. I never even communicated with anyone."

"That was due to political circumstances at the time. We never went away, you know."

Ray fidgeted in his seat, repositioning his feet under the table, which had once been a Singer sowing machine and still had the pedal and the mechanical workings in place.

"So, there're a couple of things that I need you to do, Ray. Think of them as missions," said Dermot with a smile.

Ray looked again towards Joseph, who stared back blankly.

"One," said Dermot, raising his voice to get Ray's full attention. "You are going to go now, with Joseph, and bring the weapons here."

Ray gave no reply.

"And two," continued Dermot. "We need somewhere as a command center."

Ray wasn't sure where this was going. *What could he do that could possibly help with that?*

"We need a place that's self-sufficient, with its own power."

The penny dropped for Ray.

"Your parent's farm has everything we need, and your neighbour has the radio equipment that we need to coordinate with other units around the country."

Ray let out a laugh. "Do you honestly expect my parents to let you set up base in their home? Don't be fuckin' ridiculous," he said, turning to Joseph, who gave no reaction.

"We'll put your parents up in temporary accommodation and make sure they have what they need."

Ray shifted in his seat, reaching down to scratch an itch on his leg.

"I'll get you the weapons and then that's it. I'm done. But if you think I'm gonna let you anywhere near my parent's home, then you're more insane that I thought."

Ray glanced towards Joseph again and received a stern look. A near imperceptible shake of Joseph's head warned him to be careful. Ray ignored him and brought his focus back to Dermot, who'd pushed his chair back and now sat, arms folded across his chest, staring at Ray through an arrogant, superior smirk. Ray continued to sit with his hands under the table, his elbows resting on his lap.

"I hoped you'd be reasonable, Raymond," said Dermot, before pushing himself to his feet, making a show of opening his coat to reveal a handgun tucked into his waistband.

Ray locked eyes with Dermot, then brought his hands up from under the table. He rested them on top, left over right. In his right hand, he held his own compact Glock 26. He was careful to pull his gun in as unaggressive a manner as was possible, angling the barrel away from Dermot and extending his finger along the side rather than resting it on the trigger.

"You're not the only one with a gun, Dermot," said Ray, calmly.

Dermot's smirk morphed to a deadly stare, which he levelled at Joseph.

"You let him in here with a gun?"

"I thought the guys had..."

"We'll talk about this later," snapped Dermot.

The two men turned their attention back to Ray. Joseph's stare was now as cold and fatal as his boss'. Ray knew a line had been crossed.

The whole room knew that Ray could get off two shots before Dermot could draw his pistol. The whole room also knew that Ray wouldn't get out alive if he did.

Stalemate.

"Here's what's gonna happen," said Ray, trying to keep the surging adrenaline from affecting his voice. "I will go and get your guns."

"That's a start," said Dermot.

"It's not a start. That is it! If you or any of your dogs..." he looked at Joseph, who shifted his weight slightly at the insult, "come anywhere near my parent's property, or their neighbour's for that matter, I'll shoot you on sight."

"Strong words, Mr Keenan," said Dermot, his eerily fake smile returning. "But okay, let's get the weapons and then we can talk about the rest."

Ray struggled to keep a lid on his boiling rage, but he knew he needed a way out of there and back to warn his family of what was sure to follow.

"So, how do we do this?" asked Ray, while gesturing to the gun in his hands.

It wasn't exactly a Mexican Standoff, but it was close. Any sudden movement would surely make it one.

"Joseph will go with you," said Dermot.

"He can come outside with me, but he can't come with me to get the guns."

Dermot's whole body tensed as he undoubtedly wrestled with his immediate urge to pounce.

Ray continued. "They're hidden in a place that can only be reached on a scrambler."

Dermot looked to Joseph for a moment, then back to Ray. "Ray, I hope you understand what'll happen if you don't return with the guns?"

Ray kept his eyes locked on the psychotic fanatic and nodded. "I know what you're capable of."

"Joseph, take him outside."

"The service door," said Ray, gesturing again towards his hands to imply that he wasn't putting the gun away until he was outside.

Joseph gave a nod and opened a side door, waiting for Ray to follow.

Ray push back from the table and stood. He angled, slightly awkwardly, towards the door, ensuring that he kept Dermot in his peripheral vision, only turning his back at the last moment before following Joseph out through a small storeroom.

Joseph stepped out into the alleyway and turned to face Ray. He nodded to the gun, which Ray held loose and low in front of him.

"You gonna put that away?"

"In a minute."

"So, you're full of fuckin' secrets, Rayso, aren't you?"

Ray didn't respond.

"A fuckin' covert agent?" Joseph said with a forced laugh.

"It wasn't like that, Joe."

The two men shared another moment of silence before Ray nodded towards the wooden gate. "Can you open that for me?"

"You made me look like a fuckin' fool in there," said Joseph as he approached the wooden gates.

"What do you want me to say, Joseph?" said Ray with a shrug.

"Ray," Joseph said, after Ray had ducked through the hatch in the gates. "Don't be long. I can't see him keeping his cool for more than an hour or so."

Ray nodded, then tucked the Glock into his belt and walked off towards his bike.

CHAPTER TWENTY-ONE

Lisa crouched by the side of Maria's chair and held her hand. Her aunt had come-to after about fifteen minutes, but the effects of the diabetic hypo were still obvious. She looked exhausted and weak, and had needed to be helped back into her seat.

"How're you feeling now, Maria?" asked Lisa.

Maria gave a faint smile. "Just very tired, love."

"We're gonna take you round to the hospital to get checked out."

"Ah, I don't want to be a nuisance. I'll be okay after a sleep."

"No mum, you are going to the hospital," said Conor, in a tone that left no room for debate.

"Maybe I could get a wee cup of tea and then we'll see how I feel," said Maria.

"I'll get you a fresh cup," said Lisa, lifting the untouched mug, which was now too cold to drink.

"I'll give you a hand," said Simon, following Lisa through the kitchen and out into the small enclosed backyard.

The camping stove had been positioned on the grill of an old brick barbecue, which looked like it hadn't been used in years. Lisa sparked one of the burners to life and set a pot of water on top.

"So," said Simon, drawing close to Lisa so as to keep his voice low. "What was all that about Ray and guns?"

"I don't know. She was obviously very confused," said Lisa, with a deep frown.

"Yeah, but it must've come from somewhere."

"Who do you think she was talking about? She said I, or rather Ray, needed to give him the guns because he was dangerous?" asked Simon.

"I don't know."

"And what guns was she referring to?"

Lisa shook her head. "I assume she was just completely out of it and didn't know what she was saying."

Simon didn't seem convinced. Lisa wasn't totally convinced herself.

When Maria was done with her tea, which she barely sipped at, Lisa and Conor helped her into her shoes and coat, and escorted her slowly to the car. The drama at the neighbour's house had died down, the feuding couples having parted ways. A number of other neighbours were out, however, all seemingly heading, with purpose, in the same direction.

"Hi Conor," said a middle-aged woman, as she passed carrying an empty cardboard box. "I was so sorry to hear about your friend. I hope you're okay?"

Conor nodded. "Thank you, Mrs Kennedy. Where's everyone going?"

"Have you not heard? They're giving out food at St Anthony's," said Mrs Kennedy.

Lisa and Simon stood by the car, Lisa's eyes burning into Conor, willing him to get a move on.

"Is it the army?" asked Conor.

"No, apparently Dermot O'Connor and his ones went to Lidl and managed to get a couple of truckloads of supplies. They brought them up to Father Rice for him to distribute. Anyway, better run. Don't want to miss out," said Mrs Kennedy, rushing off to catch up with a small group of other neighbours.

At the mention of Dermot O'Connor, Lisa turned to Simon, who raised his eyebrows in surprise.

"That was the guy from the meeting, right?" he asked.

"Yeah."

"That was quick."

Lisa nodded. She had to admit she was impressed.

Like before, traffic on the roads was sparse, but there was a steady stream of people all hurrying in the direction of the church.

Lisa parked as close to the hospital's front doors as possible, which was easier than expected given the almost-empty carpark. The next part looked like it was gonna be a lot harder.

The space in front of the main entrance resembled a triage area during a major emergency; nurses and admin staff worked their way through a queue of walk-in patients and anxious relatives of those already inside. The main doors to the hospital were being manned by two soldiers who only granted admittance at the direction of one of the hospital staff.

Lisa turned in her seat to see a sleeping Maria, and Conor looking anxiously at the queues. "Okay, I'm gonna go and queue up. I don't want your mum standing longer than necessary. So when you see me getting close to the front, you bring her over."

"Okay, thanks Lisa. I'll let her sleep as long as possible."

"I'll come with you," said Simon.

Lisa and Simon joined a queue in front of a foldout table, where two hospital staff sat taking details and doing initial assessments. Some people were directed through one, or other, of the main doors, whereas others were sent to another queue, which led to a smaller side door — in addition to a nurse this second queue was headed by a hospital security guard and two more soldiers.

"I wonder what that queue's for?" mused Simon.

Lisa was more focused on the queue in front of her, and with trying to estimate the speed at which it was moving.

"Don't know," she said, barely glancing in that direction.

Simon looked along the line of about twenty people.

"It must be for the pharmacy," he said.

"Humm?" said Lisa, realising that she'd been ignoring him.

"Yeah, they queue up, give some details and wait at the side until someone comes out with a package," said Simon.

"Oh, you're a real Sherlock Holmes, aren't you?" said Lisa, with a laugh and nudge with her shoulder.

"No, I was just thinking out loud," he said, defensively, then immediately laughed and returned the shoulder nudge, with a little more force than he intended, sending Lisa off-balance and into the man in front her. After a round of polite apologies and angry-faced acceptances, everyone got back to waiting.

"Oh Simon, can you wait in line here for a minute?" asked Lisa.

"Not a chance," he whispered with a smile.

"No seriously. I see a friend of mine who's a nurse here."

Lisa pointed to a guy in hospital gear, who stood propped against a wall, enjoying, what was likely, a well-earned cigarette.

"Ah, yeah sure," said Simon.

As Lisa peeled off from the line, Simon called her back. "What's your aunt's surname? In case I get to the front before you're back."

"Tobin," said Lisa. "But I'll only be a couple of minutes."

Lisa approached the nurse. "Hey Mr Abara," she said jovially.

The man turned; tired eyes suddenly alive with genuine excitement.

"Hey, Mrs Keenan," he said in his deep, heavily accented voice.

He stubbed his cigarette out and strode towards Lisa, greeting her with a strong, familiar hug.

"Jeez Lisa, it's been a long time. You are as beautiful as ever. How are you doing? Well, apart from all this, I mean," he said, waving his arm at everything and nothing.

"I know. It's great to see you, Emeka. It's been too long." Lisa kissed him on the cheek and returned the hug.

Emeka's family had moved to Ireland from West Africa when he was about sixteen, and when he joined Lisa's school, they'd instantly become friends. For a while, they were more than just friends, but Lisa had plans that didn't include her staying in Donegal, so she gradually pulled away and eventually lost touch. They'd had a couple of drunken hook ups over the years when Lisa had been back for a weekend visit, but they had dried up too and, from what she'd seen on Facebook, Emeka was now happily married with a couple of kids.

"Are you okay?" asked Emeka, holding Lisa by the shoulders.

"Yeah, yeah. I'm here with my aunt. She has diabetes and took a hypo. So, we thought we'd better get her checked out."

"Yes, good idea," said Emeka, seemingly relieved that it wasn't Lisa who needed medical assistance.

"It might be a while before she's seen though," said Emeka, with a sigh. "It is pandemonium in there. We're running on generators, but they can only power about half of the hospital, so we've been sending as many people home as possible." He leaned in. "People who really aren't well enough to go home."

"That's crazy."

"Yeah, well, over the last two days, we've started to see a lot of them coming back and trying to get readmitted. And we've been getting a number of diabetics in too. Probably like your aunt, they're finding it difficult to maintain a proper diet."

"Yeah, that's it. She just didn't have enough of the right foods."

"But I heard this morning that the electric should be back on in the next day or two. So, should be back to normal pretty soon," said Emeka, trying to reassure Lisa.

"No Emeka, that's not right. We were talking to an ESB engineer earlier, and this isn't gonna be fixed any time soon, I'm afraid," said Lisa firmly.

Emeka frowned. "Oh right, that's worrying. This place can't go on like this for much longer. We only have one operating theatre open and we can't access any of the patient records on the computers," he said, then nodded towards the queue for the pharmacy. "Plus, the pharmacy is running dangerously low on medications. Oh, keep that to yourself please, Lisa."

"Absolutely."

"What's your aunt's name? I'll be going to help with admissions when I'm finished my break. I'll look out for her."

"Thanks Emeka, that'd be great. Maria Tobin."

Lisa looked back towards the line, where Simon stood watching their exchange intently. He was now only three places from the front of the queue.

"I better go queue up again," said Lisa with a smile. "It was so good to see you."

Emeka enveloped her in another of his tight, muscular hugs, and they said their goodbyes. Lisa watched for a second as he headed off towards the staff door he'd come out of. He was still the perfect physical specimen. She shook her head and smiled to herself before turning to join Simon in the queue.

"Who was that?" asked Simon.

"An old friend of mine, Emeka. We were at school together," said Lisa.

"An ex-boyfriend?" asked Simon.

Lisa's teasing smile returned.

"He might've been. Jealous are we?"

"What? Why would I be jealous?" Simon said, too quickly, then looked away. When he looked back, Lisa was still staring at him with a beaming, genuine grin. Simon's face was flushed, but he held her gaze and returned the smile.

"Maybe a little," he said, with a raised eyebrow. "Is that a problem?"

Lisa leaned in and whispered, "Not at all." Then kissed him on the cheek.

CHAPTER TWENTY-TWO

"… so that's Operation Darkness," said Dermot, to his captivated, dumbfounded audience.

The bar was silent. Some of Dermot's followers looked at each other in confusion, not sure if what they'd just heard was some kind of joke.

One of the younger, newer recruits laughed. "Are you sure it's not Elon Musk and an army of Martians that's behind it?" he joked to the person beside him.

"What was that?" asked Dermot, singling the man out with a stare.

The young man bowed his head, reluctant to make eye contact with the top man. Joseph Kilpatrick looked at the naïve recruit, then to his twin, who stood across the room. They, and the other older volunteers, likely knew what was coming.

Dermot rose from this seat slowly, still staring at the wise-ass. He made his way around the table and stood in front of the young man.

"Sorry, Mr O'Connor," said the young man, having no choice but to look up at Dermot. "I was only joking."

"Do you not believe what I just told you?"

"No, I do. I do," said the man, his voice quivering. "It's just that it seems a bit... you know, with the French in camper vans an' all. It just sounded a bit... crazy."

"Well, I suppose I might find it crazy too if I hadn't seen the official files," said Dermot, almost sympathetically. Dermot hadn't seen the files himself, of course, but he's dad said he had, so that was good enough for him.

"Yeah, it's madness isn't it, but if you've seen the files, then it has to be true," said the young man, more relaxed now, seemingly thinking he was no longer in trouble.

But Dermot had seen something in the man's face, something he didn't like, a hint of mockery. He smiled, bobbing his head as he glanced around the room.

"Ha, Elon Musk and the Martians," he said, half turning to return to his seat.

Hesitant laughs rippled around the room, then stopped when the crack of filled-leather hitting cheekbone echoed through the bar. The young smart-ass crumpled across the lap of the guy beside him, blood already flowing from a gash below his eye. He instinctively raised his arm to protect himself as Dermot stepped closer, arm drawn up, ready to land another blow with the battle-hardened blackjack.

"Boss!" shouted Joseph as he grabbed Dermot's swinging arm.

Dermot snapped around; bulldog-rage now directed at his trusted lieutenant. "You're already on fuckin' thin ice, boyo," he spat, wrenching his arm free and pointing the blackjack in Joseph's face.

"We need every volunteer we can get, boss," said Joseph, in a hushed, more respectful tone.

Dermot glared at Joseph for a long moment, then turned back to the bleeding volunteer. He loomed over the young man, who whimpered, and squirmed to back away. Dermot's jaw worked furiously as he fought the urge to finish the young lad's lesson in respect. With a sigh and a shake of his head, Dermot allowed the fog of fury to fade. He turned, put the blackjack in his pocket and nodded to each of his inner circle, who promptly followed him into the back room.

The small, private room was now more acceptably illuminated, thanks to five new camping lanterns.

Dermot took his usual seat and the others — five men and one woman — sat where they could in a loose circle in front of him.

"Sit down, Joseph," said Dermot, without looking up at Joseph, who still stood back from the others.

Joseph hesitated for a second, then pulled a chair across and joined the group.

"So, now you all know the truth about what's going on," said Dermot.

No one spoke. Some heads nodded, some faces frowned, and some remained poker-straight.

"If we're gonna mount any kind of defence, then we need to get serious," added Dermot.

He stood and paced in the little space that wasn't occupied.

"Okay, number one. We need to set up somewhere strategic and defensible," he said. "A place that has power and is self-sustaining." Dermot looked at Joseph, expecting a comment. None came.

"Number two. We need more weapons and ammunition. And, most importantly, number three. We need to set up lines of communication with other defenders. Joseph, do you want to explain our plans for one and two?"

Joseph looked up at Dermot, his scowl suggesting he was less than happy to participate. He relented and turned to the group.

"Some of you might know Ray Keenan," said Joseph, receiving a couple of nods in response. "Well, he uncovered a weapons cache on his father's farm and has agreed to bring them to us this evening."

Excitement buzzed around the table.

"The Keenan farm is totally self-sufficient," continued Joseph, glancing at Dermot, who hovered by the table, arms folded across his wide chest. "Dermot has asked him if we can use it as a base of operations."

"And he agreed?" said the woman, incredulously.

"Well…"

"He has no choice," said Dermot sharply, growing impatient with Joseph. "We are requisitioning the property for the defence of our country."

Questioning glances between those in the room told of their reticence for the plan.

"We'll be relocating the family to somewhere suitable, and we'll make sure that they're taken care of.

They'll have plenty of food and whatever they need. I'm actually hoping that they'll agree to keep working the farm while we're there," he added.

This seemed to afford some measure of justification, at least enough for the members to set aside their moral concerns.

"And then the third issue becomes a lot easier," said Dermot, taking his seat again. "The Keenan's neighbour is a radio enthusiast." He spun one of the walkie-talkies on the table and looked to Joseph for a name.

"Michael Foy."

"Yes, Michael Foy," said Dermot. "We'll be taking over his place too."

"And are we relocating him too?" asked someone in the group.

"Do you know how to work all the equipment?" asked Dermot, sarcastically.

"Ah, no."

"No. So Mr Foy will be staying to work it for us," said Dermot.

A knock on the door drew the room's attention. Joseph rose from his seat and opened the door to the main bar. After a short, whispered exchange with another of the volunteers, he ushered in a red-faced, red-haired man in his thirties, and nodded towards Dermot.

"I'm sorry Doc, but we just got word that the hospital is critically low on medications," said the newcomer.

"And what do they expect us to do?" asked Dermot.

"No, no. They haven't asked, but I was thinking we could hit all the pharmacies in town and bring everything up to the hospital," said the man excitedly.

"*You* were thinking?" asked Dermot, rising from his seat.

The young man took a half step backwards, but Dermot was too fast. He grabbed the man by the arm and pulled him in.

"Brilliant idea," said Dermot, beaming. He put his arm around the man, whose expression had turned from terror to hesitant-joy in an instant. "You see?" he said, turning to the rest of the room. "This is what we need; people to show initiative, to think outside the box."

"Okay, what's your name, lad?" asked Dermot, taking his seat and gesturing for the man to sit in Joseph's empty spot.

"Ah, are we supposed to give our real names?" asked the man, looking to the other faces around the table.

There was silence for a few seconds, then the entire room erupted in laughter. All but Joseph.

Even Dermot was awkwardly belly laughing, as if it pained him to do so.

"Lad," said Dermot, when he'd composed himself. "We're in a fight for our country. It doesn't matter if people know your name."

"My name's Damien."

"Okay Damien, let's see what we can do. Kevin here will go with you," said Dermot, gesturing to one of the other men at the table. "Kevin, pick a couple of volunteers and take the van. I want you to try to find the owner of each pharmacy. If you can, explain the situation and get them to give you access to their supplies. They can then keep a track of what's being moved to the hospital."

"And if we can't find the owners?" asked Kevin.

"Then you get access whatever way you can."

"Okay boss," said Kevin, working his way out from behind the table and nodding for Damien to follow him."

"Right, back to business," said Dermot when Damien had left the room. "When Ray arrives with the weapons. Which better be soon," he said, flashing a stern look at Joseph. "We'll talk to him again about the farm, and hopefully he'll see sense. Either way, we're gonna move to the Keenan farm tomorrow night."

CHAPTER TWENTY-THREE

Simon stood off to the side as Lisa and Conor dealt with getting Maria checked in. Conveniently, the body-building Black Adonis was back on the scene and was now helping Maria into a wheelchair.

Ha, I am jealous, thought Simon, as he realised he was allowing himself to feel something for another woman. He looked away and shook his head, then smiled.

The line for the pharmacy was growing, as was the number of people who were standing to the side waiting for their prescriptions to be filled. He watched as a security guard appeared at the small door carrying a number of paper medication bags. Behind him came a nurse, who placed a tray of small paper cups on the table and began to hand out the bags; calling and confirming names. When all the bags were handed out — to the irritation of those still waiting — the nurse turned to a clipboard and started calling other names. Four men, two of them barely adults, shuffled forward when each of their names was called. They had a gait and manner that Simon recognised. He'd remembered the sunken faces, the agitated mood and the disorientated movements.

A flash of anger and remorse shot across him as he watched each heroin addict step forward and receive his single dose of methadone. Each newly medicated addict then slopped off, leaving their friends, whose names had yet to be called, to wait for their turn.

Those in the pharmacy queue eyed this sorry band of unfortunates with suspicion and contempt.

"What about the rest of us?" shouted one of the addicts, when the nurse had finished giving out her current batch of methadone.

"We're getting through the list as quickly as we can," she said, the irritation clear in her voice.

"I was supposed to get my Done at five o'clock," the addict replied angrily.

"Seamus! You behave yourself now," said the burly security guard, who'd obviously got to know the daily visitors over the years. "You only gave your details a few minutes ago, so just be patient."

"Well, I've been fuckin' queueing for ages," said Seamus, in a sulk.

The security guard tilted his head and raised his eyebrows at the young man. Seamus mumbled some profanities before hunkering down beside the wall. He hugged his knees and rocked back and forth. Even from a distance, Simon could see that he was soaked with sweat.

"Okay so," said Lisa, startling Simon, "they're gonna keep her in for observation and to get her levels right."

"Ah okay. That's good," said Simon, looking at Conor as he approached.

"Yeah," said Conor, glumly.

"They won't let anyone in to sit with her," said Lisa. "Emeka says..."

Simon forced himself not to have any facial reaction to the handsome ex-boyfriend's name, which was ridiculous, but now that he was thinking about it...

"... that they had to squeeze extra beds into the wards, so there's no space for visitors," continued Lisa.

"So, you're coming back with us then, mate?" asked Simon with a smile.

"Yes, he is," said Lisa, putting her arm around Conor and starting towards their car. "Emeka said he's gonna take care of her."

Simon glanced back at the pharmacy station where the nurse was now calling the next set of names for the methadone tablets. The agitated loud-mouth, Seamus, was now back on his feet and shoving his way through the crowd to get his dose. He bounced from foot to foot as he waited for his turn, and when he got to the front, he scribbled his name on something, took the little paper cup from the nurse and dumped the tablet into his mouth. He turned to leave, then stopped. Before the next person in line could move forward, Seamus spun around and grabbed at the tray of tablets. He came away with a handful of paper cups, each with a little white tablet bouncing around inside. He bounded through the queueing people towards the carpark and the exit.

Simon watched as the addict sprinted towards him. There were so many tablets tumbling along behind him that Simon wondered if there'd be any left if he did get away.

"Stop him," shouted the security guard.

Simon tensed up, ready to spring at the fleeing man, but Seamus was too fast and changed direction, which put him just out of Simon's reach. He took a half step after him, before realising it was futile, he'd no chance of catching him.

Seamus's new escape route took him past a middle-aged man on crutches, who was struggling to get into a waiting car. He'd set his prescription bag on the roof as he manoeuvred the crutches into the back seat. The opportunistic Seamus barely broke stride as he swiped the bag from the car roof and sprinted on.

Lisa and Conor were a few feet ahead, and Conor was quicker to react. He lunged towards the sprinting stranger — probably for no reason other than someone had shouted 'stop him'. It looked like the game was up for Seamus as Conor grabbed a handful of his jacket sleeve, but the fleeing youth managed to tug free and, after a couple of floundering strides, regained his balance.

Seamus sprinted on towards the carpark exit, with Conor hot on his heels. Seeing Conor pursuing the man, made Simon's mind up for him — he knew he couldn't catch them unless they stopped, and if they stopped, it meant that Conor had caught him, and Simon didn't want Conor confronting this guy on his own — so he joined in the chase, followed closely by the security guard, who probably should've been in better shape.

As Simon rounded the large stone pillar at the exit to the carpark, he saw that Conor had indeed caught the guy. The two were now trading blows, Conor with his back against the railings as the skinny, malnourished drug addict summoned strength from somewhere in a desperate attempt to escape.

Simon slowed for a second, then quickened his pace again as he stooped and speared the guy with a perfectly timed rugby-tackle. A rush of air burst from Seamus' lungs and they both went sprawling, Simon's weight pinning the man to the ground.

The security guard arrived on the scene, soon followed by Lisa, who stood with her hands over her mouth. With a grunt, the guard hoisted Seamus to his feet and held him tightly by the arm. Paper cups lay all around, but not a single tablet could be seen. Conor straightened himself and lifted the stolen bag of medication, which lay at his feet.

"Do you want me to take this back to the guy?" asked Conor.

The security guard held out his free hand. "It's okay, I'll sort it. Thank you, lad."

Conor handed him the package, then he and Simon joined Lisa. The security guard spoke, unheard, to Seamus, then gave him a nudge to encourage him on his way.

Lisa frowned as the guard moved to return to his post. "You just letting him go?"

"Nothing else I can do," said the security guard with a shrug. "The cops won't come, and even if they did, they'd just let him go, anyway."

He strode off, leaving Lisa, and the two panting pursers bewildered.

"Jeez, you're fast," said Simon, with a broad smile.

"I assume you played rugby," laughed Conor.

"If you two are finished playing hero, maybe we can go home now," said Lisa with a smirk.

CHAPTER TWENTY-FOUR

Lisa craned her neck to look past Simon and out through the passenger window.

"What is taking him so long?" she asked from beneath a pinched brow. She was keen to get home before darkness fell – it was already past the time when the street lamps would normally have come on and the light was starting to fade.

"Do you want me to go see where he is?" asked Simon, looking towards Maria's house for Conor, who'd gone in to put an overnight bag together. Just as he reached for the door release, he spotted the young man emerging from the house. He had a large green rucksack on his back and was carrying the camping stove that they'd delivered earlier that day, in one hand and the grey gas bottle in the other. He lumbered awkwardly along the path and used his foot to pull open the gate.

"For frig sake. He should've just left those," sighed Lisa with an exaggerated shake of her head.

Conor placed the gas bottle and stove on the footpath and shrugged out of his rucksack. The lack of urgency only adding to Lisa's exasperation.

"Lisa, do you mind if I give the stove to Marty, our next-door neighbour?" he asked, as he leaned in to place his bag on the back seat. "He really helped us out over the past few days."

"Yes, not at all, go ahead," said Lisa, suddenly disarmed and feeling a little guilty for losing her patience. "But try to be quick, will you? I don't fancy driving in the dark."

"Okay, two minutes," said Conor, ducking away and lifting the gas and stove.

"He's a good kid," said Lisa, twisting in her seat and watching Conor stride up the neighbour's path. "Very thoughtful for his age."

Simon turned to her and gave a rueful smile without replying.

"What?" Lisa asked, returning the smile.

"You blow hot and cold, don't you?" said Simon. "You were wanting me to go in and drag him out by the neck a minute ago."

"What?" asked Lisa, with a hint of fake indignation. "Ah, fuck off you." She laughed and gave him a playful punch on the arm. "I didn't know he was getting them for his neighbour."

Simon laughed and held his hands up in surrender.

"Here he comes," said Lisa, shifting in her seat and clicking her seatbelt on.

"Right, okay, sorry," said Conor when he returned and shuffled into the back seat.

The town was quiet again; the newly created relief station at the church was likely now closed for the night. The roads looked alien in the enveloping darkness, the rows of dormant street lamps only noticed for their absence of light.

As the sky drew darker, the yellow-tinted beam from the car's headlights soon became the only source of illumination. Lisa focused, white-knuckled, on the road ahead as they drove, at a cautious speed, through the town. Rounding a bend leading out of town, Lisa leaned forward and squinted. A red light danced and bobbed in the distance ahead of them. She slowed further, the car now all but crawling towards what was clearly a roadblock.

"You think these are the same guys from this morning?" asked Simon.

"Yeah, probably," said Lisa, eyes still straight ahead.

"Who are they?" asked Conor, wedging himself forward through the seats.

"They were stopping cars earlier," said Simon. "But they knew Ray, so they let us through."

Simon looked at Lisa, who met his stare for a moment.

"Yeah, should be okay," she added. "Sit back in your seat please Conor."

As the car drew to a stop beside the man in charge of the red flashlight, it was clear that the militia's dress code had changed. One guy was in some mis-matched ensemble of khaki green and camouflage, the others just in normal everyday clothes, but all were absent of the balaclavas that the earlier group had worn.

Lisa buzzed her window halfway down as the torch-bearer stepped in to address her.

"Where're you heading to?" asked the man, in a not unfriendly tone.

"Home," replied Lisa curtly.

"And where's home?" pressed the man, stooping and craning his neck to get a better look at Conor and Simon.

"I'm sorry. Who are you? And why are you stopping traffic?"

The man's attention snapped back to Lisa, his face suddenly stern.

"We've volunteered to man these checkpoints to keep the community safe," he said, clearly annoyed by Lisa's questioning of his authority.

Lisa opened her mouth to reply, when another member of the roadblock crew called the leader over. They huddled for a moment, then both looked back at Lisa — she was obviously the topic of their conversation. The leader said something inaudible to his colleague, then pointed towards the front of the car.

"What's going on?" asked Conor in a hushed tone.

"Don't know," said Lisa as she watched the guy tuck his flashlight into his combat trousers and pull out a small handheld radio.

"Fuck this," said Lisa as she put the car into gear and revved the engine slightly, intending to drive off.

The man who'd moved to the front of the car had now been joined by another, and they both sprang to life at the sound of the engine. Lisa froze as one of the men produced a handgun and pointed it directly at her through the windscreen.

"Turn the fucking car off!" the man with the gun shouted.

At this, the others manning the checkpoint edged closer, their expressions a mix of anger and excitement.

The main guy finished his conversation on the radio and strode back to Lisa's window.

"Turn the engine off," he said firmly, emphasising each word in turn.

Lisa reluctantly did as ordered and switched the engine off, letting out a slow breath, her attention still fixed on the gun.

"Are you Ray Keenan's sister?" asked the man.

"What's this about?" asked Simon, leaning over to look up through Lisa's side window.

The man stooped down and glared across at Simon.

"You're not from around here, are you, lad?" asked the man, his eyes narrowing. "Where you from?"

Simon paused before replying. "Belfast."

"Are you trying to be a smart-ass?"

Simon stared back defiantly.

"What part of England are you from?"

"None of your fucking business," snapped Lisa. "You've no right to stop us, and you've certainly no right to question where we're from."

"Englishman, step out of the car," said the man before straightening and directing two of his colleagues to Simon's side of the car.

Lisa turned to Simon, his look of defiance turning to one of trepidation. Two more figures stepped from the shadows and darted across the strip of daylight at the front of the car on their way to Simon's door.

"Don't get out," she said, her heart pounding.

"Don't think I've much choice."

"Lock the door," she shouted, as she snatched at the keys and started the engine again.

When she moved to put the car in gear, the whole world erupted around her. Shouts came from all directions as angry faces barked orders. Four or five men had closed in around the car, at least two of which were pointing guns.

"Turn the fucking engine off. Now!"

Lisa stared straight ahead, straight into the barrel of one gun while sensing the presence of another protruding through her open window, inches from her head.

The leader extended his free hand, palm up. "Keys!"

CHAPTER TWENTY-FIVE

Dermot sat pensively in the back of the car. His new *Communications Chief* — or at least the guy currently in possession of the walkie-talkie — sat up front beside the driver. Although quiet, Dermot was not relaxed. His mind darted from one thought to the next; from an opportunity to a threat, from an ally to an enemy, piecing together fragments of ideas to formulate his plan. He wanted to run his ideas by his father before the old man retired for the night. Not that he needed his blessing, but a good leader considers the council of his wisest advisers.

A squelch from the radio in the front passenger's hand drew Dermot's attention. He couldn't hear the report, as the audio went straight to the operator's ear via a cheap set of wired earphones plugged into the top of the handset.

"What's happening?" said Dermot, his voice weak and dry from a period of non-use. He coughed to clear his throat and reset a more commanding tone. "Has Ray Keenan turned up yet?"

The radio operator held up a hand, one finger extended, in a *shut up I'm trying to listen* gesture which he immediately regretted and retracted, instead rotating in his seat and pointing apologetically to his ear.

"Hold on a second, Barry," he finally said when the man on the other end had taken a breath. "That's Barry out at one of the checkpoints. He says he's stopped Ray Keenan's sister."

Dermot twitched an eyebrow.

"He says she tried to run them over."

"Is that right?"

"Her and some English guy."

Dermot frowned deeply. "Does he still have them there?"

"Are they still there?" asked the comms guy into the handset. "Yes, he got them out of the car."

"Good. Tell him to bring them to the bar."

The radio operator hesitated and glanced at the driver before relaying the order.

"Wait for me here," said Dermot as the car pulled to a stop outside his house. "But come and get me if you hear any news about Mr Keenan."

Dermot closed the front door behind him and stepped into the small living room. One of the newly acquired camping lanterns provided the only illumination, but its charge was all but gone and the dim yellow light that it struggled to emit did little to chase the growing gloom.

"So, things are moving fast, Da," said Dermot. "We're nearly ready to..." He stopped mid-sentence and stared at his father for a long moment, then moved to the sofa and wearily lowered himself to perch on its edge rather than settling into the familiar indent that years of habit had inflicted on the old couch. He rested his elbows on his knees, his head bowed and his hands clasped together in a tight embrace.

Dermot Senior sat across from him, unmoving, in his well-worn wingback armchair. He faced the lifeless television, his head resting against the left-hand wing which protruded from the tall back of the chair. Although designed to keep drafts from their — often elderly — occupants, the wings also provided a convenient support for weary heads that would often nod-off mid-soap opera. The rest of his body sat rigidly straight. His thin, moated hands gripped the arms of the thread-bare seat, as if preparing for the arduous feat of dragging their frail owner to his feet. The bones and tendons of his hands stretched the near-translucent grey skin tight as his fingertips dug into the fabric.

Dermot continued with his report, telling his father of his plan to arm his volunteers and set up base at the Keenans' farm, and how he would use the radio at their neighbour's to coordinate a country-wide campaign.

"That's a great plan, son," his father's words came clear and strong, despite the lack of movement from the old man's lips. "I'm very proud of you, Dermot."

Dermot didn't look up. The uncharacteristically kind words from his father did little to remove his solemn expression.

"It's your turn, son," the voice of his father continued. "It's your time to show what you're made of. You need to seize control from these weak idiots and drive the invaders out of our country."

Dermot rubbed the back of his of neck, but still he couldn't look towards his father.

"These bastards have always thought they could just take what they wanted from the Irish people," his father continued. "They stole our food and starved us during the great hunger, and now they're here to take our electricity and leave us in darkness. You can't let that happen, son. It's all on you now. You need to do whatever it takes to drive them out."

Dermot's head bobbed gently as he listened to his father's words.

"Some people won't believe you son, they might even stand against you. You need to be strong. Sacrifices will need to be made. Harsh decisions taken. You have what it takes, Dermot, don't you?"

"Yes," said Dermot, the sound barely making it past his wringing hands.

"What? Speak up."

"Yes, I have what it takes."

"Will you make the hard decisions? Will you do what needs to be done?"

"Yes. I will," replied Dermot through teeth clenched in determination. "I'll do whatever it takes, Da. I won't let these bastards take our country. I'll fuckin' kill every last one of them, and any traitor who stands in my way."

He pushed himself to his feet, finally forcing himself to look at his father. The death-throes of the lantern cast a harsh yellow hue across the old man's cold and greying skin. The flicker of the artificial flame seeming to bring movement where there was none. Dermot stepped closer, his hand coming up to reach out to the man he'd feared, and loathed, and loved, only to retreat and clinch into a fist.

"I won't let you down, Daddy. I promise."

As the lantern consumed the last of its charge, Dermot turned and strode purposefully to the door, leaving his father to the darkness.

CHAPTER TWENTY-SIX

Ray cut the engine. Both he and his once-pristine bike were now caked in mud. He climbed off and flicked the kickstand down, rocking the scrambler backwards onto it. Ray shook his head and sighed when the bike rolled forward, failing to catch on the stand, before trying again. No luck.

"For fuck's sake!" he huffed, and tried for a third time. The stand held for a teasing second, then folded in, causing the bike to lurch forward again.

"Fuuuuuuuck!" Ray screamed, before flinging his beloved bike to the ground and kicking the front tire.

He pulled his gloves off and threw them at the bike as punishment, then slumped back onto a mound of grass and buried his head in his hands. *What the fuck was he gonna do?*

He thought he had a plan, but the more he considered it, the more stupid it seemed. *What'd he think would happen after he gave O'Connor the guns? That he'd just leave him and his family alone? No chance! His family! How was he gonna explain this to his family, and to Derek? Derek probably knew by now that he'd taken half of the guns.*

"Fuck, fuck, fuuuuuck!" he screamed, the last 'fuck' echoing across the open fields, not that anyone would be in earshot. That's why he'd chosen this spot to hide the bag while he went to see O'Connor. He'd been coming here for years, ever since he got his first dirt bike, which was really the only way to get across the bog-like terrain. The only landmark for miles was the remains of a small stone structure. A local landlord had built the 'Prayer House', as locals called it, in the 1700s for one of his favoured servants, its only window facing east towards Mecca, allowing the Muslim servant to practise his daily prayers. The roof was now gone, the moss and ivy and shrubs enveloping what was left, but it was the best hiding place Ray could think of for the bag of weapons.

Digging his fingers into his scalp, Ray clenched his jaw in anger. He'd been taken advantage of by O'Connor and by his own aunt. He'd been young and impressionable and always looked up to his aunt Maria. He knew she'd strong Irish Republican views, but she'd always played it down to him, nevertheless he was surprised when she'd encouraged him to apply for the prison service job. He thought about the day when he'd found out he'd been accepted to the course. She was so excited for him. At least he thought she was excited *for him*. How naïve! She was excited about what it meant for her and for O'Connor, and *the cause*. The first time he'd ever met O'Connor was at her house later that same week.

Ray had been surprised when he'd walked into Maria's and found Dermot O'Connor sitting at her kitchen table.

"Ray, this is Dermot," said Maria, when Ray followed her through to the kitchen.

"Hello Raymond," said Dermot.

"Ah, hi," said Ray, a little taken aback. He'd heard the rumours about the older man, and his supposed involvement with the IRA, but Maria had never spoken about him.

"Have a seat, lad," said Dermot, a congenial smile fixed, somewhat uncomfortably, on his lined face.

Ray had been excited to show Maria his letter of offer for the prison service course, but on seeing Dermot O'Connor he thought it wise not to mention it, and before sitting, he slipped the envelope into his back pocket, assuming that his aunt wouldn't have mentioned his plans to this stranger.

He took a seat opposite Dermot and looked nervously up at Maria.

"It's alright Ray. Dermot's a close friend," she said with a reassuring smile. "I told him your good news."

Ray shifted uneasily. "Right?"

It'd been Maria who'd advised him to keep the whole thing a secret from everyone apart from his immediate family.

"Don't worry, lad," said Dermot. "It's not a problem. Your aunt just wanted to make sure it wouldn't be an issue, you know, with the movement."

"Okay," replied Ray, looking sheepishly from Dermot to his aunt, transmitting a – *What the fuck, Maria* – with his eyes. He wanted to be anywhere else in the world but here, sitting across from this man.

"It's okay, Ray," said Maria. "I thought it was better to be up front with Dermot from the start, you know, so that there's no misunderstanding."

"As I'm sure you know, Raymond, normally we wouldn't be over the moon about people going to work for the British state," the statement hung for a moment as Dermot took a sip from his mug of tea. "But times are changing."

Ray managed a weak smile and looked to Maria again, who smiled back and nodded.

"It's just better that we know these things," continued Dermot. "And it's always good to have a friend in these places. We've a lot of comrades spending time at Her Majesty's pleasure, and as I'm sure you can imagine, some of the old-school prison guards wouldn't be very hospitable towards our lads. It'll be good to just level the playing field a bit. You know what I mean, Raymond?"

"Not really, no," said Ray, his mouth dry.

Dermot took another sip of his tea, "Well, there's a certain bias within the British prison service. It'll be good to balance that out a bit."

Ray nodded slowly, glancing occasionally towards Maria.

"It's not as if we'll be wanting you to spy for us or anything like that," said Dermot, turning to Maria and laughing.

Ray forced out a laugh. "Ha, that's good. I don't think I'd be cut out for something like that."

"No, no. We'd never ask you to do something like that," said Dermot. He turned to Maria and held up his cup. "I couldn't get a wee top-up there, Maria, could I?"

"Yes, no bother," said Maria, lifting the stewing teapot from the stove. "Do you want a cup, Ray?"

"No, thanks. I'm okay. I can't stay long, anyway. I've to go and help my da."

Dermot kept his focus on his mug as Maria added more tea from the pot. "But you know Raymond, sometimes we might need to pass on a wee message to some of our guys or something like that. Nothing that'd get you in trouble or anything." He put his mug to his lips again and turned to look at Ray, icy eyes peering through the steam.

Ray needed to get out. "Well, I better go. My da will be looking for me," he said, rising from the table and fixing a stare at Maria.

"It was good to meet you, Raymond," said Dermot. "I hope everything works out for you."

Maria followed Ray through the living room and out to the front door.

"What the fuck, Maria?" whispered Ray, when they stepped out onto the front path.

"Don't worry about it, Ray," said Maria with a smile. "It was better to let them know, rather than them find out down the line."

"Yeah? And what if he asks me to do something for them?" asked Ray, his excitement for the role now tainted.

Maria laughed. "He was only joking. That's the way he is. He just likes winding people up."

In the days and weeks that followed, Maria had continued to reassure Ray that Dermot had only been joking, and that they'd no interest in his position, but the whole situation felt wrong to Ray. He'd had no intention of ever working for them or even relaying messages, and there'd been many times in his first few weeks on the course when he'd been close to quitting because of it. It'd been Derek who'd convinced him to stay — not that Ray ever told his roommate of the true reason for his cold feet. The IRA ceasefire came soon after he'd completed the course, and so he'd never heard from Dermot O'Connor again, and Maria never brought up the meeting, either. Ray put it to the back of his mind and threw himself into a career that he grew to love.

Drawing in a long breath, Ray slowly emerged from his hiding place behind his hands and raised his head to the darkening sky. A slow, purposeful exhale steadied him for what he planned to do. Good or bad, his plan was now set. He'd appease O'Connor with the weapons, and warn him to stay away from his family. He'd then go home and explain everything. His parents and Derek might be a bit pissed off, but they'd understand.

CHAPTER TWENTY-SEVEN

Lisa's nose crinkled as the acrid aroma of the room caught in the back of her throat; a stale mix of beer, tobacco, and sweat. The hint of cheap disinfectant did little to mask the stench, instead adding a sickly sweet tang to the offending cocktail. The tingling sensation in her fingertips was becoming more noticeable as the plastic cable ties restricted the circulation to her hands. Simon and Conor sat on either side of her, perched on small wooden bar stools, hands similarly restrained behind their backs.

After being wedged into the back of Lisa's car, they'd been driven to the run-down bar at the edge of town, where they were to wait for Dermot O'Connor who, *'wanted to have a word'*. They now sat in silence, their earlier protests and resistance harshly subdued by threats, and finally quashed when Simon received a blow to the face as he tried to resist being dragged from the car. The promise of more severe treatment succeeded in keeping the three captives quiet.

One of their captors stood guard by the door, the other having gone through to the main bar.

"Are you okay?" whispered Lisa, frowning in concern at the reddening bruise under Simon's eye.

"Yeah, I'm alright," said Simon, glaring angrily at the man who'd earlier cold-cocked him.

"I fuckin' told you to shut up, didn't I?" snapped the guard, stepping towards them threateningly. The creak of a door stopped him and he turned to see his partner reappear from the main bar, followed by a bigger, older man with a twisted nose and a head half-covered in wispy fuzz that should've been shaved long before.

"This prick's mouthing off again, Barney," he said to the more senior new-comer.

The balding man stopped in front of Simon. "Is that right?"

Simon looked up at him, expressionless.

"That looks sore," said Barney, reaching out and prodding Simon's swollen cheek.

Simon jerked his head back, twisting away from the man's touch.

"Leave him alone," shouted Lisa.

Barney turned to Lisa with a smirk. "Where's your brother?"

"I don't know where my brother is," spat Lisa defiantly. "What do you want with him, anyway?"

"He's got something of ours," said the man, before returning his attention to Simon. He leaned in, stopping inches from Simon's face. "You're a long way from home, aren't you lad?"

Simon tensed, but resisted the urge to protest.

"What are you doing here?"

"You fuckin brought us here," said Conor under his breath.

"You'd do well to keep your mouth shut, son," hissed one of the other men.

A rough hand gripped Simon by the chin. "Who are you working for, you British bastard?" Barney bellowed, speckles of spittle hitting Simon's face as he leaned in. "Where are the rest of your forces? Where are the French?"

Simon's face scrunched in total confusion. "What forces? What the hell are you talking about?" he said, flicking his head to free himself from his inquisitor's grip. He looked at Lisa as if for some thread of explanation.

"We don't know what you're talking about. He came with me from Belfast to get out of the city," she shouted before turning to the other men in the room, appealing for some sanity, assuming the first had lost his mind. "We don't work for anyone. What the fuck is this guy talking about?"

"I know *you* don't," said Barney with a sarcastic smile, before turning back to Simon and taking him by the chin again, "but do you expect me to believe that it's just a coincidence that your English friend here happens to show up at the same time as his country's invasion?"

"Invasion?" asked both Simon and Lisa simultaneously.

Lisa looked at each of their captors in turn, shaking her head, face scrunched in disbelief. "What the fuck are you talking about? What invasion? Who's invading?"

"Ask your friend here," said Barney, rising from his crouch and releasing his grip on Simon with a rough flick of his hand. He stepped back and folded his arms across his chest.

Lisa raised her eyebrows in disbelief at what she was hearing. Her mouth opened but she couldn't find words, and instead just continued to shake her head. *It must be some strange, sick joke,* she thought.

"So, are you gonna tell her about operation Darkness?" asked Barney, towering over Simon.

"I have no idea what you're talking about," said Simon, voice quivering.

"Shouldn't we wait for Doc, Barney?" asked the guy by the door.

Barney held a hand out to quieten his comrade. "I want this fucker to tell me his plans."

"I don't have any fucking plans," shouted Simon defiantly. He looked pleadingly at the other two men in the room. "I don't know what he's talking about."

"Barney, let's wait for Doc," said the man at the door again.

"Shut the fuck up," Barney snapped, levelling an angry glare at the younger man.

"Operation Darkness! We know all about it," growled Barney. He sprang forward and grabbed Simon by the hair, pulling his head back.

"Leave him alone," screamed Lisa as she sprang to her feet.

Barney released Simon and slapped Lisa with the back of his hand, sending her flailing over her stool. She landed heavily on her side, a stab of pain shooting through her shoulder as it absorbed the brunt of the fall.

A guttural roar erupted from Simon as he propelled himself upward, driving his head into Barney's chin. There was an audible thwack as skull met jawbone, and the thug toppled backwards, Simon's momentum carrying him down on top of him.

The two other men hesitated for a second, surprised by the sudden explosion of violence, then, as one, they lunged towards Simon. Barney was out cold before he'd even hit the ground, but Simon wasn't going to stop. He shuffled and rolled to his knees beside the unconscious thug, and with hands still secured behind his back, he used the only weapon he had. He reared up, then dove forward, driving his head into the man's face. Before he could right himself to repeat the attack, one of the other men grabbed him and threw him to the side. Simon's head connected with a table, sending a stack of pint glasses tumbling to the ground. Broken glass and stale beer shattered and sprayed across the room.

Lisa squirmed on her side in the corner where she'd landed, straining against her restraints, desperate to get free. The plastic cut deep into her skin as she twisted and pulled in a frantic attempt to snap the ties. They wouldn't budge. Rolling onto her back, she brought her knees in tight to her chest. Thankful for her flexibility, from years of yoga practise, she arched backwards onto her shoulders and worked her hands down behind her knees. The plastic straps dug into her wrists as she stretched her hands down to her left foot. Water filled her eyes, her injured ankle burning with pain as she pulled and strained to force her hands past her heel. All around her the shouts and grunts erupted.

Conor had joined in the fight, charging at one of the men. He barged into him with his shoulder, momentarily throwing him off balance. His futile attack was soon ended when the man righted himself and spun, revealing a hand gun. He swung his arm, catching Conor on the side of the face with the butt of the hard metal weapon.

As Conor fell to the side, Lisa appeared behind him, her face wild with rage. She charged forward, a squat wooden stool held firmly in front of her like a battering ram. She drove the stool into the man, catching him on the arm as he tried to bring the gun up. The gun clattered to the floor and skidded away, a Lisa propelled herself forward, one of the protruding legs of the stool connected with the man's sternum, prompting a heavy grunt and an explosion of air from his lungs.

The other guard was now on top of Simon, pinning him with a knee and pressing his face into the beer-soaked, threadbare carpet.

Everyone in the room, including Lisa, jumped at the deafening gunshot as it reverberated through the small space. The yellow-stained polystyrene ceiling tile disintegrated as the bullet torn through it, raining dust and fragments down on the tangle of bodies on the ground.

"Get the fuck off him," screamed Lisa, her own voice barely audible through her ringing ears. "Get back!"

She took a step towards Simon's attacker, jabbing the gun forward to emphasise her seriousness. The man stood slowly, his hands instinctively rising to a surrender position.

Lisa's hands shook, her grip on the gun made awkward by her restraints, but she'd proved that she was willing and able to pull the trigger.

"Get the fuck back!"

"Okay, okay love, take it easy," pleaded the man as he stepped away, nearly trampling on Barney, who was groaning and cupping his face as he gradually regained consciousness.

She contemplated shooting the prick for calling her *love*, but firing the gun into the ceiling had been hard enough. The door to the adjoining bar swung open and a collection of faces tentatively peered in, only to pull back when Lisa levelled the gun at them.

Conor shuffled awkwardly onto his knees, then stood, unsure what to do next, the shock of his cousin's actions clear on his face.

"Stay back," Lisa ordered again before bending and using her little finger and thumb to lift the remnants of beer glass. She straightened again, resetting her aim at the men now huddling in the corner, to dispel any thoughts they might have of rushing her.

"Come here, Conor. Turn round," said Lisa, without taking her eyes off the men.

Conor took an unsteady step towards Lisa and turned, extending his bound hands out from his body. Lisa readjusted the broken glass in her grip, allowing her aim to drop momentarily, before snapping it back to the group of aggrieved, bruised and stunned men.

"Don't you fucking move!" she shouted.

With an awkward sawing motion, and trying not to cut Conor's wrists, she finally heard the satisfying crack as the plastic restraints snapped.

"Here do me," she said, presenting her hands to Conor while trying to keep the gun pointed in their captors-turned-captives' direction.

"Now help Simon up," she said, when her own restrains broke and fell away.

With Conor's help, Simon staggered to his feet, his now freed hands wiping at his beer and blood-soaked face. His pained and fearful expression gave way briefly to an awestruck smile as he sidled up beside Lisa.

The door to the bar creaked open again and a brave face inched through to assess the scene.

"Get back," Lisa bellowed again, and the door swung shut.

"What now?" whispered Simon.

"We get the fuck out of here," said Lisa. She addressed the men again, the gun bobbing in her hands as she spoke. "Where's my car keys?"

Barney sat with his back against the wall, still clutching his face. The others glanced at each other nervously.

"Who's got the fucking keys?" shouted Simon.

"I have them," said one of the younger men, as he slowly reached into his pocket and retrieved the keys.

"Throw them ov—"

"No wait," interrupted Simon. "Do you have the cable ties too?"

The young man looked to his partners, then nodded tentatively.

"Put them on your mate, then put the keys in his hands," ordered Simon. "Do them tight!"

The man hesitated.

"We'll need him to get out of here," said Simon quietly.

"Do it!" shouted Lisa, gesturing with the gun.

"Walk backwards towards us. Slowly!" ordered Simon, when the man's hands were secured.

Simon intercepted the man and gripped him roughly by the back of his neck before tugging on the ends of the cable ties to ensure they were tight. Lisa stepped up beside him and took the man by the elbow, holding the gun close by his head. Conor tucked in beside them.

"Now, we're gonna walk out that door," said Lisa, nodding to the side door leading to the alley. "If any of you come out after us—"

The door that they'd been edging towards suddenly opened. Lisa instinctively pointed the gun in the direction of the movement, sharing the aim between Dermot O'Connor and the two men who followed him.

Dermot surveyed the scene. "You're a fuckin useless bunch of pricks, aren't you?" he said, directing an icy glare at Barney, before returning his attention to Lisa. "Okay, look, I think there's been some misunderstanding. We just wanted to have a chat about your brother, Ray."

"A misunderstanding?" fumed Lisa. "You think you can just snatch people of the street and hold them captive? The police will be hearing about this, you crazy bastard."

"These aren't normal times, Lisa," said Dermot, his voice strangely calm for the situation. "You may not realise it yet, but we are at war."

"War?" asked Lisa, her mask of confusion returning as she looked from Dermot to Barney. "What the fuck are you people talking about? What war? What invasion? Have you all gone mad?"

"I'm sorry to tell you, love, but it's true."

I'll shoot the next fucker that calls me love, thought Lisa.

"What do you think has caused the power cut?" continued Dermot. "It's part of a plan by the British and the French."

"The British and French? Do you hear yourself? You're fucking insane!"

Lisa looked at Simon, who mirrored her look of disbelief.

"A solar flare caused the power cut. A natural phenomenon," said Simon. "And it's not just limited to Ireland."

"That's what they want you to believe. It's fake news," said Dermot with a condescending smirk and a slow shake of his head.

"You've all lost your fucking minds," said Lisa. "Move!" She gestured with the gun for Dermot to move away from the door. "I've had enough of this shit."

"I think you should wait for your brother, Lisa," said Dermot, standing his ground in front of the exit.

"And why would my brother be coming here?"

"He's bringing us the weapons we need to mount a defence of our country."

"Weapons? What weapons? Where would Ray get weapons?" asked Lisa.

"They were hidden on your parent's farm a while ago. Just for a situation like this," said Dermot.

Lisa looked at Simon and frowned. She thought about the holes dug out by the old house. "Even if that was true, how would Ray know anything about them? He's been living in Belfast for years."

"Ah, we know all about Ray's life in Belfast, and his job at the prison."

Lisa stiffened. Ray's job was supposed to be a secret, and certainly not known to people like Dermot O'Connor.

"Who do you think got him the job?" said Dermot with a smile. "He's on our side, Lisa. He's always been one of our volunteers."

Lisa felt her stomach churn.

"That's fuckin' bullshit," snapped Conor. "Ray's not in the IRA. There is no IRA anymore. You and these bag of pricks are just a bunch of fuckin' drunks who hang out in holes like this pretending to be someone."

"Is that right, Mr Toner?" asked Dermot, clearly angered by the comment. "Who do you think suggested the location for the cache? Who do you think talked your cousin into working for the British Queen?"

Conor looked at him blankly.

"How *is* your mother, Conor? I hear she's in the hospital."

"What the fuck are you talking about? You fat prick!" shouted Conor.

"Your mother has been a key member of our organisation since long before you were around, Conor," said Dermot with a wry smile. He seemed to be enjoying enlightening his guests. "She was one of our main recruiters."

"Right, I've had enough of listening to this madman," said Lisa. She nodded to Simon and together they tugged their captive towards the door. "You either move or I'll fucking shoot you."

Lisa pointed the gun directly at Dermot's head, the look on her face convincing Dermot and his men to stand aside.

"If anyone comes out after us, I'll shoot this prick," said Lisa, as they backed out through the exit.

They made their way along the alley and out through the wooden gates. Dermot and his men followed cautiously.

"You drive, Simon," said Lisa, as they made their way across the road to where her car had been parked. "Conor, open the front door for me, then get in the back."

Simon took the keys and wiped at his bloody forehead with his sleeve before climbing into the car and starting the engine. Conor opened the door for Lisa, then stood beside his own, ready to jump in once Lisa had released her prisoner. The small group from the bar filed through the wooden gate and fanned out, some of them taking a bold step out onto the road.

Dermot O'Connor stood to the side by the small brick wall of the neighbouring property, his hands buried in his pockets, face as cold as stone.

"Ready Simon?" asked Lisa.

"Yes, let's go."

"Get in, Conor," ordered Lisa before giving her captive a shove and jumping into the front passenger seat. "Go!"

She watched as the man they'd used as a shield stumbled towards his group of comrades, the shame something he wouldn't soon live down. Beyond him, she saw Dermot O'Connor. He was still standing by the wall, but he now had something in his hands. He raised them, pointing directly at her. A gun!

"Go, Simon," she screamed.

She ducked instinctively when she saw a flash mushroom from the end of Dermot's gun. A split second later, hearing the metallic clack of a bullet hitting the car.

"Fuck, they're shooting at us, go go go!"

There was thankfully only one shot, and with Simon's foot to the floor, they were soon far enough away to feel a measure of safety. Lisa let out a deep sigh and let her head flop forward, suddenly felling like she was gonna throw up.

CHAPTER TWENTY-EIGHT

"Drop it!" Ray screamed into Dermot's ear as he pressed the barrel of his Glock into the older man's temple and grabbed him roughly by the back of his collar.

Dermot stiffened as Ray yanked him backwards, barking the order again and digging the gun into the soft tissue in front of the man's ear. The older man complied, tossing his snub-nosed revolver on the ground in front of him.

Ray watched as his father's car sped off. He'd arrived just in time to catch a glimpse of his sister in the passenger seat, Dermot O'Connor having already taken a wild shot at it and preparing a better aimed second.

"Was that my sister?" Ray growled through clenched teeth as he twisted the gun against Dermot's skin. "Did you just fire a fuckin' gun at my sister?"

Dermot squirmed, trying to angle his head away from the increasing pressure, but Ray tugged him back and held him in close. Rage tightened Ray's finger against the trigger as he fought the burning urge to put a bullet through the deranged thug's head.

The rest of Dermot's men had already turned their attention from the escaping car and now stood wide-eyed and impotent, unsure of their next move. Anthony Kilpatrick stepped forward, seemingly the only other person with a weapon, which he now levelled at Ray.

"Stay the fuck back," shouted Ray, rotating to keep Dermot between him and Kilpatrick's gun. "Tell him to put the gun down."

"I don't think I will," said Dermot coldly.

"If you want your fuckin' guns, you'll tell him to put it down."

Dermot extended his hand, palm forward, halting his men but stopping short of ordering Anthony to lower his weapon. "Where are they?" he asked, over his shoulder to Ray.

"They're close," replied Ray. *He'd have to play this very carefully if he was gonna get away with his life.*

"Give me the weapons, Raymond, and we'll talk," said Dermot, gesturing for Anthony to lower his gun.

"No. We'll talk, and if I like what I hear, then I'll give you the weapons," said Ray, as he tugged Dermot away from his cohort and began to edge backwards up the street.

"Where're we going, Raymond?"

"You want the guns, don't you?" said Ray. "Tell them not to follow."

"It's okay. Just stay where you are," Dermot instructed Anthony and the others. "Raymond knows what'll happen if he does anything stupid."

Dermot lowered his voice, talking over his shoulder as Ray shuffled him backwards. "Don't you Raymond? Don't you know what'll happen to your family if you do anything to me?"

Ray ground the barrel of his Glock into the side of Dermot's head, "Are you seriously fuckin' threatening my family again? With a fuckin' gun to your head?"

Every muscle in Ray's body tensed as he fought the urge to pull the trigger. He bit his bottom lip and continued on until they reached the alley where he'd leaned his bike against a wall. He glanced back at Dermot's group of followers, none of whom had dared to move, before releasing him with a shove. Dermot stumbled forward into the alley, needing a couple of steps to gain his balance and steady himself. He turned and gathered himself, straightening his jacket before slipping both hands into its pockets.

"Keep your hands where I can see them," said Ray, holding the gun at a low ready.

Dermot smiled and withdrew his hands again, opening his palms to show he was no threat.

"You're making a mistake, Raymond," said Dermot, his voice quiet and cold.

Ray positioned himself at the mouth of the alley, ensuring that he could still see Dermot's men outside the bar and that they could see that he still held the gun on their boss.

"So what happens now, Raymond?"

"That's up to you."

"I like you, Raymond," said Dermot, "and I think if you knew what was really going on, you'd join us."

Ray huffed and shook his head, then glanced back towards the bar. Dermot took a small step forward.

"Stay back!" ordered Ray, raising the gun again.

"You don't understand, Raymond," said Dermot, retreating again. "This is much bigger than you realise."

"No, I think I understand alright," said Ray with a slow nod. "You're a washed up old drunk, desperate to have people think you *are* something. Taking advantage of the situation, riling people up, making them think you're some kind of local hero. You're only out for yourself."

"This is not about me, Raymond. This is about a fight for our country."

Ray rolled his eyes and shook his head. He glanced again towards the bar, checking again that the others hadn't moved. *If it wasn't for his reputation, Ray would actually pity this old fool.*

"What do you mean, a fight for our country?" he asked, disdain thick in his voice.

"When you know the truth, I'm sure you'll join us, Raymond."

"Join you? Join you in what?"

"Join us in the fight."

"What fight? Who do you think you're fighting against?"

"The Brits, Raymond. The Brits."

"Fuck me," Ray muttered with a shy.

Sensing movement in his periphery, Ray took a step back and turned to see that Anthony and a couple of others had edged forward. "Stay fuckin' back!" he shouted, stabbing the gun towards them before returning his aim to Dermot.

"The British are invading, Raymond," said Dermot. "This whole blackout is their doing. Them and the French."

Ray physically recoiled, his eyes narrowing to slits as he tried to process what he'd just heard. He shook his head, "What?" he asked, stuttering to get the word from his lips.

Dermot tilted his head and nodded, "That's right, Raymond. And we have proof."

Ray's heart was already racing. Now he could feel his pulse thumping in his ear. He blinked slowly and tried to clear his thoughts with a sharp shake of his head.

"So, let me get this straight," said Ray, stretching his eyes wide and trying to find the right words. "The British and — did you say the French?"

Dermot nodded.

"The French, right," said Ray, drawing the last word out, eyebrows raised high on his forehead. "So, the British and the French have caused a power cut in order to invade Ireland?" He narrowed his eyes again. "That's what you're saying is happening?"

"That's exactly what's happening, Raymond. And we need to stop them."

"Have you any idea how absolutely insane that is?"

"We have pr—"

"And these half-wits," interrupted Ray, gesturing towards the group outside the bar, "believe this shit?"

Ray drew his hand slowly through his hair.

"You see, Raymond, that's how they've been able to do this," said Dermot, his face reddening. "There're so many small-minded people in this country, all too willing to believe the propaganda that they're fed."

"Enough!" snapped Ray. "You're a bunch of deranged, paranoid, fuckin' madmen."

"Where's the guns Raymond?"

"You expect me to hand weapons over to you and your crazies after what you've just told me?" asked Ray with a humourless chuff.

Dermot glared at him.

"Okay, I'll give you the weapons," said Ray. "You wage your war against the non-existent British and French invaders. But if you come anywhere near my family, I will not fuckin' hesitate to put a bullet through your head. Do you understand me?"

Dermot tilted his head. "Where are they?"

Ray looked again to make sure the others had heeded his warning to stay back, then nodded towards a large green wheelie bin half way along the alley. "Behind that bin."

Dermot turned to look towards the bin.

"Go get them," said Ray.

As Dermot moved towards the bin, Ray took his chance to mount his scrambler. He turned the key and kick-started the engine. Still holding the gun, he rolled the bike along the alley to where Dermot was dragging the holdall of weapons from behind the bin.

"Where's the rest, Raymond?" said Dermot as he crouched and unzipped the bag. "There was a lot more than this."

"The rest were too badly corroded. That's all I could save," said Ray.

Dermot straighten and fixed Ray with a chilling stare.

"And, I'm telling you, if I see you anywhere near my family I will fuckin' kill you," said Ray, emphasising the point by levelling his gun at Dermot's head as he released the brake and allowed the bike to roll forward before twisting the throttle and tearing off down the alleyway.

CHAPTER TWENTY-NINE

Simon had slowed the car to maximise his chances of keeping it on the road, the immediate danger having subsided after they'd turned the first bend. He wiped at his brow with his sleeve and winced as the rough material of his sweatshirt caught on the torn skin above his right eye. The blood cascaded through and around his eyebrow, turning his world a blurred red. The swelling on his left cheek had risen to a purple mound, restricting that eye to a watery slit.

"Shit!" cried Simon as he jerked the steering wheel to the right, having barely seen the next sharp bend. After a couple of counter adjustments on the wheel, and a prudent application of brake, he brought the car to a stop straddling the centre line.

"I can't see," he said, trying again to mop the blood from his eye with his bicep. "Are you okay to take over?"

Lisa looked vacantly at the stolen hand gun cradled in her lap, eventually catching up with Simon's request. "Yes, okay," she said, turning to Simon and grimacing at the sight of his battered face. "Shit, that looks bad. You need to stem the bleeding until we get home."

She dropped the gun onto the floor by her feet and dragged open the glove compartment. The tiny light illuminated nothing but a service manual and a little orange bag, presumably containing the special key for the locking nuts on the wheels.

"Okay, switch seats," she said, throwing her door open and jumping from the car.

Simon wasn't so sprightly. He groaned as he stumbled from the car cradling his ribs, every joint and muscle burning with pain.

"Here, hold this to your head," said Lisa, removing her shirt and handing it to Simon.

He took the shirt and rolled it into a ball before pressing it to the wound on his forehead.

Lisa had the engine started again by the time Simon lowered himself into the passenger seat. The building clouds that'd been threatening all day finally began to open. The first few spats of slow but voluminous rain drops slapped against the windscreen and Lisa flicked the wiper lever up to intermittent.

"Fuckers!" she hissed through gritted teeth.

"What's wrong?" asked Simon, alarm returning to his voice.

"Lisa," came a muted voice from the back seat.

"The fuel light's blinking," she said, ignoring or not hearing Conor. She squinted at the fuel gauge which teetered at the bottom end of the red warning band.

"There was half a tank when we left the house. They must've syphoned it off when we were in the bar."

"Is there enough to get us home?"

"Just about, I think," she replied, putting the car into gear and moving off.

Simon adjusted Lisa's shirt, finding a less blood-soaked section, and wiped the blood from his eye before reapplying pressure to his throbbing wound.

"Lisa," the voice from the back seat, although still quiet, came with more urgency.

"You okay in the back there?" asked Lisa without looking round.

"I don't think so…"

Simon twisted in his seat. "Jesus! Lisa!"

Conor sat in the middle of the back seat, his head bowed. He had one hand over the other clasped against his stomach, blood seeping through his fingers. He raised his head slowly, his disbelieving, tear-filled eyes meeting Simon's. It was clear he was in shock.

"I think I've been shot," he said, almost nonchalantly.

"What?" cried Lisa, twisting in her seat and almost taking the car off the road. She slammed on the brakes, causing Conor to lurch forward, prompting a first groan of pain as his initial trance wore off.

Simon managed to cushion Conor's movement with a palm to his chest as he wedged himself between the seats. The agony from his own ribs was forgotten for the moment.

"Don't stop! We need to get to the hospital," he said, turning to Lisa, who was rising to her knees and trying to get a view of the wound past Simon.

She dropped back into her seat and grabbed for the gear stick. "Move your leg!" she yelled, roughly shoving Simon's trailing foot.

"Don't move yet," said Simon, repositioning himself and carefully easing through the gap and into the back seat beside Conor. "Okay, go!"

Lisa pressed on the accelerator, moving off with less abruptness than when she'd stopped.

Simon unfolded the jumbled shirt that he clutched in his hand, re-balling it as best he could. "Okay Conor, I need you to move your hands a second."

"I can't, it hurts," Conor groaned.

"It's okay, I need to get pressure on it."

He coaxed Conor's bloodied hands away and tried not to react to what he saw. Blood had begun to pool in Conor's lap and a dark, wet mess spread across his once-white t-shirt. He tried to peel the sodden top away from Conor's skin, but a cry from the young lad forced him to reconsider and he instead pressed Lisa's shirt on top of it, tentatively at first before applying more pressure.

"Ahhhh, it burns. It burns," cried Conor as he grabbed Simon's arm, digging his fingers into his bicep.

"It's gonna be okay, Conor," said Simon, forcing some reassurance into his voice.

He remembered how he'd used those same words only a few days before as he tried in vain to stem the bleeding from one of Martin's many wounds. *Was he also lying to this young man?*

Conor's groaning became more intense, only punctuated by periods of panting and hissing through gritted teeth.

"How long to the hospital?" Simon asked.

Lisa didn't reply.

"Lisa, how long?"

"We're not going to the hospital. We don't have enough fuel," she said with a quick glance into the back seat. "We have to get him to my mom. She'll know what to do."

Simon fixed her with a stern, questioning look when she turned again. He was in no position to argue. He could only hope she was making the right decision."

"How does it look?" she asked, stealing another look back.

"I can't really see it, but I've got pressure on it. Hurry Lisa."

CHAPTER THIRTY

Lisa leaned on the horn as she eased to a stop outside the front door. She hoped the noise would prompt those inside to come and help.

Turning in her seat, she surveyed the carnage in the back. She was met with a scene from a horror movie. Simon was awash with blood, both his own from the gash on his head, and Conor's as he tried to stem the blood flow from the bullet hole in his stomach. Conor was barely conscious. He looked up at her with heavy eyes, his skin pasty and deathly pale.

"Okay, I'll go get help, I'll be two seconds," she said, then jumped from the car and sprinted up the steps to her parents' house.

She burst through the door into the kitchen and froze. Her parents, Derek and Jenny, clearly already had reason for concern as they sat, grave-faced, around the table, on which lay a large collection of weapons; hand guns, and rifles and two cloth bags, one of them open, showing its contents of hundreds of loose bullets.

Her mum lifted her head from where it'd been resting heavily in her hands. "Oh my God, what happened? Are you hurt?" She was focused on Lisa's white vest, which was streaked with Simon's blood from where she'd rubbed against the steering wheel.

Lisa followed her mum's eyes then shook her head as she backed out of the room, beckoning for them to follow. "It's not me. Conor's hurt. He's been shot."

A chorus of gasps and questions accompanied the scraping of chairs as the room sprang to life. Whatever stresses and concerns relating to the arsenal on the kitchen table were instantly shelved.

"Where is he?" asked Derek, rushing to catch up to Lisa.

"In the car. We'll need help to get him out."

Moira grabbed Lisa by the arm. "Where's he been shot?" she asked, before Lisa had finished her first reply.

"In the stomach I think," Lisa replied, her worry intensifying when she saw the grave expression on her mum's face at this fact.

Derek reached the car first and pulled open the back door. He recoiled at the scene inside before being squeezed out of the way by Moira. She pulled Conor's rucksack out and dumped it behind her, then climbed in to assess the situation.

"Okay Conor love, let's have a wee look," she said, her frantic urgency now replaced with a calm, reassuring professionalism.

Derek had climbed into the driver's seat and was now kneeling up trying to get a better look.

Lisa stood with her dad and Jenny, waiting for Moira's instructions.

"What the hell happened, Lisa?" asked Vinnie.

"It was Dermot O'Connor," she said, without looking at him. She paced from one spot to another, trying to get a view into the car. "He fuckin' kidnapped us and brought us to that wee hole of a bar at the edge of town. He was looking for Ray."

Moira emerged from the car. Despite being retired, her thirty-odd years of paramedic training kept her calm and focused. "Vinnie, clear the kitchen table and get my first aid kit out."

Vinnie gave a curt nod and strode up the steps.

"We need to get him out and into the house with as little movement as possible," Moira said, turning and looking around her, searching for inspiration.

"What about a chair?" asked Jenny. "We could slide him out on to it."

"Yes! Can you get one from the kitchen please, Jenny?"

Jenny was already moving when Moira called after her, "One of the ones with no arms."

"What do you need me to do, Moira?" asked Derek.

"I need you and Simon to try to ease him out onto the chair," she turned to Lisa. "Lisa, can you reach through from the front and keep pressure on the wound as they move him?"

Derek climbed into the back seat beside Conor. "Okay, mate, we'll need to move you inside, okay?"

Conor gave no response other than a low moan.

Stretching through from the front, Lisa replaced Simon's hands and pressed her, now sodden, shirt down on Conor's wound.

"Okay, everyone ready?" asked Derek, positioning one hand under Conor's thigh and the other behind his back.

Simon manoeuvred himself into a kneeling position beside Conor and nodded. "Ready."

"Are you ready, Moira?" Derek asked over his shoulder.

Moira took the kitchen chair from Jenny and placed it a couple of feet from the car. "Yes. Now, as gently as you can."

The first movement roused Conor back to consciousness, and he cried out, gritting his teeth against the pain.

"Nearly there, mate," said Derek. He edged backwards through the door, Simon doing his best to take some of Conor's weight as he shuffled awkwardly on his knees across the back seat.

They lowered him onto the chair then, as a group, lifted it up the stairs and through to the kitchen where Vinnie was finishing clearing the table. Conor's moaning had stopped by the time they laid him down, and his head lulled to the side. Lisa feared the worst.

"Is he gonna be okay mum?" she asked frantically, blood-stained hands pressed to her face.

Moira took a pair of blue latex gloves from the first aid kit, which Vinnie had unzipped and placed on the kitchen counter. "Pass me the scissors," she ordered.

Jenny stood closest to the medical kit, and so became Moira's assistant. Her hands hovered over the kit as she tried to locate the scissors among the multitude of compartments and divided sections.

"They should be in the top section on the underside of the lid," Moira instructed. "Vinnie, get me some tea towels. The new ones from the second drawer."

She took the scissors and, with practised hands, cut a long line up Conor's t-shirt, before carefully folding the flaps back to reveal the source of the bleeding. She wiped at the area, clearing away the pooling blood. A small hole about the size of a pea became visible for a second before being obscured again by a fresh oozing of blood.

"Help me turn him on his side," said Moira, as she bent Conor's leg up at the knee and rolled him into a recovery position. "There," she said, pointing to another small hole further back on his waist.

She wiped the excess blood away and pressed a freshly opened gauze to both wounds.

"How's it look, Moira?" asked Vinnie.

"It's not as bad as I thought," said Moira. "It went through his side. I don't think it's hit anything vital. I'll clean it, but we'll have to get him to the hospital. I'm more worried about infection at this stage."

Lisa let out a relieved sigh and slumped into a chair, the weight of the ordeal suddenly hitting her.

Derek helped Simon into the chair beside her and pressed another of the fresh cloths to the gash on his forehead. "Jesus, you look like shit, mate. What the fuck happened?" he asked.

"They stopped us on the road and forced us out of the car," Simon replied.

"Who were they?"

"Dermot O'Connor," said Lisa, answering Derek's question but looking up at her father.

"IRA," said Simon at the same time.

Derek flashed a stern look at Vinnie. It was confirmation of what they'd suspected from the haul of weapons Derek had revealed to them earlier.

Simon looked at the guns that'd been hastily stacked by the wall beside him. "They said Ray was bringing them guns," he said. "Is this them? Where is Ray? What the fuck is going on?"

"Daddy, what's going on?" asked Lisa, her voice wavering. "Where is Ray?"

"I don't know," replied Vinnie dryly.

"They said Ray was one of them," Lisa said, staring up at her father.

Vinnie stared at the stack of cloths in his hands but didn't reply.

"Yeah, but they also said that the British and French were behind the power cut and were invading," said Simon with a snort.

"What?" said Derek.

"Yeah, they're fucking insane."

Lisa persisted, "They said Maria hid the guns, and that she got Ray to apply for the prison job."

Derek's head snapped to Vinnie, and he straightened, leaving Simon to hold his own cloth to his head wound.

Vinnie met Derek's stare, then looked to the floor, his shoulders slumping. "Did you hear that? Moira?" he shouted.

Moira looked back at him briefly, but said nothing.

Simon put his hand on Lisa's elbow. "Lisa, they're completely insane. I wouldn't listen to a wor…"

"Stop doing that, Simon," Lisa snapped, jerking her arm away. "Stop trying to be peace maker all the time. You don't know what you're talking about." She stood and stepped in front of Vinnie. "Mum? Dad?" she said, looking between her parents. "Do you know something? Tell me!"

"Moira! For fuck's sake," shouted Vinnie.

"Will you stop with that language," said Moira, still working on Conor.

"Fuck me, woman! If there's ever a time to fuckin' curse, this is it," fumed Vinnie. "And if this is true, then it's your fuckin sister's doing." He stormed from the room, leaving Lisa and the rest looking to Moira for answers.

"Mum? Was aunt Maria in the IRA?"

"Lisa, we'll talk about this later," said Moira sternly. "Now you all need to give me space to work on your cousin."

Lisa looked in turn to each of the others, tears welling in her eyes before turning and running from the room.

CHAPTER THIRTY-ONE

By the time Simon had finished cleaning the worst of the blood from his hands and arms and face, his small adjoining bathroom looked like a murder scene. The sink and taps were streaked in red, as was the mirrored cabinet above. Even the toilet bowl had somehow failed to escape the spray.

With a wadded handful of toilet paper, Simon did his best to return the bathroom to its former state. He feared that the towel, however, which had once been pale blue, was now well beyond salvage, and so he let it fall to join the heap of blood-stained clothes that lay by the door. This was now the second time in a week that he'd had to peel himself out of blood-drenched clothes. *Was plugging people's wounds, and being covered in their blood just par for the course now?* He thought of Martin and the terror in his friend's eyes as he looked up at him, pleading for help through the iron gate that separated them. Help that Simon couldn't give him.

Simon gripped the sink and leaned heavily over it, the urge to empty his stomach hovering just out of sight. With a slow breath, he closed his eyes and tried to usher the sensation away. When the danger had passed, he opened his eyes to see a stranger staring back at him from the mirror. A stranger with tired, hopeless eyes, set into a broken and swollen face that was not his own. How quickly his life had changed; within two weeks he'd gone from having a comfortable existence; with a nice apartment, a top-of-the-range car, and more money than he knew what to do with, thanks to him investing his wife's life insurance payout in Bitcoin at just the right time. Now his apartment was abandoned, his car was locked in a garage he couldn't open, and every satoshi of his digital fortune had evaporated in a mist of ones and zeros along with the entire internet.

Pulling on his last remaining pair of jeans and a less than fresh t-shirt, he steeled himself to return downstairs to his adopted family, who now found themselves broken by betrayal and violence.

As he descended, he could hear voices raised in anger coming from the front sitting room. Lisa and Vinnie were arguing again, Lisa demanding to know the truth about her aunt Maria.

Derek met him at the foot of the stairs, a grave expression etched on his face.

"How's Conor?" Simon asked.

Derek nodded. "Moira thinks he'll be okay. She stopped the bleeding and patched him up, but we'll need to get him to the hospital to be seen to properly, and to make sure his wound doesn't get infected. He was very lucky."

"That's good," replied Simon. He gestured to the sitting room. "How are things in there?"

"Not great," said Derek, looking towards the sitting room, then back to Simon before lowering his voice. "From what I can piece together, their aunt Maria is, or at least was, in the IRA. It seems she hid the weapons out by the old house in the nineties, before the ceasefire. And it looks like she was the one who persuaded Ray to join the Prison Service."

"Jesus, so it's true then? That Ray's in the IRA? Fuck!"

"Fuckin' looks that way, doesn't it?" said Derek.

"You two were close, weren't you?"

Derek stared at Simon without reply, then looked away. "Best mates for nearly twenty years."

"Fuck. And you'd no idea?"

Derek snapped his head back to Simon. "Yeah, I knew all along that Ray was an IRA spy and I said nothing."

"I didn't mean it that way," said Simon apologetically.

Derek moved to the front door and peered through the small side window. The rain — now heavy and cascading down the glass in small rivulets — obscured most of his view. "I knew he wasn't being straight with me these last couple of days. Since we found the weapons. He promised me he knew nothing about them, and told me to trust that he would sort it out." Derek shook his head and let out a snort.

The voices in the sitting room fell silent and Lisa came storming out, eyes wet and cheeks red. She paused for a second when she saw Simon at the foot of the stairs.

"Hey, are you okay?" asked Simon gently.

"No. I'm not okay," she said, before pushing past and running up the stairs.

Simon turned to Derek and shrugged. "I don't know what *I've* done."

"I don't think it's about you, mate," said Derek.

Simon nodded. "Yeah, I suppose," he said, suddenly feeling like an idiot. "So, what happens now? Do you think Ray will turn up?"

"I really don't know. He'll have some serious fuckin' questions to answer if he does," said Derek, turning and looking out through the window again towards the front drive. "I'd be more concerned about this O'Connor guy turning up. If Ray only gave him half the guns, he might come looking for the rest."

"If that fucker O'Connor steps a foot on my land, I'll take his fuckin' head off," said Vinnie, emerging from the sitting room, red-faced and agitated. He opened the small cloakroom door and came out with a large shotgun. "Do you know how to handle a gun?" he asked Simon.

"Me? No!" said Simon with a nervous laugh.

"Well, it's not fuckin' rocket science," Vinnie snorted. "Derek, you show him, will you?" he added, before striding through to the kitchen. No sooner had the kitchen door closed behind him that Simon heard the muffled voices of another heated argument between Lisa's parents.

"Right. Crash course in firearms it is then," said Derek, peeling away from the window and beckoning for Simon to follow him into the sitting room.

"Seriously Derek," said Simon, reluctantly following. "I've never even held a gun."

"It's easy; take the safety off, point, and pull the trigger," said Derek, as he hefted the recovered guns on to a small oval coffee table which sat between two armchairs.

The guns, which were now stacked in a large translucent-plastic storage box, were of various sizes; Simon could see a couple of handguns and at least two different kinds of rifles. It was only when Derek clicked the curved magazine into place on one of the larger guns that he recognised it as the ubiquitous AK47.

Derek turned and held the assault rifle out to Simon. "You think you could handle one of these?"

Simon hesitated, then tentatively held out his hands to take the gun. "I don't know, but I'll give it a try."

Derek pulled it away and laughed. "On second thoughts, I think you might be better with a handgun." He placed the assault rifle on one of the chairs and lifted a handgun from the box, then removed the thin plastic wrapping. "I think this'll be better for you."

Simon held out his hand and took the gun. He bobbed it up and down. "It's lighter than I thought it would be."

"There's no clip in it yet," said Derek. He removed two black magazines and unwrapped them. "Here, hold these," he added, before returning to the box and lifting out a heavy cloth bag filled with loose bullets.

"Bloody hell," said Simon, eyeing the contents.

"There's a lot more than that," said Derek. "These are just the nine millimetres for the handguns."

"Did Ray give them any bullets with the guns?"

"He must have," said Derek with a shake of his head. "There was definitely more than this." He placed the bag on the table and lifted one of the bullets. "Do you know how to load a magazine?"

Simon shook his head.

"Okay, so you hold the clip like this," said Derek, taking one of the magazines. He held the bullet up to Simon. "Tip of the bullet pointing like this. You push the bullet down and slide it back." Derek demonstrated with the first bullet and then lifted another and did the same again. "Now it will get harder the more bullets you put in, as the spring compresses."

"How many does it hold?" asked Simon.

"I'm not sure," Derek said, holding the magazine up to inspect it more closely. "Maybe twelve or thirteen. We'll see in a minute," he added, handing the magazine to Simon and gesturing to the bag of bullets. "Give it a go."

Holding a fresh bullet between his finger and thumb, Simon attempted to copy what Derek had just done. It was harder than it looked, but he soon got the hang of it.

Derek lifted the AK47 again and turned it over in his hands. "They're in some condition for being in the ground for so long," he said, as he ejected the magazine and peered into the gun's various openings. "It'll have to be cleaned, though. And that Beretta too," he said, pointing to the gun he'd given Simon.

"Do you know how to do that?" Simon asked.

"Yeah, Vinnie has some cleaning rods and oil in the shed. I've helped Ray clean their shotguns before," said Derek, already making for the door. "Come on, we'll do it out there. Bring the two clips as well. We'll need to oil those, too."

Simon gathered up the Beretta and the other magazine and followed Derek out to the shed. They paused for a moment in the kitchen to ask Moira how Conor was, but there was no change and he was still sleeping, so they didn't linger.

Once outside, Derek jogged towards the tractor shed, his shoulders hunched and chin tucked into his chest in a futile attempt to protect himself from the now deluging rain. He made for a large wooden bench with an ancient-looking vice bolted to the side and laid his rifle down. Simon sidled up beside him and, using the back of his hand, brushed away a small mound of metal fillings to clear a space for his Beretta. The rumble of millions of violent rain drops reverberated through the corrugated metal roof and amplified in the expanse of the shed.

"We need to find the gun oil and the brushes," said Derek, having to raise his voice, even though Simon stood shoulder to shoulder with him. Derek scanned the workspace, then opened and closed various containers and drawers to find what he needed.

"What are you looking for?" came a shout from behind them.

Both Simon and Derek spun to see a figure standing on the threshold of the shed, silhouetted somewhat by a spotlight on the wall opposite. It was only when he stepped further into the shed and lowered his hood, that Simon realised that it was Ray.

CHAPTER THIRTY-TWO

"Where the fuck were you?" Derek shouted, pushing past Simon. "Is it true?"

"Is what true?" asked Ray, shaking the rain from his coat.

Without breaking stride, Derek shoved Ray, sending him toppling backwards to land on his back in one of the many developing puddles.

"Is it fucking true? Has the friend I've known for nearly twenty years been an IRA spy the whole time?"

Ray stared up at Derek, stunned, unable or unwilling to answer the question. Derek towered over him, oblivious to the rain that thundered down around them.

"It's not that simple, Derek," said Ray eventually, as he scrambled to his feet.

"It *is* that simple," bellowed Derek as he surged forward and shot a left jab into Ray's face. It was a short, sharp, stinging punch that'd bust a nose or incite a black-eye, but there was restraint there too. It wasn't a jaw-breaking hay-maker that would take Ray off his feet.

"Fuck!" Ray cried as he clenched his nose and staggered backwards before steadying himself.

Simon stepped in front of Derek, his back to Ray. "Derek, stop!" he said, grasping the bigger man's arm as he moved towards Ray again.

"Get the fuck off me, Simon," said Derek in a low, grizzly voice without taking his eyes from Ray, who now stood a few feet away, one hand extended in front of him as a separator, the other pinching the bridge of his nose.

Derek stepped in again, fists clenched.

"Stop!" shouted Ray, taking another step back. "They'll be coming here. O'Connor is fucking insane. He's convinced the idiots that follow him that this power cut is all the doing of the British, as part of an invasion of Ireland," Ray paused, probably expecting that statement to cause some bemusement. "Aided by the French, for fuck's sake."

"So I've heard," said Derek.

"Well, O'Connor plans to take this farm as his base to lead his resistance against these imaginary invaders," said Ray.

Derek glanced to Simon, his question from earlier, as to what would happen next, seemingly answered.

"And you gave them the fucking weapons they needed to do it," Derek shouted, as he took another step towards his once friend.

"Don't worry about the guns," said Ray.

"Don't worry about the guns? Are you fuckin' serious?" Derek felt an added surge of rage fill him, and he stalked closer. "My family is in there and you just gave a bunch of mad bastards an arsenal."

"Stop!" shouted Ray as he took a step back, "I don't wanna to hurt you Derek."

"You already have, Ray," said Derek. "And not just me, your cousin is lying in there with a bullet in him."

"What? Conor?" Ray looked back towards the house, his concern for Conor evident on his face. "What the hell happened? Is he okay?"

"He'll live. No thanks to you and your fuckin' lies," said Derek. "They know everything Ray. So unless you're gonna start telling the fuckin' truth, I wouldn't go in there."

"What do you mean, they know everything?"

"They know about the guns," spat Derek. "I told them, when you fucked off."

Ray looked to the ground and nodded.

"And your friend O'Connor told Lisa everything else," Derek added. "All these years, pretending to be my colleague. My friend! And all along you were working for the IRA."

"He's fucking lying. I was not working for them. I have *never* been involved with the IRA, in any way."

"So you didn't just give them the weapons?"

"I did, but…"

"So your aunt Maria didn't get you to apply for the Prison Service?"

Ray paused before answering, and stepped backwards again as Derek stalked closer, his anger coiling him like a spring.

"It wasn't like that, Derek," said Ray.

"So what was it like, Raymond?" asked Vinnie, as he splashed towards them from the back of the house.

Ray turned to see his father approaching, his shirt already soaked and clinging to his skin, "Look Daddy, it's not that simple, you have to listen to me..."

"I've heard all I need to," said Vinnie, his voice breaking. "I never thought I'd ever say this, but I am ashamed of you. Take yourself off. I don't want to even look at you."

"But Da—"

"Go! Get off my land, now!"

Ray took his father's words like a slap and started to edge backwards. A thin trickle of blood that ran from his nose was soon diluted by the pelting rain. He looked briefly at Derek and to Simon, his wounded eyes pleading for support. When he saw that no one was prepared to come to his defence, he gave one more adjuring look towards his father before turning and running off into the darkness.

CHAPTER THIRTY-THREE

Dermot handed the duffel bag of weapons to one of his men and turned to see Joseph Kilpatrick duck through the hatch in the wooden gates.

"Ray came-through then?" asked Joseph, eyeing the bag.

Dermot glared at him. "Where the fuck were you?"

"I needed to go home for a bit to make sure my folks were okay," said Joseph unapologetically.

Dermot paused for a moment, fixing his lieutenant with a stare. "Well, you missed a bit of commotion here. The boys brought the Keenan girl here, with her English fancy-man."

"Are they still here?"

"No, those useless pricks let them get away," said Dermot. *How was he supposed to win this war with this bunch of idiots?* He rested his hands in the pockets of his coat and found the familiar, cold-leather handle of his grandfather's blackjack. "But it's alright, Ray turned up with our weapons, or at least some of them. We'll get the rest."

"I assume he didn't agree to letting us use his parent's farm?" asked Joseph.

"No, he didn't," said Dermot. "Which is something he'll regret."

"Look Dermot, I really don't think this is the way to go," said Joseph.

Dermot's jaw clenched, and he closed his eyes. He was getting tired of this insubordination.

"I mean, I understand that we need the use of Foy's radio," Joseph continued, "and I'm sure he'll see reason, but the Keenans..."

"Enough!"

"They're not gonna give up their home, boss."

"They'll have no choice."

Joseph clearly had more to say on the issue, but an icy stare of determination from Dermot persuaded him to hold his tongue.

Dermot turned and made his way through to the main bar where his group of volunteers had already gathered. The air was heavy and dull, the light from the many candles and a handful of camping lanterns being stifled by the sheer number of bodies in the small space.

Muted laughter immediately fell silent as Dermot entered. The subjects of the banter, the three embarrassed *guards* of their recent guests, hung their heads or nursed their injuries. The young lad who'd been held at gunpoint by Lisa sat at one of the tables, rubbing his arm. Dermot moved into the room and stood behind the injured man.

"Telling jokes, are we?" said Dermot, a smile breaking through his normally stern expression.

"Here's one. An Englishman, a farmer's daughter and a kid walk into a bar…"

The chorus of laughs rippled through the room as the group, spurred on by their leader, began to rib the three disgraced volunteers again.

"… the men inside had one job," Dermot continued, raising his voice to quell the crowd, "to keep them there until their boss got back."

Dermot snatched the man with the injured arm by the hair and yanked his head back violently. "But you fucked it up," he shouted, immediately silencing the group again. He gave the man's head another jerk. "Didn't you?"

The young man stared helplessly up at Dermot, the pain from his arm, or from his boss' grip on his hair, causing his eyes to water. A single teardrop escaped and trickled down the man's cheek.

Dermot held his head back as he withdrew the blackjack from his pocket. The entire room took an expectant breath. Starting at the young man's forehead, Dermot ran the blackjack slowly and gently down his face; over his nose and down to rest on his chin, where he tapped it lightly. The man quivered in his seat, his petrified eyes pleading with Dermot.

Dermot looked at Joseph, daring him to say something, daring him to try to intervene. His stare lingered for a long moment and when no objection came, he raised the blackjack high above his head. "We need better from you, from all of you, going forward," he said, then lowered the cudgel and returned it to his pocket. He released the man's hair and looked around the room, fixing his stare on Barney, who sat massaging his jaw. "I expected better of you, Barney."

Barney made to respond, likely with some excuse but Dermot silenced him with a raised hand. "Now that we have what we need," he said, gesturing to the bag of weapons which sat unopened on one of the larger tables, "we can move on to the next phase of our plan. This next phase is crucial. We need to set up a proper base of operations and make contact with other resistance cells."

There was a mixed reaction in the room, some verbalising their enthusiasm, others remaining quiet and reticent. Dermot noticed some of the group glancing towards Joseph. "So, tonight we will take control of the Foy and Keenan properties," he turned to Joseph and paused until his lieutenant raised his head and made eye contact, "hopefully peacefully," he said with a slight nod, before turning again to the rest of the group, "but, if we need to use force, then we will. In war, there are always casualties. It is a sad truth. Some of these casualties will be our own countrymen and women; some of those will be deserving of their fate — traitors and turn-coats who have helped the enemy in the hope of benefiting in the future for their treachery — others may be normal everyday people who, by no fault of their own, get in the way of our mission. There'll be time in the future to mourn these unfortunates, but it is not today, we cannot let anything prevent us from defending our land. We've tried to reason with the Keenans and they've refused to listen. But we will appeal to them again, and to Mr Foy, but be under no illusions, we *will* take control of the radio equipment and the farm tonight, and tomorrow we will begin the most important military campaign that our country has seen in over 100 years."

A chorus of cheers erupted from the crowd, to Dermot's delight. This was his chance to make a difference, to make his father proud, and he wasn't gonna let it slip.

Anthony Kilpatrick lifted the bag of weapons and carried them through to the back room, followed by the usual senior members. Once inside, Joseph voiced his concerns again, "Boss..."

"Mr Kilpatrick, I'm starting to think you don't want to be here," said Dermot.

"It's just that I think tonight is too soon," Joseph pressed on. "We'll need to get these weapons ready and train some of the guys on how to use them."

As Joseph spoke, his brother unzipped the bag and started removing the contents; there were three AK47s and three handguns, along with magazines and a cloth bag about half-filled with an assortment of bullets.

"They look okay to me," said Anthony, holding up one of the AKs and rotating it in his hands. "They've already been cleaned."

Joseph frowned at his brother, then looked at the weapon in his hands, if anything, his frown deepened.

"See?" said Dermot, taking the rifle from Anthony for closer inspection. "Mr Keenan has done a great job on them. And we do not have the time, or the ammunition, to train everyone on them. A few of us have handled AKs before and the Berettas are straightforward to use."

"Why'd he bother cleaning them?" asked Joseph, to no one in particular.

Dermot turned to Joseph. "We go tonight, Joseph," he said, keeping eye contact until Joseph responded with a nod. "Okay, now get these loaded and handed out to whoever you think can handle them."

CHAPTER THIRTY-FOUR

Derek showed Simon how to clean the guns and after a, less than ideal, servicing, they returned to the house.

They shook out of their wet coats in the boot room and found Lisa and Moira in the kitchen tending to Conor.

"How's he doing?" asked Derek.

"The bleeding's more or less stopped, but I don't like the colour around the wound," said Moira. "We need to get him to the hospital."

"Can we take him by car?" asked Simon.

Moira replaced the dressing around Conor's wound and covered him with a blanket. "I'd rather he went in an ambulance."

"Are the ambulances even running?" asked Lisa. "How do we even call for one?"

"Michael might be able to get through on the radio," said Vinnie from the doorway. He'd changed out of his wet shirt, but he still wore the face of a broken father.

"I'll go and ask him," said Derek. He handed Simon the rifle and reached for his coat again. "Simon, can you load the magazines like I showed you?"

Simon nodded and headed for the sitting room.

"Is that really necessary?" asked Moira.

"It's just a precaution, in case your sister's friends come calling," said Vinnie, fixing Moira with a frosty stare.

"Will you stop Vinnie?" said Moira.

Derek pulled his coat on and ducked out through the back door, leaving Vinnie and Moira to their argument.

The spotlight at the back of the house illuminated the path to the small wooden fence which separated the two properties, but beyond that the going was difficult and slow in the pitch darkness and still-heavy rain. A dim light from a window at Michael's house kept him on track.

After a short wait on the front porch, a surprised Michael inched the door open and peered out.

"Hi Michael."

"Derek."

"We need your help, Michael. Are you able to raise the emergency services on your radio? We need an ambulance."

"I'll try, but I can't guarantee it. Come on in."

Derek was a little surprised that Michael hadn't asked for details, but he followed him through to the kitchen, one half of which was taken up by an impressive collection of radios and electronics.

Michael dropped into a swivel chair in front of the equipment and rotated to face it.

"Also, Michael, it's not safe for you here. Dermot O'Connor and his men will be coming back. They want to take control of your radio equipment, and take the Keenan's house as their base."

"I know," said Michael, continuing to work at his equipment, the news seemingly coming as no surprise.

"Yeah, but it gets crazier."

"Yeah, I know. They think that the British and French are invading," said Michael. He turned and looked up at Derek. "He's fucking insane."

Derek frowned. "How'd you know that?"

"I told him," said Ray.

Derek spun to see Ray standing in the doorway, a towel draped over his shoulders.

"I told him everything."

Derek ignored Ray and turned back to Michael. "Are you able to get through?"

"I'll try," said Michael.

"Derek, can we talk?" asked Ray.

Derek's focus remained on Michael and the radio. "I've nothing to say to you, Ray."

"I just need you to listen to me for two minutes."

"So that you can spin more lies?" Derek turned to face Ray, the venom in his voice returning.

"Give me two minutes. I'll tell you everything."

"You've got until Michael gets through to the ambulance," said Derek, as he moved to the adjoining living room to give Michael some space, he wasn't confident that he'd be able to keep his cool once Ray started with his lies.

"I was telling you the truth. I have never been involved with the IRA," Ray started.

Derek shook his head and looked away.

"Yes, my aunt did encourage me to apply for the prison job, but I didn't know she was connected in any way. After I received word, saying that I'd been accepted, I went to Maria's, and Dermot O'Connor was there. I'd never met him before. I knew who he was, or at least what the rumours were, but I'd never spoken to him before that."

"And that's when he recruited you?"

"No! He never recruited me. No one did."

Derek raised a disbelieving eyebrow.

"Look, I was an eighteen-year-old kid, sitting across from a senior IRA man. I was shitting myself. He was coming across as if he was my friend, and like he was giving me permission to work for the British. He said it was a good thing because it'd even things out. He then joked that he might ask me to pass on a message or something at some stage."

"And there it is," said Derek.

"I didn't fuckin' agree, okay?" said Ray. "He put it across as a joke, but I didn't say anything. I just wanted to get out of there. So, I left, and that was it. I never heard anything from him after that. The whole peace process thing happened, and I assumed it was just all forgotten about."

"And?"

"And nothing. That was it. I never heard from him, I never passed any messages, and no one ever mentioned it."

"And you didn't tell anyone?"

"Who the fuck was I gonna tell?"

Derek perched himself on the edge of the sofa opposite Ray, watching him intently, considering what he'd just said. "And what about the weapons? And the guy at the gate? Kilpatrick right?"

"The first I knew anything about the weapons was when *we* found them."

"And Kilpatrick? You saying you didn't know he was IRA?"

Ray looked away.

"Well?"

"Are you telling me that there aren't people from your past who went on to be involved with Loyalist paramilitaries?"

"Not friends, no."

"Joseph Kilpatrick is not my friend. We hung around together when we were kids, but we drifted apart. I hadn't spoken to him in years. You have to believe me, Derek."

"You've done nothing but lie to me since I got here, Ray," said Derek. Although the hostility was starting to subside, he still didn't know what to think.

"I just thought I could sort it out without getting you or my parents involved."

"And you thought handing over assault rifles to a madman was the way to do it?" said Derek. He rose from the seat and ran his hands through his hair. "For fuck's sake Ray, what were you thinking?"

"I thought it would buy us some time, and that maybe the power would be back on and things would get back to normal. Anyway, the guns are no use to them."

"What do you mean?"

"I filed down the firing pins on all the guns," said Ray with a hint of a smile. "They won't fire."

Derek stopped pacing and turned to face his friend. He'd been hoping that Ray'd have some plausible excuse. *Maybe this was it.*

"They can still dry-fire them, but they won't know anything is wrong until they actually try to fire a bullet," said Ray, as he stood and approached Derek, taking him by the arms, "I need you to believe me Derek."

Derek stared intently into Ray's eyes, searching for something to sway him one way or the other.

"Do you believe me?"

Derek could hear the desperation in Ray's voice.

"Derek?"

"Fuck sake Ray. Yes. I believe you."

Ray smiled. "I wish you had've let me tell you that earlier, instead of punching me in the face."

Derek chuffed a muted laugh, then got serious again, "But I'm telling you Ray, if I find out you're lying to me, and you put my family in danger," he paused, "I'll put a fuckin' bullet in you myself." He gave a curt nod for affirmation.

"Okay, that's fair," said Ray with an accepting nod. "So, how's Conor? Why's my mum calling for an ambulance?"

"She says he's okay, but she's afraid of infection."

"Lads," Michael called from his desk in the kitchen. "I got through. They're asking what the nature of the emergency is."

Derek and Ray re-joined Michael in the kitchen. "Tell them it's a gun-shot wound," said Ray.

Instead of a free-standing microphone or handset on a coiled lead, Michael wore an expensive-looking headset with a mic protruding from the side — like you'd expect to see an air traffic controller wearing — so Derek and Ray could only hear Michael's side of the conversation.

"Tell them it's Moira Keenan's nephew, and that she's the one calling for the ambulance," said Ray. He lowered his voice and turned to Derek, "She used to work with them, so hopefully that helps."

"Okay, I understand, but whatever you can do please, over," said Michael, after relaying Ray's message and receiving a lengthy response.

"Well? Did they say how long they'll be?" asked Derek.

"They said they'll do their best, but they're running a skeleton crew, so it might be a while. She couldn't even give me an estimate."

Derek shook his head, but he wasn't entirely surprised. "Thank you, Michael. Now I think we should all go to the farm, just in case."

"I'm not going anywhere," said Michael, rotating his chair and folding his arms across his chest. "And what makes you think they'll come here tonight?"

"They might not come tonight, but I do think they'll come," said Ray.

"So what? I've to stay at your parents' indefinitely?" asked Michael with a scowl. "No chance. This is my home. I'm not leaving. I'll be ready for them this time."

"They'll have guns, Michael, and as you said yourself, O'Connor is insane," said Derek.

"It's alright, Ray says he's got a gun, so we'll be okay," he turned to Ray, "isn't that right?"

Ray nodded. "But Derek's probably right. It'd be better for us all to be in the same place."

"Right," said Derek.

Ray turned to Derek with a sombre expression, "Although I don't think I'm welcome, given what my father said."

"Well, he was angry, and we didn't have the full story," said Derek, placing a hand on Ray's shoulder. "You just have to tell him what you told me."

"I don't think he'll listen. My ol' man can be a bit of a hot-head sometimes."

Derek let out a laugh. "Ah, pot, black."

"Yeah, I suppose," said Ray with a smile.

"Okay, I'll head back and talk to him first and explain the situation," said Derek, leading Ray by the arm to the door. "Convince Michael to come with you and follow me over. Don't leave it too long, though."

"Okay."

“Right Michael, I’m heading back. Thank you for that,” Derek called from the hall. “You really should come over, for tonight at least.”

“I’m staying here,” replied a defiant Michael.

Derek exchanged a worried look with Ray before heading back out into the rain.

CHAPTER THIRTY-FIVE

"Right, kill the engine here," instructed Dermot.

Anthony Kilpatrick switched off the engine and let the car freewheel for the last few hundred yards, the slight downslope helping to keep their momentum. As he flicked the headlight selector to sidelights, the darkness of the night squeezed in around them and the car fell silent. The chatter from the back seat ceased with the cutting of the engine as the occupants contemplated the task at hand, leaving only the swishing of the wipers and the muffled patter of the rain above their heads.

Dermot twisted in his seat to confirm that the van carrying the rest of his crew had followed suit. It had. Its weak lights now barely visible through the squalling rain.

"Okay, this is close enough," said Dermot. "Pull in here."

The car eased to a stop in a lay-by under a crop of trees just short of Michael Foy's gate. The Keenan's entrance was another fifty feet further on. When the van pulled in behind them the occupants of both vehicles exited and gathered behind it. In all there were twelve men, all but two of them armed with either new guns — thanks to Ray — or with the handguns that Dermot himself had supplied.

Anthony Kilpatrick had made his way further along the road to where he could get a view of both properties and was now returning with an update, "Boss, I just saw someone cutting across the field from Foy's to the Keenan's."

"Could you see who it was?" asked Dermot.

"No, it was too dark, but it was probably Michael Foy."

"Okay, so his place is likely empty," said Dermot. "You take young Oisin here and check it out. Remember, if Foy is there, he's not to be harmed."

Dermot watched as Anthony withdrew a handgun from his waistband. He'd pulled-rank back in the bar and upgraded from the revolver that Dermot had given him, to the more modern semi-automatic Beretta. He double checked the clip, then racked the slide to put a bullet in the chamber. With a nod to his young partner, who now carried Anthony's hand-me-down revolver, the two of them moved off through the trees towards Michael Foy's. The rain was still falling heavily; the wind wiping it in at an angle, and although it would make the trek through the field a little harder, it would certainly help to conceal their approach.

"Joseph, you take two men and circle around to the back of the Keenan's from the left," said Dermot, reiterating the plan that they'd discussed in the bar.

"Barney, you and your guys go around to the right. I'll go to the front door and give them one last chance to make the right decision."

Barney nodded and set off with two others.

Joseph hesitated. "Maybe I should go to the front with you?"

"No, I want you round the back," said Dermot, without making eye contact.

"Ray might listen to me."

Dermot looked up and glared at Joseph. "You had your fuckin' chance to make him listen, and he didn't."

"But..."

"But nothing! We do it my way now. You've got your orders, now go!"

Joseph turned and beckoned for two others to follow him.

With a clenched claw Dermot watched as Joseph disappeared into the darkness. "We'll give them a few minutes to get into place," he said, turning to the remaining volunteers.

###

Simon's face had turned as red as his aching thumb as he wrestled with the magazine. The movies made it look so effortless, but loading bullets into a clip was difficult. *Maybe he wasn't doing it right.* The first five or six of each clip were easy enough — push down, slide back, done — but after that, the resistance increased as the spring tightened, and it took all his might to get the bullet down far enough to be able to slide it into place.

"Fuck's sake," he spat, as his latest reluctant round escaped, bounced and skidded across the floor.

"Hey," said Lisa, appearing in the doorway. The bullet came to rest by her foot and she bent to retrieve it.

"Hi," said Simon with a cautious smile.

"Having trouble there?" she asked, handing him the errant round.

"Thanks," he said. "It's harder than it looks."

Lisa lifted one of the empty magazines for the Beretta and looked at it absently as she turned it over in her hands. "Listen Simon, I'm sorry for snapping at you earlier. I just..."

"Lisa, you don't need to apologise," said Simon. He stood and took a tentative step towards her. "I think you're allowed to be upset on a day like this."

"But I shouldn't have taken it out on you," she said, lowering her head.

"Hey, it's okay," said Simon, as he opened his arms and enveloped her in a hug. "Most people would've crumpled given what you've been through this past week."

Lisa returned the embrace and rested her forehead on Simon's chest.

"And," said Simon, "you saved my life today."

Lisa looked up and smiled. "Well, that's us even then."

"I suppose so," said Simon, and he leaned in to kiss her.

"For fuck's sake, get a room, will you?" said Derek with a laugh.

Simon and Lisa turned and released their embrace.

"Can you come through to the kitchen?" said Derek, more seriously. "I need to talk to you all about Ray."

CHAPTER THIRTY-SIX

Ray dried off his hair and pulled-on the fresh t-shirt that Michael had given him. With his finger and thumb, he gently wiggled his nose. It was tender, but he was thankful that nothing was broken. Pulling on the draw-strings of his borrowed tracksuit bottoms, which were at least two sizes too big, he stepped into his still-damp boots. He looked ridiculous, like the kid in school who tried to get out of gym class by 'forgetting' his trainers, only to be made to participate in his school brogues.

He tilted his head and listened, thinking he'd heard his name being called. As he opened the bathroom door, he heard it again.

"Raymond."

"Coming now," he called down to Michael. *He'd never heard Michael call him anything other than Ray.* Brushing it off, he finished tying his shoelace and made his way downstairs and through to the kitchen.

"What's up?" asked Ray as he entered the kitchen.

Michael sat stiffly in his swivel chair, facing the door as if waiting for Ray to enter. He didn't reply.

"Any update on the ambulance?" asked Ray. His sentence trailed off when he noticed how strangely Michael was behaving. He was sitting bolt-upright, his hands grasping the arms of his chair. His face was stern and eyes wide, as if attempting to communicate telepathically.

"What's wrong?"

In the instant that Ray saw Michael's eye dart to the right, towards the sitting area, he felt the hard steel of a gun being pressed to the back of his neck, just behind his ear.

He closed his eyes and cursed to himself.

Michael's face morphed to a wordless apology as Ray was urged forward into the room. The cause of Michael's strange demeanour came into view; a young, nervous-looking lad stood a few feet away, both hands clasped around a revolver which he pointed shakily at Michael. It wasn't one of the guns Ray had delivered.

Ray's hands had reflexively gone into surrender mode — not up in the air, but high enough — and with palms open and fingers spread to show compliance. A mirror on the wall gave him a view of his assailant.

"Anthony," said Ray, with the slightest of nods.

"Ray."

Ray stared at Anthony's reflection. "So, what's the plan here Anthony?"

"We need use of the radio equipment," said Anthony. "We need to be able to communicate with the rest of the resistance."

"Resistance?" asked Ray.

"We're being invaded, Ray, and the sooner people realise that, then the sooner we'll all be fighting on the same side," said Anthony.

"For fuck's sake, mate, are you really believing that fuckin' mad man's bullshit?"

"It's not bullshit, the British and…"

"Yeah, yeah. The British and the French are invading Ireland," interrupted Ray. "Can you not use that single braincell in your head to think about how fuckin' stupid that sounds?"

A sting of pain pierced Ray's head as he was rewarded for his insult with a sharp jab with the barrel of the gun.

"You're a fuckin' traitor, Keenan," hissed Anthony.

"He's telling you the truth," said Michael, pleading for the men to see sense. "I've been talking to people all over the world," he added, tossing his head towards the array of radio equipment. "The blackout is worldwide, it's not just here. It was caused by a solar flare, nothing else."

"Where else is the power off?" asked Oisín.

"You shut the fuck up, Foy," shouted Anthony, momentarily shifting the gun to Michael before pressing it roughly against the back of Ray's head again. "That's what they want you to think. It's all misinformation."

Ray could feel and smell Anthony's foul breath on his neck, but he also smelt the familiar and welcome scent of his father's gun oil. He couldn't see Anthony's weapon in the mirror, but he now knew it was one of the Beretta's that he'd cleaned and delivered to O'Connor. As Anthony continued to recant the invasion theory, and the fact that there were supposed documents to prove it, Ray slowly shifted his weight on to his left foot. He looked at the younger man and the *real* danger that his gun posed. The lad had relaxed his stance a little and now held the gun a little lower, although Ray could see that his finger still hovered over the trigger. That was a problem, but he couldn't wait.

Ray raised his right foot and stamped down with his heel, driving his weight into the small bones on the top of Anthony's foot. As he ducked and spun, he heard a yelp of pain and the click of the gun by his ear — he knew that if the gun had been functional, he would already be dead — but his filing of the firing pin had worked.

Ray took advantage of Anthony's momentary distraction and in a single movement he rotated, slapped the gun from Anthony's grip and spun him, so that he and Anthony were now blocking the younger man's sight of Michael.

Ray pulled Anthony in tight and clamped him in a vice-like sleeper hold, all the while jostling and adjusting to resist the man's clawing attempts to free himself and ensure that he kept him between him and the younger man, who was now aiming his gun trying to get a clear line of sight to Ray.

"Let him go! Let him go or I'll fuckin' shoot you," screamed the young man.

Ray could see the fear in the lad's face, the sense of empowerment of being handed a gun now washed away by the abject terror at the prospect of actually having to use it.

"You don't want to do that, son," said Ray, grunting as he continued to struggle to keep his forearm pressed against Anthony's carotid artery. A few more seconds and the lack of blood-flow to Anthony's brain would render him unconscious.

"Let him fuckin' go!"

"It's all lies," said Ray. "O'Connor has lost his mind. There is no invasion."

"He's got proof."

"He's lying," said Ray. He could feel Anthony's grip on his locking arm start to weaken. "We can prove it."

"How?"

"Michael," said Ray, without turning. "Can you get someone from another country on the radio?"

"Maybe," said Michael.

Ray had hoped for a more definitive reply, but he heard Michael spin his chair and start to fiddle with his equipment.

Anthony's body went limp, and Ray was suddenly burdened with the man's full weight. He hoped Michael could get through to someone before the weight became too much to bear. There was no way that he could get to the gun in his ankle holster in time, and even if he could, he really didn't want to shoot this young man.

"I've got someone," said Michael with breathy urgency.

"Ask them where they're from and if there's a power cut there," said Ray, the burden of holding Anthony's unconscious body up evident in his voice. "And put it on speaker."

"...zis is Franz, I am in Germany, and yes, of course ze power is still off, it is off everywhere..."

CHAPTER THIRTY-SEVEN

Dermot strode proudly up the Keenan's driveway, his five men following a little less assuredly, some of them in a crouch, all watching the windows for movement. They aimed themselves towards a car which sat abandoned at the foot of the steps leading to the front door. It would conveniently give them cover while they negotiated a peaceful outcome. Three of the four doors of the car lay open, the cabin light illuminating the interior.

"Look at this, boss," whispered one of the men. "looks like you hit one of them earlier."

Dermot peered into the back of the car. The cloth covering on the seat showed a dark stain, obviously blood, more severe in the middle but also streaking across to the opposite rear door.

"Looks like it," said Dermot.

He tried to remember who'd gotten into the back of the car before he'd fired at it. *Maria's son.* The feeling of regret lasted but a moment before he shook it off, putting it down to an unfortunate consequence of war.

"There's someone at the top window," said one of the younger volunteers, as he instinctively ducked behind one of the car's wheels. "I saw the curtain move."

The other men followed suit and crouched behind the car. Dermot remained upright, resting his hands in his coat pockets, his left hand caressing the blackjack, his right gripping his trusted revolver.

He cleared his throat. "Hello in the house," he shouted, knowing that the Keenans were already aware of his presence.

###

Derek stood by the kitchen door and relayed what he'd learned from Ray to the rest of the group. The Keenan's seemed only too happy to grasp on to Ray's explanation. The relief, that Derek himself had felt after hearing Ray's side of the story, played across each of the Keenans' faces.

"Oh, thank God," said Moira, cupping her face in her hands. "I knew it couldn't be true."

"Did ye, aye?" said Vinnie under his breath. He leaned against the worktop, arms folded and head bowed. Derek could imagine the avalanche of emotions that he must now be feeling; relief, shame, regret, but most of all, anger.

"It sounds like they really took advantage of him," said Lisa. She fixed Moira with an accusatory frown. "And Aunt Maria was part of it?"

Moira avoided eye contact with her daughter and stood to check on Conor, who was still asleep.

Vinnie slammed his fist down on the counter and straightened. "That fucker O'Connor is gonna answer for this."

"Hold on," said Derek, extending his hand to quieten Vinnie. "there's something else."

"What?" snapped Vinnie.

"Ray says that O'Connor wants to take this farm," said Derek.

"Take this farm?" Vinnie spat. "He'll need to step over my body to do it."

"Take the farm? What do you mean?" asked Moira, folding her arms and looking up at Derek. "Why would they want our farm?"

"Power and food, Moira," said Vinnie curtly. "And they'll want the rest of their guns."

"Ray doesn't know when they'll come, if they even do, but I think we need to be prepared just in case," said Derek.

"Oh, we'll be prepared alright," said Vinnie, lifting his shotgun from its resting place against the wall.

"Derrrrek!"

Derek heard Jenny's call through the closed kitchen door. "I'll be back in a minute," he said, slipping out into the hall.

"Everything okay?" he called, from the bottom of the stairs to Jenny, who'd been nursing the baby.

"Derek, come up here," said Jenny, the urgency in her voice enough to make him bound up the stairs, two at a time. "There's a group of men coming up the drive."

"What? Where?" said Derek, easing past his wife at the top of the stairs and darting into their bedroom, which overlooked the front of the property. He crouched as he approached the window, then slowly peeled back the edge of the net curtain and squinted to focus through the wet glass. He immediately turned and sprinted for the door.

"Okay love, take the baby and go into the en suite," he said, pointing Jenny towards a bathroom off one of the rooms at the back of the house. "Close each of the doors and keep the light off."

Although Jenny wasn't aware of the latest threat, she knew that someone might come looking for the rest of the guns, and so she did as instructed. They'd had to take their security very seriously over years due to Derek's job, so she knew to trust his judgement.

Derek ratcheted down the stairs and into the kitchen. "They're here!"

Vinnie snorted and stomped past Derek into the hall.

"Wait, Vinnie!" said Derek frantically. "Moira, Lisa, can you go up to Jenny? She's in your room Lisa."

"I'm not leaving Conor," said Moira emphatically. She adjusted the blanket over her sleeping nephew, as if to reinforce the fact that she was needed there.

"I'm not hiding upstairs," protested Lisa. "I can handle a gun."

Derek took Lisa by the arm. "That's why I need you up there, Lisa. I want you to protect my family."

Derek placed his foot on one of the chairs, hiked the leg of his jeans up, and removed his Glock from its holster. "Take this, and if anyone, other than one of us, tries to get through the door, you shoot."

Lisa glanced at Simon, but Derek cut off her argument before she'd a chance to verbalise it. "This guy barely knows where the trigger is. He's staying down here with me."

Simon pressed his lips together and nodded a reluctant acknowledgement.

Lisa seemed less than happy, but accepted her role and pushed past her father before scrambling up the stairs.

Lifting the AK47 that he'd cleaned earlier, Derek slotted a magazine into place before following Vinnie to the front door. Keeping the bulk of their bodies behind the solid wooden door, they peered out through the long windows at either side, squinting to focus through the rain-blurred and distorted view.

"I can't see anything," said Vinnie.

"There were five or six of them," said Derek. "There! I can see movement behind the car."

"Fuckers!" spat Vinnie as he reached for the door handle.

"Wait, Vinnie!" Derek jammed his foot against the bottom of the door and put his hand on Vinnie's wrist. "Let me go upstairs again. I'll have a better view and can talk to them from there. Don't open the door!"

Vinnie scowled at Derek, resisting the grip on his arm, before finally relenting, sense seemingly trumping his rage.

"Simon," Derek shouted, as he turned and started up the stairs, "stay at the kitchen door and make sure nobody comes through the back."

Derek scrambled in a crouch to the bedroom window and slowly rose over the windowsill to get a view of the men outside. He could make out five figures hunkered behind Vinnie's car and another – presumably Dermot O'Connor – standing in plain view. Derek reached up and twisted the handle, then, using the barrel of his rifle, he pushed the window open a few inches. He ducked back into cover as some of the heads turned to look up.

"Mr Keenan," O'Connor called towards the front door, "we just want to talk. We don't want anyone else to get hurt."

Derek pulled the charging handle on the AK47 and adjusted his position so that he was in a low squat, then slowly rose again, bringing the scene back into view. As he rested the barrel of the rifle on the window frame, the attention of the men below snapped to the front door.

"For fuck's sake, Vinnie," Derek muttered. He couldn't see Vinnie from his vantage point, but he knew what was coming.

In an instant, the scene below turned to chaos. O'Connor dropped into cover with the rest of his men just as the flash and thundering boom of Vinnie's shotgun brought any thought of a negotiation to an end. Dermot O'Connor was the first to return fire. Without lifting his head, he reached up with a handgun and started to fire blindly towards the front door. The others followed suit, although only one other gun actually fired.

Derek could see confused and panicked faces as frantic hands wrestled with impotent weapons. Another flash and boom, and the drivers-side window of Vinnie's car exploded in a shower of glass, sending the attackers into hiding again.

Pressing the butt of the rifle tight to his shoulder, Derek aimed for just in front of the car and squeezed the trigger. He'd only fired an AK47 once before, at a tourist firing range in Florida, when on holiday, but he remembered how the recoil kicked the barrel up and to the right when set to full auto, and even though he tried to compensate for it, he watched as a flurry of rounds stitched across the gravel in front of the car.

He hoped that his presence, and the sound of the automatic weapon, coupled with the realisation that most of their guns didn't work, would be enough to dissuade the attackers. He really didn't want to have to take another life. At the very least, he prayed that Vinnie had the sense to get back inside.

CHAPTER THIRTY-EIGHT

Simon pulled the slide back on the Beretta — the way Derek had shown him — and held the gun flat in his hand, trying to remember what Derek had said about the thumb-activated safety switch. He flicked the switch up, exposing the little red dot underneath. *But did the red dot mean it was ready to fire, or that it was safe? Shit, I really should've been paying more attention,* he thought. He considered asking Vinnie, who paced by the front door, but didn't want to move from his position where he could keep an eye on the back door. *Okay, red dot means it's ready to fire. If you can see a red dot on the gun, then you can make a red dot on a person's head,* was what he'd told himself during Derek's hastily delivered crash course. He flicked the switch back to — what he was reasonably sure was — the safe position, with the red dot hidden.

His position on the threshold of the kitchen gave him a view through to the back porch, and along the hall to the front door. Moira was busy tending to Conor, who seemed to be coming round from his shock-induced sleep. Simon wondered what he would do if someone did try to come in through the back. He was pretty sure he couldn't just shoot them on sight. A voice from the front, somewhat muted by the heavy door, pulled him from his macabre musings.

Without warning, or consultation, Vinnie grabbed the sliding bolt of the front door and swung it open.

"Vinnie…" Simon tried to protest, but before he could, Vinnie was out the door, shotgun at the ready.

The boom of the shotgun reverberated down the hall, causing Simon to drop instinctively into a crouch, his hearing dulled for a moment, only to be replaced by a high-pitched whistle. He stretched his jaw wide, trying to clear the noise from his ears. A handful of less-deafening shots followed, at least one of them shattering the window beside the front door, sending shards of glass skidding along the hall's wooden floor.

Simon pressed his back against the wall and sank as low as he could. The second of Vinnie's shots seemed muted, but for an instant, the scene outside flashed into view.

"Fuck, fuck, fuck," Simon muttered, although he could barely hear his own words.

Vinnie stumbled backwards through the door and landed on his side as a flurry of cracks added to the melee.

"Vinnie!"

Simon pushed himself away from the wall and sprinted towards Vinnie who was attempting to crab backwards away from the door. He crashed into the door, slamming it shut, and turned to see Vinnie lying on his side, fumbling to reload his shotgun.

"I'm alright," Vinnie snapped.

Simon moved to help him to his feet, but before he could, a figure appeared in the kitchen doorway. It was Barney, the man from the bar, the man who he'd pounced on, and tried to kill with his head. In the chaos he must've come through the back door, ignoring Moira in the kitchen and coming straight for the source of the gunshots.

Simon froze, the sight of the assault rifle in the man's hands paralysing him. Murderous recognition flashed in Barney's eyes as he raised the rifle and pulled the trigger. Simon's body tensed, and he closed his eyes, only to open them again to the sight of Barney pulling frantically at the charging lever on the rifle.

Stepping over Vinnie, Simon raised the Beretta and squeezed the trigger. Nothing happened. Cursing to himself, he flicked the safety switch up, but it was too late. Barney closed the distance and swung his rifle, catching Simon on the forearm and sending the Beretta sailing through the open door to the sitting room.

Ignoring the burning pain in his arm, Simon gripped the rifle with both hands and slammed Barney against the wall. The bigger man's reddened eyes screamed of revenge, and as he drove his weight into Simon, the two men tumbled through the sitting-room door, landing in a heap on the floor. A sharp pain spasmed from the small of Simon's back as he landed on something hard.

Barney hissed and grunted, spittle spraying from his snarling mouth and the veins on his forehead pulsing as he bore down. They wrestled for control of the rifle, but Simon knew it was only a matter of time before he would feel it across his throat; he could maybe match the man for strength, but being on top gave Barney the advantage as his weight helped to edge the barrel of the gun closer to Simon's neck. It was like bench-pressing a bar that just kept getting heavier. Simon had to try something different; he released the tension in his left arm — momentarily upsetting the equilibrium — then drove upward again. At the same time, he twisted and bucked with his hips, but it was futile. He felt like a boy pinned by a bully twice his age. The feel of cold metal on his neck brought a final surge of primal fear. A guttural roar began in his throat as he released his grip on the rifle with his right hand and reached up through Barney's flexing arms. His roar turned to a stuttering croak as the pressure increased on his windpipe. Gripping the side of Barney's head, he stabbed his thumb into the man's eye. Barney screamed in agony and tried to pull his head back out of Simon's range. It was a momentary relief, but it was enough to let Simon twist and arch his back. He reached behind him into the gap, searching for the object he'd been lying on. His hand closed around the grip of the Beretta. Pulling it free, he jammed it into Barney's ribs and pulled the trigger. Three muffled cracks reverberated against Simon's chest and in an instant, the pressure on his neck ceased.

Barney's dead eyes starred through Simon as his twisted face flopped onto Simon's chest. A sickeningly claustrophobic wave flooded Simon, and he writhed and squirmed to escape the macabrely intimate embrace. As he used his last ounce of strength to roll the man off, he saw another armed figure appear at the door. Simon raised his gun, but before he could pull the trigger, the man was gone, propelled backwards as if yanked by a stuntman's rope. The force from Vinnie's shotgun sent the man tumbling backwards into the kitchen from where he'd emerged.

Panting and coughing, Simon dragged himself weakly to his feet and stumbled to the door, nearly colliding with Vinnie. They regarded each other; terrified, angry eyes flashing relief. Another movement at the kitchen door drew their attention, their weapons rising to level on another of O'Connor's followers. But this one held Moira in a tight grip in front of him, a gun pressed to her head.

"Drop the guns. Drop the fuckin' guns," the man screamed.

Simon glanced at Vinnie, then bent and placed his gun on the floor in front of him. Vinnie held the shotgun at a low ready.

"Don't be stupid, old man, put it down," said the man holding Moira. He jerked her by the arm and glared at Vinnie.

"Take it easy, son," said Vinnie, as he slowly bent and placed the gun beside Simon's.

A noise behind the man made him turn, dragging Moira round with him.

"We got them, Joe," he said, triumphant excitement in his voice.

Joseph Kilpatrick stepped into view and crouched beside the body of the man Vinnie had just blasted with the shotgun. He shook his head slowly, "This has got outta hand," he muttered, as he pressed his hand to his forehead and ran it slowly back through his hair. "Move them in there," he said, nodding to the sitting room.

The young volunteer waved Simon and Vinnie into the sitting room with a flick of his gun, then escorted Moira in behind them.

"Go and tell Doc we have it under control," Joseph ordered the excited young man.

The man seemed eager to relay the news of their victory and skipped out of the room and down the hall towards the front door.

"Hey!" yelled Joseph, stopping the man in his tracks. "Not out the front door, you idiot, unless you want a bullet in the head. Go out the back and round, and make sure you shout that it's you before you step out."

The man's face dropped, and he reversed direction and headed out through the kitchen, pushing past the other men who'd come in with Joseph.

Another burst of automatic gunfire rang out from upstairs, causing Joseph to turn instinctively and point his own gun in that direction. "Who's up there? Is that Ray?" he demanded, bringing the gun back to the three captives.

No one replied.

"Who is it?"

"It's not Ray. His name's Derek," said Vinnie.

"You," said Joseph, pointing at Simon with his revolver. "You go up and bring him down. Tell him to throw the gun down the stairs, and then both of you walk down with your hands on your heads." He stepped into the sitting room, shaking his head again at the sight of Barney lying face-down in the middle of the floor.

Another burst of fire rang out from above.

"Go!" said Joseph, gesturing with his gun. "And don't do anything stupid. No one else needs to get hurt here tonight."

CHAPTER THIRTY-NINE

Ray cursed the rain as he sloshed and slid his way across the muddy field. He'd heard the gunfire as soon as he'd stepped out from Michael's back door. He recognised the sound of a shotgun, and the unmistakable bark of the AK47 on full auto, and given that the only *operational* AK47s were inside the house, he was pretty sure that it'd be Derek behind the trigger.

Approaching the back yard with caution, Ray extended Oisín's relinquished revolver in front of him. It hadn't taken long for the kid to see sense when he'd heard the truth about the power cut, firstly from Franz in Germany, and then confirmed by a lady in Norway. Ray had given him the option to put the gun down and go home; an option which he was only too happy to take. Anthony, however, wasn't so easily persuaded; he'd heard the same testimony from the Norwegian operator — albeit while bound, gagged and strapped to a chair — but Ray knew that he was too deeply indoctrinated, and would follow O'Connor's lead, no matter what. So Ray wasn't gonna take the chance of letting him go free.

He negotiated the fence between the properties and made his way across the yard, ducking behind the rear tyre of his father's trailer at the sudden appearance of a figure by the back door. His heart pounded in his chest as dread gripped him. *Were they already inside*?

He watched as the man ran along the back of the house, then turned, heading for the front. The sound of Derek's controlled bursts from the assault rifle echoed off the enclosed yard, and the individual cracks from those returning fire, which were, thankfully, sporadic – either they were being pinned down by Derek, or not many of them had weapons that actually worked.

Ray almost lost his footing on the wet concrete as he sprinted for the back door. Coming to a skidding halt, he pressed his back to the wall beside the door to the back porch. The outer door was ajar, so he edged forward, the revolver held in a compressed-ready position with his elbows tight to his sides. Using his foot, he eased the door open and tried to get a view of the inside. The inner door was closed, so he stepped quickly into the small boot room and listened for a clue as to who was inside. He couldn't risk rushing in and potentially shooting, or being shot by, one of his own people inside. Maybe the guy who'd run from the back door had been repelled by his dad or Lisa – his sister knew how to handle a gun, and he was sure she'd be doing her part to defend the house – or maybe even by the city-boy Simon.

Tilting his ear towards the door, he listened. He could hear nothing from inside the house, but he suddenly realised that he could hear nothing from outside either; the gunfire had stopped.

Slowly twisting the handle, he began to ease the inner door open. The fact that the door opened into the small porch didn't help, as he had to pull it back towards himself to even get the slightest of views into the kitchen. The first thing to come into view was the kitchen table with Conor stretched out on top. He was conscious, which Ray was immediately thankful for, but he looked dreadful. He was propped up on both elbows — a position which was obviously causing him considerable pain — and facing away from Ray towards the hallway.

"Conor," Ray whispered, with a volume that he hoped would reach his cousin but go no further. There was no reaction.

"Conor," he tried again, a little louder.

Conor's head turned slowly towards the sound of his name and his eyes stretched wide when he recognised Ray through the small slit he'd made in the door. Conor began a slow shake of his head, his eyes fixed and stern.

Before Ray could register the warning, a familiar, but unwelcome, voice called his name.

"Is that you Ray?" called Joseph Kilpatrick. "Don't do anything stupid now. We have your family here, Ray. No one else needs to get hurt."

Ray closed his eyes and muttered a curse. *Was his family okay?*

"Throw your weapon through, and come in slowly with your hands on your head," ordered Joseph.

Ray fought back his panic and searched for another option.

"Please Ray, do it now," said Joseph, "before Doc comes in."

"Joe, you know this isn't right," said Ray, through the gap in the door. "The stuff O'Connor's been telling you is all bullshit. He's lost his fucking mind."

"Ray, throw your gun down, mate."

"This is my family, Joe," pleaded Ray. "You can't let this madman do this."

"Ray, throw the fucking gun in and come out," said Joseph with urgency.

Ray gritted his teeth and raked his hand down over his face.

"Ray!"

"Okay, okay," snapped Ray, as he bent and placed the revolver on the ground, before sliding it through the opening.

"Now come in with your hands on your head."

Ray placed his hands on his head as ordered, and pulled the door open with his foot, before stepping slowly into the kitchen.

"Are you okay Conor?" he asked, giving his cousin a forced smile.

"I'm okay," said Conor, despite the fear in his eyes telling Ray otherwise. "What's going on Ray?"

"It's gonna be okay, Conor," said Ray. His eyes fell on the body sprawled out by Joseph's feet. He swallowed hard, then met his once-friend with an icy glare. "Where're my family? Are they okay?"

"They're all fine, Ray," said Joseph with a hint of compassion.

"Where are they?"

Joseph stood in the doorway, his hands folded lazily in front of him over a revolver similar to the one Ray had just surrendered. "Damien," he said to a red-haired man standing by the sink.

The man looked like he was about to throw up. He was staring, glassy-eyed, at the dead body on the floor.

"Damien!" said Joseph, getting the man's attention, then nodding towards Ray's discarded gun.

The man took a tentative step forward and snatched up the revolver before quickly retreating to the sink again. He held the gun in shaking hands and looked at it vacantly before turning to Joseph. "This isn't…" he struggled to find the words, "I didn't think…"

"You didn't sign up for this, did you lad?" said Ray.

Damien turned to look at Ray, tears filling his panicked eyes.

"Ray, shut up," said Joseph.

"I thought we'd be helping people," said Damien. "No one else was doing anything to help."

"You know all this stuff about an invasion is complete fantasy, don't you?" said Ray, keeping eye contact with the man.

"Joe?" said Damien, pleading for confirmation.

"You both know it's all in O'Connor's head," said Ray, turning back to Joseph. "He's having some kind of breakdown. You must see it Joe?"

Joseph didn't reply.

"I shouldn't be here, Joe," said Damien.

"Okay, just stay calm Damien," said Joseph. He nodded towards Conor. "You just stay here and keep an eye on *him*."

"Joe, you need to stop this," said Ray.

Joseph looked between Conor, and the body at his feet, and then back to Ray. "Let's go Ray," he said, flicking his head, and the gun in his hand, towards the sitting room.

Ray stepped over the body and out into the hall, then stopped at the door to the sitting room. Inside, Derek and Simon were kneeling in the middle of the floor with their hands behind their heads, another of O'Connor's men standing behind them. Beside them lay the body of another man, face down and motionless. Relief washed over Ray when he saw his parents huddled together on the small settee by the window. Each of their faces wore a grave expression, and Derek gave Ray a quick tilt of his head, which Ray took as an apology for letting the house be taken so easily. Although Ray knew it was no one's fault but his own. *But where were Lisa and Jenny?*

Prompted by Joseph, Ray moved to join the rest in the sitting room, only to be stopped by a sound at the front door. The door swung open and, with an absence of caution, Dermot O'Connor strode in. He paused momentarily at the sight of Ray's subjugated form, his red-faced scowl flashing a smug grin of victory.

"Ah Raymond," he said with a sigh, as he crunched forward over the broken shards of glass. "Nice try with the guns." His grin morphed to a vicious snarl and, without breaking stride, he produced the well-worn blackjack and delivered a scything blow which caught Ray on the jaw, sending him toppling into the room.

To the sound of gasps and protests, and a motherly scream from Moira, Ray staggered forward, tripping on the dead foot of Barney and careering into Derek and Simon, who toppled like bowling pins. He came to a stunned stop, wedged between an armchair and the coffee table.

###

Simon added his own rasping voice to the melee of protests and pleads as he tried to right himself, only to be wrenched back to a kneeling position by a rough hand.

Vinnie pounced to his feet with surprising agility, and put himself between Ray and the advancing mad man, whose arm was raised ready to deliver another sickening blow to his defenceless son. A slap from the blackjack crumpled Vinnie back onto the settee beside Moira.

"Sit the fuck down, you fucking traitor," growled O'Connor, froth and saliva spilling from his lips. He spun and swiped at Derek, narrowly missing him. "You're all fucking traitors," he screamed, spinning on the spot and looking for a target within his reach. "You're all working for the British. And you," he spat, rounding on Simon, "do you know what we do with fuckin' spies?" He withdrew his revolver and jammed it against Simon's forehead.

"Stop!" shouted Joseph.

O'Connor turned his head and snarled at his second in command. His eyes narrowed, rage causing his sweat soaked cheek to twitch.

Simon shook uncontrollably, his life balancing on the edge of a half-pulled trigger.

The creek of a floorboard, somewhere above them, drew O'Connor's attention, "Who's upstairs?" he demanded, turning to Vinnie and Moira, who cowered in a protective embrace on the settee. "Where's the sister?" he asked, turning back to Joseph.

Joseph didn't respond.

"You!" said O'Connor, turning and pointing the gun, like a finger, at one of the men who'd entered the house behind him. "Go and see who's upstairs."

The man hesitated and looked at Joseph.

"What are you fuckin' looking at him for? Go!" screamed O'Connor. "Go!"

Simon caught movement in the corner of his eye as a semi-conscious Ray stirred. The world moved in slow motion and he willed the rest of the room not to notice as Ray's hand strained to reach towards his ankle. Simultaneously, Simon watched as O'Connor turned to complete the task of his execution. His reprieve rested with Ray's ability to draw his weapon from its holster and fire.

O'Connor's hate-filled eyes met Simon's for a millisecond before registering Ray's intent. His revolver arched past Simon's head and levelled on Ray's prone form.

Both guns exploded as one.

Ray summoned the strength to pull the trigger only once, but O'Connor's gun flashed twice before he was spun around by the force of a round to the thigh.

Ray's arm dropped as O'Connor's bullets punched into his chest.

Submerged screams and shouts swam through the mud in Simon's ears, only to be drowned again by another solitary blast.

O'Connor's legs folded beneath him, and he crumpled in a heap. Simon met his lifeless stare and watched as a single trickle of blood escaped from the penny-sized red dot on his forehead.

Joseph Kilpatrick's arm was still extended, pointing at the space where O'Connor had stood half a second before, the faintest wisp of smoke drifting towards the ceiling.

The rest of O'Connor's men stood like robots, motionless, their connection to control severed.

"Out!" said Joseph, almost absently. "Everyone out. Now!" He dragged and pushed the men from the room and began to back away, then stopped and stared at Ray, “I’m sorry. I’m sorry,” he said, then he was gone.

CHAPTER FORTY

Simon placed his hand on Lisa's shoulder and she turned and buried her tear-streaked face in his chest, another wave of sobbing smothered by his embrace. She felt she was to blame, castigating herself for hiding upstairs. But Simon knew the truth. It'd been his job to watch the back door and to make sure no one got past him, and he'd failed.

Derek and Jenny stood a few feet away, heads bowed, comforting their son, and each over. The handful of neighbours, who'd been able to attend, stood at a respectful distance and waited for the priest to finish his blessing before taking their turns to approach the family to whisper their condolences.

They had chosen a small hill overlooking the river for Ray's temporary resting place. The police — who'd eventually arrived hours after Michael had radioed for them — had insisted that Ray's body must be removed with the others, but Vinnie had made it clear to the Sergent that under no circumstances would his son be taken and *stored*, like so many others, in a makeshift morgue. The arrival of Father Rice, and the presence of Vinnie's shotgun, had finally persuaded the Sergent to relent, under the agreement that Ray would be moved to a grave in the cemetery once things were back to normal.

Vinnie stood at the foot of the grave, Moira clinging to his arm. He looked exhausted, broken. The last time he'd spoken to his son, he'd told him he was ashamed of him. Simon felt a lump in his throat every time he thought of it. It was something that Vinnie would never have the chance to take back. Simon couldn't begin to imagine the anguish such a legacy would cause. In the three days since Ray's death, Vinnie had barely spoken a word, other than to lament the fact that he'd turned his back on his son when he needed him the most.

As if by way of penance, Vinnie had taken it upon himself to dig his son's grave by hand, and even constructed a coffin of sorts, vehemently rejecting all offers of help. Moira too had busied herself with mundane tasks, overcoming her shock, and adjourning her grief for future, quieter, times.

Simon hadn't known Ray very long or very well, but he'd grown much closer to Lisa since her brother's passing and, in comforting her, he'd felt her pain. He'd found some time for his own grief too, and during walks through the fields, he and Lisa had shared stories and reminisced about their respective lives with Ray and Martin.

Lisa continued to bob on a sea of emotions; inconsolable despair giving way to periods of vacant introspection. He knew things would eventually get easier, someday.

The current circumstances had, for one reason or another, robbed the family of the usual comfort of a traditional Irish wake, and so the house endured a cold, dark silence — occasionally punctuated by the ironically joyful noises of Derek and Jenny's new-born son.

News that Conor was recovering well in the hospital was welcomed and, although Maria had also reportedly been sent home to recuperate, her name had not been spoken.

A muted gathering for tea, and egg and onion sandwiches, continued into the evening, although it lacked the usual, borderline-inappropriate joviality that such an event usually attracted; there were still too many tell-tale signs of the recent violence; a boarded window, a splintered door frame or an empty space where a blood-soaked rug had been removed and discarded of.

The day's light was fading by the time the last of the visitors finally bid their farewells and repeated their sorrowful condolences. Moira had insisted, despite many protests, that each person left with a package of eggs, or vegetables, or leftover sandwiches, and even Father Rice had gratefully accepted.

Lisa and Simon walked with the priest to the bottom of the lane, graciously accepting his practised words of spiritual wisdom, designed to bring a measure of comfort.

They watched as he mounted his bike and squeaked off along the country road.

Lisa took Simon's hand and rested her head against his arm. "Can we sit for a while?" she said, pointing to the benches at the lay-by across from the gate. "I just think I need a break from the house for five minutes."

"Sure," said Simon. He put his arm around her and they crossed the road, perching themselves on a picnic bench beside an out-dated telephone box. They sat in silence, each other's presence comfort enough.

"That's a strange place for a phone box, is it not?" said Simon, eventually filling the silence with a mundane observation.

"Ha, yeah," said Lisa with a chuff, "it's been there for about twenty years. My dad had a big fight with the council when they first put it in. I've never seen anyone using it."

"I'm not surprised."

Lisa sat forward, with her elbows on her knees, and rested her face in her hands. Simon rubbed small, comforting circles on her back.

"I can't take much more of this, Simon," she said, looking up at him with tearful eyes.

Simon bobbed his head in agreement, and put his hand on her shoulder, pulling her in tight. "I know," he said with a deep sigh. "We just have to keep going. And hope that things get back to normal."

"I don't even know what normal is anymore," she said quietly. "What kind of future is there after all this?"

"I don't know," said Simon. "But we're still here, and it's up to us to live life as best we can. We'll help those that we can, and we'll remember those we've lost."

Lisa nodded. "Yeah, you're right," she finally said, with a measure of determination. She then stood and held out her hand for Simon. "Let's head back up. I think we should all be together."

They crossed the road, secured the gate behind them, and turned their backs to the picnic area and to the antique phone box. If they'd sat for just a few more minutes, they might've noticed as the florescent light, recessed into the roof of the old phone box, flickered and buzzed to life, momentarily bathing the area in a soft yellow glow, before returning to the darkness of the world around it.

The End

ACKNOWLEDGEMENTS

I'd like to thank Catherine, Steve and Jane for all their help and advice, and for the many hours spent wading through pages of gibberish.

I would also like to mention two people who, likely unbeknownst to them, encouraged me at a couple of crucial times in my life. My school life, at St. Mary's Christian Brothers' Grammar School in Belfast, was a strange one. I lived for the Maths and Science subjects, but lived in fear of the English classes or any class in which I may be asked to read aloud. In English, I was the kid sinking as low as I could in my seat at the back of the room, hiding from the gaze of the teacher searching for the next reader. Dyslexia was a bad word in those days, whispered under-breath between sniggers, and avoided in fear of contagion.

My 1st Year English teacher (Year 8 in new-speak), Mr Séamas Crilly, was an intimidating, formally spoken, Sergent Major of a man (at least to his 12-year-old students) but despite his strict exterior and his militant insistence that we memorise WB Yeats' The Lake Isle of Innisfree, Mr Crilly showed an understanding and empathy for my situation which helped me to survive the horrors that the subject held for me. I remember him even encouraging me to take on a Latin class, which strangely helped my Dyslexia and gave me a love for the origins of words.

Jump forward a few years and a now 16-year-old me is still hiding at the back, trying not to be seen by Mr Dermot Campfield. Mr Campfield was one of those teachers who treated his students (certainly the older ones) as adults. His tweed jacket and sense of humour gave each lesson that Dead Poets Society vibe. He too showed an unspoken understanding and compassion for my plight, and on the occasions when I could no longer avoid my turn to read aloud, he would give an apologetic nod, and mercifully keep my stumbling recital as brief as possible.

To both, I thank you.

Reviews

I hope you enjoyed Control, if you did, perhaps you would consider leaving a short review.

Links to the various sites can be found at

https://linktr.ee/pmcmurrough

No matter how short, reviews are very important for independent authors.

Thank you, I look forward to reading your review.

Printed in Great Britain
by Amazon

20152459R00202